Praise for the

LOUISA MAY ALCOTT
MYSTERY SERIES

Louisa and the Missing Heiress

"This thrilling mystery reads like one of Alcott's own 'blood-and-thunder' tales. The colorful characters and long-held secrets will keep you guessing until the final page."
—Kelly O'Connor McNees, author of *The Lost Summer of Louisa May Alcott*

"An adventure fit for Louisa May Alcott. A fine tribute to a legendary heroine."
—Laura Joh Rowland, author of the Adventures of Charlotte Brontë series

"Your favorite author takes on a life of her own, and proves to be a smart, courageous sleuth."
—Victoria Thompson, author of the Gaslight Mystery series

"Charming and clever amateur sleuth Louisa May Alcott springs to life."
—Karen Harper, national bestselling author of *The Queen's Governess*

continued . . .

Louisa and the Country Bachelor

"Anna Maclean has created an entertaining period piece around Louisa May Alcott and her adventures as an amateur sleuth before she becomes a well-known author. . . . Those readers who enjoy mysteries set in the past, like the Irene Adler series, will want to add this series to the list of their must-reads."
                                        —Roundtable Reviews

Louisa and the Crystal Gazer

"In *Louisa and the Crystal Gazer*, Louisa continues to grow as a character. . . . This self-growth and self-awareness help keep the book from becoming simply another historical cozy. . . . By relying on her own personal strengths and those of family and friends, Louisa has the ability to find the criminal regardless of the circumstances."
                                        —Reviewing the Evidence

Other Louisa May Alcott Mysteries

Louisa and the Missing Heiress

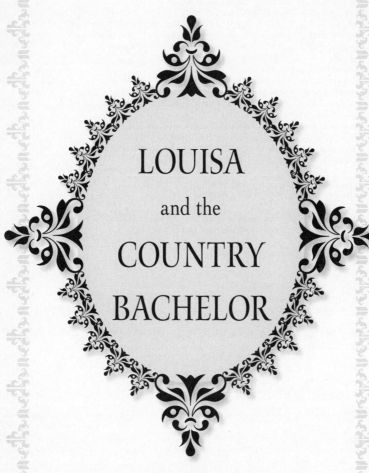

LOUISA
and the
COUNTRY
BACHELOR

A Louisa May Alcott Mystery

ANNA MACLEAN

AN OBSIDIAN MYSTERY

OBSIDIAN
Published by New American Library, a division of
Penguin Group (USA) Inc., 375 Hudson Street,
New York, New York 10014, USA
Penguin Group (Canada), 90 Eglinton Avenue East, Suite 700, Toronto,
Ontario M4P 2Y3, Canada (a division of Pearson Penguin Canada Inc.)
Penguin Books Ltd., 80 Strand, London WC2R 0RL, England
Penguin Ireland, 25 St. Stephen's Green, Dublin 2,
Ireland (a division of Penguin Books Ltd.)
Penguin Group (Australia), 250 Camberwell Road, Camberwell, Victoria 3124,
Australia (a division of Pearson Australia Group Pty. Ltd.)
Penguin Books India Pvt. Ltd., 11 Community Centre, Panchsheel Park,
New Delhi - 110 017, India
Penguin Group (NZ), 67 Apollo Drive, Rosedale, Auckland 0632,
New Zealand (a division of Pearson New Zealand Ltd.)
Penguin Books (South Africa) (Pty.) Ltd., 24 Sturdee Avenue,
Rosebank, Johannesburg 2196, South Africa

Penguin Books Ltd., Registered Offices:
80 Strand, London WC2R 0RL, England

Published by Obsidian, an imprint of New American Library, a division of Penguin
Group (USA) Inc. Previously published in a Signet edition.

First Obsidian Printing, October 2011
10 9 8 7 6 5 4 3 2 1

LOUISA

and the

COUNTRY
BACHELOR

Dunreath Place
Roxbury, Massachusetts
March 1887

Gentle Readers,

It was the summer of 1855 when I first began to
associate potato cellars with corpses. Dear. That does
sound strange, doesn't it? Especially coming from the
famous Miss Louisa May Alcott. But in 1855 I was still the
unknown Louy Alcott and I was badly in need of
wholesome air, sunshine, and serene days, having spent the
previous Boston winter investigating the murder of my
close friend Dorothy Wortham and being almost run over
by carriages and threatened at knifepoint by a
blackmailing valet.

I was twenty-two years old and that sad and dangerous
winter had awakened in me pleasant childhood memories of
Concord, of racing through meadows, climbing trees and
spending entire days out-of-doors, reading and
daydreaming—activities impossible to fulfill in the narrow
lanes and busy streets of Boston. Moreover, I wished for
more time and energy to write. I had sold two "blood and
thunder" romance stories under a pen name and a collection
of stories for children, *Flower Fables*, but I had a nagging
sense of nonarrival, of not yet writing what was most
important for me to write, what only Louisa Alcott could
write. There was a name, Josephine, and an image of a
tomboyish young woman surrounded by a loving but

1

difficult family, but I had no more than that. *Little Women* was still quite a way from its conception.

I remembered that restless time again today, when Sylvia visited. She has grown plump with the years, and looking at her now, with her cane and her several chins and her strict schedule of naps, it is amusing to remember her as she was decades ago, lithe and eager for adventure, my companion in danger.

Perhaps her perceptions of me are similar. I am no longer the unknown, struggling authoress in her chilly and dark attic. I look a bit "the grande dame," I fear, though my cuffs are still ink-stained.

When Sylvia arrived today she was carrying a package that had been waiting for me downstairs on the hall table.

"It's from London, Louy." Sylvia gasped, breathing somewhat heavily from her climb up the stairs. She sat opposite me and leaned forward with such eagerness I thought she might open it herself. The brown package almost disappeared into the folds of her bright green plaid dress. Sylvia has buried two husbands, but refuses to wear black.

"London! Yes, I know the handwriting," I said, taking the package. "It is from Fanny Kemble. Dear Fanny. There is a letter, and another volume of her memoirs."

Fanny Kemble, if you are of that group that does not recall names easily, was, in her day, the finest Shakespearean actress on both sides of the Atlantic. She was one of the few of her profession who could play both wicked Lady Macbeth and girlish Juliet with wondrous credibility. To see Fanny onstage, wringing her hands and sobbing,

"Out, damned spot! out, I say . . . Yet who would have thought the old man to have had so much blood in him?" why, that was to know great acting. Especially when she gave us a private enactment of that scene, in Walpole, where there was indeed a considerable quantity of blood in the cellar.

She was a great friend of the family, and one of the joys of my girlhood was to see pretty Fanny standing behind Father, hands on hips or pointing at invisible causes, and perfectly mimicking his expressions and mouth movements as he earnestly expounded on his principles.

"Fanny visited you in Walpole, didn't she?" asked Sylvia, bringing me back to the present. "I think I remember her there, in that summer of 'fifty-five. This morning I have been thinking of Walpole, and potatoes."

I patted Sylvia's hand with great affection. Only a friend so old, so true, could say, "I have been thinking of potatoes," and feel confident I would understand exactly what she meant.

"Yes," I said, reaching for the scissors in my sewing basket. "When we had our little theater." I cut the string and the brown paper fell away. On top of the volume (so new I could smell that wonderful fragrance of printer's ink!) was a likeness of Fanny. She looked much the same, except that like Sylvia her chins had multiplied and her hair looked unnaturally colored. I passed the photograph to Sylvia and a moment later the maid arrived with a tea tray. "Four lumps?" I asked Sylvia, picking up the sugar tongs.

"One. I'm trying to be slim. But you are too thin, Louisa," she said sternly. "You must eat more." She stirred her tea and eyed the little cakes beside the white teapot. They had been frosted with pink icing, which I found very disagreeable but Sylvia obviously found tempting.

"I need little," I protested, "and eat as appetite demands."

"Not like the old days," said Sylvia. "Remember those breakfasts you put away in Walpole? Bacon and ham and porridge and toast. Then eggs. You ate like a field hand and stayed slender."

"Perhaps because I had to eat quickly before Father returned from his morning ramble and found me in the kitchen gorging on forbidden meats."

We laughed, thinking of Father's stern vegetarianism and the ruses the rest of the family had used to avoid that strict regimen. Our laughter turned from bright to sad when we also thought of the iniquitous crimes of that strange summer, the sense of loss and waste that accompanies memories of premature death. Sylvia eyed the pink cakes again and looked so wretched that I put one on a plate and handed it to her.

"If you absolutely insist, Louy," she said, eagerly attacking it with a fork.

Outside the window, past the shoulder frills of Sylvia's plaid frock, I watched the gardener clear away a thick mass of last year's leaves from the lavender beds in preparation for spring, and it reminded me of the lavender bed beside the kitchen door in Walpole, New Hampshire, and just steps away from that country garden, the ravine where I ran each morning.

I was revisiting in my memory those granite cliffs, the

clear blue sky with hawks circling overhead, when I heard Sylvia sigh and was brought back to the parlor, to the red plush chairs and carved table and striped wallpaper.

"I can't quite remember, Louisa. That summer, did you perform your comic scene before or after the body was found in the potato cellar? What a strange place to find a body! I still feel faint when I think of it." Sylvia shivered.

"It did put us off potatoes for quite a while, as I recall. Another cake?"

"I couldn't. Well, maybe a small one. Perhaps you should write about that summer in Walpole," she suggested. "Do you still have your journal from that time?"

I did, but even without my diaries I remembered clearly what I had written about that summer. It was an abbreviated entry, which meant, of course, there was much I did not say. I had written of the ease of the journey and the kindness with which my cousin and uncle greeted me, and of country pleasures and friendly neighbors.

Friendly neighbors, indeed. Except for the occasional murderer.

Louisa May Alcott

CHAPTER ONE

The Curtains Are Hung

"Is it straight, Louisa?" asked Sylvia Shattuck, holding a framed watercolor of Kilburn Mountain against the blue sprigged wallpaper of my new parlor. She stood precariously on a footstool, stretching to place the picture over her head against the wall, and displayed to advantage the graceful arm movements and balance achieved during her private lessons with an Italian dancing instructor.

"A little higher on the left corner," I said, considering. "There. Now it's perfect."

We had just swept and dusted the parlor and equipped it largely with leftovers from my cousin Eliza Wells's amply stocked attic. The two blue brocade settees were of that style known as "worn"; the lace curtains were gently moth-eaten; the thick braided rug had sentimental burn holes from the hearth.

To make up for any deficiencies of decor, Sylvia and I had added jars of wildflowers to the mantel and a special "Abba's corner," consisting of a comfortable chair close to the hearth, a footstool, and a table and lamp, so she could sew and knit in comfort in the evenings.

And because this cottage, given to us rent-free by Abba's brother-in-law, Benjamin Willis, was soon to hold my beloved family, it did come close to being perfect.

In June of that year I had received a letter from Cousin Eliza and Uncle Benjamin, inviting me to come spend time with them. Yes, he was the unfortunate owner of the already mentioned potato cellar, but I must not rush the story. Pacing is important.

Abba, my mother, had been concerned for me, since in the weeks before, I had endured far too many hours exploring the darker and often dangerous side of family life when large fortunes are at stake. We Alcotts, at that time before our removal to Walpole, lived in a little run-down house on Beacon Hill, though even the rent for that modest residence was becoming difficult to meet. It had been a winter of hard work and frugal vegetable broths.

That day the invitation from Uncle arrived, Abba was cooking potato soup, I'm afraid to say, though I did not yet know the association I would soon make with that vegetable. "I haven't had a letter from them for years, I believe," I said. "What can this be about?" I sat on a stool near the stove to warm myself and tore open the envelope. "I have no idea," said Abba, stirring the pot and looking, to use a phrase, like the cat that swallowed the canary.

The letter was on old shipping letterhead, for Eliza's father, Benjamin, had done well in that industry before settling in Walpole with his books and various hobbies and family members. It was also brief. *Come visit, my dear,* Eliza had scrawled. *Fine weather up north, though I understand it's sodden in Boston. I've a litter of kittens for you to play with.*

"Does Eliza know my age, Abba?" I asked, looking up.

"She has a houseful of young children and two grown men to care for. I doubt she knows her own age," Abba said. "But there's more, Louy. She wrote on the back side, as well."

I turned the paper over. "It's a postscript. She says 'There's a theater here.'" The spidery writing with the arabesque capitals continued. "'The Walpole Amateur Dramatic Company, a flock of young people who would look kindly upon your joining them.'"

Abba was humming as she stirred and looked up at the cracked, flaking ceiling.

"You've arranged this," I said, giving her a quick hug.

"You need time away." With her free hand, Abba sketched a circle in the air that encompassed my household duties, the young students I taught in our parlor to earn money, my baskets of take-in sewing with which I earned a little more money. Father was a philosopher, and while they make for very interesting conversation, philosophers do not provide much leisure time for their offspring.

In my mind, I was already thinking of the plays I would write and help produce with the Walpole Amateur Dramatic Company, for I have always loved the stage. My plays would all be comedies. I'd had enough of tragedy and death.

It would seem, though, that they hadn't had quite enough of me.

I accepted the invitation with alacrity, believing as I often did in those earlier days that what I most needed was time away from my beloved family, time alone, to be simply me, not daughter or sister. I thought I wanted privacy, solitude. Indeed, I had risked Father's impatience by quoting a little too frequently from Charles Dickens's *Bleak House*: "I only ask to be free. The butterflies are free."

"Be a butterfly," said Abba.

I had tried. But in Walpole I had grown lonely without my family.

And now they were joining me, and Sylvia and I were putting the final touches on the new Alcott parlor. Her voice called me out of my reverie.

"Is it straight?" she asked again. "Maybe another picture over the doorway," she suggested. "There's plenty of room for an embroidered motto or something long and narrow."

I pretended to consider so as not to hurt her feelings, but the answer was no. Sylvia, when she wasn't with me, lived in her mother's Commonwealth Avenue mansion amidst a plethora of embroidered mottoes, watercolors, bronze gargoyles, chinoiserie cabinets, and other clutter. When it came to decorating, the Shattuck women did not know when to cease. In that, they were indicative of the times. Abba, however, and my father, Bronson Alcott, the philosopher of Concord, preferred simplicity in their immediate surroundings, less rather than more, so that when one walked into a room one did not feel quite menaced by the many fragile objects lurking within. It was a question of finances as well as aesthetics. The Alcotts could not afford fripperies.

Sylvia read my expression and grinned. "No embroidered mottoes," she agreed. "No shelves of porcelain shepherdesses. Then we are done. I don't think I have ever worked this hard."

"We are done, and your labor will be rewarded," I promised. I sat on the blue settee and looked around, sensing those other rooms that could not be seen. They were waiting, as was I, for the three-o'clock omnibus that would bring the rest of the Alcotts to Walpole.

I admit, dear reader, to feeling a certain pleasure and even pride, though Father would have disapproved of such a lack of humbleness. The cottage on Main Street was the first house I had ever prepared for habitation without Abba's guidance. All the while, as I had mopped floors, wiped windows, placed furniture, I had been guided by Abba's invisible presence, and I was certain she would approve.

This was what a house for the Alcott family must contain: one room with wall-to-wall bookcases for Father, who often forgot to pack his hairbrush but never traveled without at least five trunks of books; a little room with a rented piano for shy Lizzie, who had no ambition other than to master the more difficult Chopin preludes; a mudroom for fifteen-year-old May to contain her paint boxes and smocks; a lady's room with a desk stocked with writing paper and envelopes for older sister Anna, who had friends in many parts of the country; a sewing room for Abba and myself, since our income often came from that occupation. However, I was on vacation that summer. *Flower Fables* had earned me forty dollars. Not a fortune, like the fortune that would come many years later, but a goodly sum nonetheless, one that purchased new afternoon dresses for all the Alcott women and allowed me a little more time for my writing.

So, of course, the new household also contained my writing room—no longer in the attic, as in our Beacon Hill house, but in a little outdoor shed that I shared with a solitary pitch-fork and several handsome spiders. My desk was a plank set on two sawhorses; my rug was the graveled floor under my feet. The only decoration was three topsy-turvy umbrellas dangling from the roof to catch the seeping raindrops. The shed was a paradise.

Out of an empty house I had, with Sylvia's help and Ab-ba's unseen guidance, created a home.

"There was mention of a reward for my labor," said Sylvia, sitting on the other settee. Her blond hair had escaped its snood and curled around her face in rascal ringlets; there was a smear of dust on her nose and grime under her nails. Her costume was strange, with a high, tight collar and long bell sleeves that had been trailed through mopping buckets and looked much the worse for wear. Sylvia, when she had arrived the week before, had announced she was now a student of Confucius.

She had quarreled with her mother over her marital status, which remained single despite several proposals; hence her flight to join me in Walpole. She had also become disillusioned with the Roman Catholic faith, abandoned the idea of joining a convent, and now quoted the Chinese philosopher whenever possible.

This moment seemed to offer such a possibility.

She folded her arms in those strange long sleeves and tried to rearrange her face in what she thought was a serene expression. How anyone with such unruly curls and such highly arching brows could achieve serenity was beyond me.

"Confucious said: 'A greater pleasure it is when friends of congenial minds come from afar to seek you because of your attainments.' That's me, come up from Boston. Will you grant a wish for greater pleasure?"

"As you wish."

Sylvia's gaze landed on my dress pocket, from which peeked a corner of white paper. "My reward shall be a reading," she said. "Is that a new story, Louy?"

"It is." I took the papers from my pocket and gave them a caress, for luck. "A story about the true nature of woman."

"Read on," ordered Sylvia, resting her feet on an ottoman and making herself quite comfortable.

I shook out the paper, which had gotten damp from the mopping activities of the morning. "It is barely begun," I explained. "But there is a young woman, Kate, who has suffered much adversity and learned to be both strong and independent. She herself describes the ideal woman: 'I would have her strong enough to stand alone and give, not ask, support. Brave enough to think and act as well as feel. Keen-eyed enough to see her own and others' faults, and wise enough to find a cure for them. I would have her humble; self-reliant; gentle though strong; man's companion, not his plaything; able and willing to face storm as well as sunshine and share life's burdens as they come.'"

Sylvia was silent for a while. Then: "I feel quite fatigued from the responsibilities. But it is nicely stated, Louy. Very nicely said."

A knock sounded on the front door, which caused us both to sit up straighter, alert, since we were expecting no one until the arrival of the omnibus. The front door creaked open. A man's voice boomed down the hall to where we sat.

"Is anyone at home?"

"In here!" I called back, wondering.

Dr. Peterson Burroughs stuck his long, red nose into the doorway.

"Ah," he said. "The two young ladies are at home. I have come to see that all is well. Two women alone often encounter difficulties, you know, without a man for guidance and protection. Have you overexerted yourselves? Do you need salts?"

Sylvia's face was so screwed up with displeasure I almost laughed. She had met Dr. Burroughs once before, in the town square, when he had stopped us with similar statements about the dangers of two young ladies shopping alone, unescorted.

I had more knowledge of the man, as he had been my accidental companion during the train journey from Boston to the depot south of Walpole where the train tracks ended, since the railroad company had not yet finished the line that would connect Walpole with the more southerly cities. Dr. Burroughs was a tall gentleman of some seventy years, dressed in the stern black suit and white stockings of an earlier generation. A shock of white hair sprang out from under his hat, and during that journey his hair had trembled with constant disapproval. "Don't see why we need trains t'all, t'all; coach do just fine," he had said over and over.

During that trip, I had restrained from asking why he had journeyed by train, if such were his feelings, and had surmised that his Boston daughter-in-law (the topic of most of his conversation, for according to him she was lazy, ambitious, slatternly, and overly refined, all at once) had wished him a hasty removal to his Walpole daughter-in-law.

He had one wonderful saving grace—many years of experience as a medical examiner. He had assisted in piecing together the dismembered remains of Dr. George Parkman, who had been murdered by his debtor, Professor John Webster of Harvard Medical College, some nine years before. "I myself found the right thigh," Dr. Burroughs had told me. "Skinny, you know. The professors at Harvard don't eat enough to put meat on their bones. These colleges will turn out paupers."

Dr. Burroughs had talked at great length about the process of reconstructing a corpse as part of the process of finding the murderer, and I had found this even more interesting than the scenery.

We had met in the Walpole town square several times since our concurrent arrivals in that pleasant village, and I had learned to feel some affection for the man, since it seemed no one else cared for his company. He wandered the town square for most hours of the day seeking conversation and rarely finding it.

"Come in, Dr. Burroughs," I said. "Have a chair and make yourself at home. Would you like a glass of water? I can't offer tea; we haven't purchased any yet."

I hadn't told Dr. Burroughs that I was moving from Uncle Benjamin Willis's house to his cottage, to live there with my own family. Yet I should have known Dr. Burroughs would know. Such men—old, unwanted, but still filled with vigor and curiosity—are better at garnering news than the best newspaper reporters.

"Ah." He took a package from behind his back. "A housewarming."

I opened the brown paper–wrapped parcel. It contained a box of Ceylon tea, a tin of biscuits, and a cone of sugar.

"Well," said Sylvia, smiling. "Now we can offer tea."

"Offer accepted. May I?" He stepped over the threshold into the parlor, making a pantomime of stepping highly as if over a fence, and wobbled a bit, having challenged his sense of balance. Obviously he, unlike Sylvia, had never benefited from an Italian dancing instructor.

I took his arm to steady him and put his coat and hat on a free chair. Sylvia went into the pantry to heat the kettle.

"Your color is good," he said, sitting on the settee and peering closely into my face.

"I spend much time out of doors," I said.

"Good, good. Cannot stand those pasty, fragile females. My daughter-in-law seems to think she is more appealing with white powder all over her face." He sighed heavily at the sins of youth. "Your family arrives today?" he asked. "Good, good. Do not like the thought of young women on their own. It's an evil world." He sighed heavily again.

"It is also a beautiful world," I protested. "Look out the window, Dr. Burroughs, at the mountains. Aren't they glorious? And Walpole. So friendly, so filled with neighbors looking after neighbors. It is quite a change from Boston, I assure you."

"Bah," he said, thumping his walking stick on the floor. "Walpole has gone to the dogs. That railroad line has sent property prices to the sky, and everyone is looking to buy or sell for profit, even the foreign laborers. Time was, a man bought a house and knew his children and his grandchildren and great-grandchildren would grow up in it. Now they buy only to sell later for more money in the bank. Bah. I never."

Sylvia arrived just then with the tea tray.

"Coming by train, are they?" he asked, changing the topic.

"As far as the depot. They travel often by train," I said. "At least, Father does."

"Bah! Trains!" he muttered, thumping his cane again. His beautiful thick white hair, free now of its hat, shook as if a sudden breeze had captured it.

"It is progress." I poured tea into three only slightly chipped cups. "They say that soon we will be able to travel from Atlantic to Pacific in three weeks or less, and from Walpole to Boston in less than a day."

"Harrumph. Such speed is not good for the constitution. People will be dropping like flies should that happen. No, a strong horse's steady pace is as fast as man was designed to travel." Dr. Burroughs sipped his tea and glowered.

"Think of hot-air balloons," I said. "Soon we may all fly in the air."

"It will never happen. In the air, underground. Bah. I suppose you, like other young people, approve all this digging about for fossils and dead elephants. Geology. I never."

"You mean the mastodon they found nearby in a farmer's bog last year," Sylvia corrected.

"I mean that dead elephant." Dr. Burroughs knitted his brows. I bit my lip to keep from quarreling with him and stared determinedly out the window at the lovely mountains. Who knew what secrets could be found in those hazy peaks and vales, if mastodons could be found in bogs?

A few minutes later the hall clock (also on loan from Benjamin's daughter, Eliza) chimed two o'clock.

Sylvia cleared her throat. "Shouldn't we be leaving soon, Louisa?" she asked.

Dr. Burroughs took the hint and rose stiffly from his chair.

"Thank you for the housewarming," I told him. "I hope you will come again, and meet Mother and Father and my sisters."

He looked at me somewhat cross-eyed. Obviously it had been so long since he had received an invitation that he didn't quite know what to say.

"Well," he muttered, confused. "Well."

AT TWO THIRTY, dressed in freshly washed and ironed frocks (Sylvia, unaccustomed to such work, had scorched hers, but the brown patch was covered nicely by a summer shawl), we made our way down Main Street to the central square.

Walpole at that time was a large village of some fifteen hundred souls, twelve thousand sheep, and four hundred horses, perched on a high plain surrounded by the Cold and Connecticut rivers. Main Street ran tidily from north to south and was lined with beautiful old elms and maples, and behind those trees were very handsome residences. Children played at tag or with marbles, being careful to avoid the tidy, brightly planted front gardens of roses, foxglove, and iris that marked the homes. Walpole, with reason, was proud of itself. The town had excellent schools with almost universal literacy, a dozen shops, two shoe manufactories, and one shirt factory. White church spires darted into the cloudless blue sky, and in the near distance, Kilburn Mountain loomed in hazy shades of lavender and green.

Father, I knew, approved of Walpole in particular and New Hampshire in general.

"It is restful," agreed Sylvia, reading my thoughts. "And Mother seems so very far away." For as much as I admired my materfamilias, Sylvia spent much of her time trying to avoid hers.

But then I saw the row of idling men leaning against fences and walls, the burly laborers whose work had been halted because of property disputes. Some of the men and boys spit great gobs of tobacco that made walking a hazard; they all wore the tweed caps and collarless linen tunics that marked the new Irish immigrants.

There was a second group of men farther down the street, men with white-blond hair and wooden clogs: the Dutch workers who had arrived even before the Irish. The two groups shot glances of dislike back and forth, and occasionally one would venture over to shake his fists, mutter an insult, or snarl, before returning to the safety of his own group. It is ever this way, I have observed, that one group of low-wage immigrants will despise the next to come after them; there is a hierarchy of suspicion and employment rivalry.

Each day, when I had walked to the square, I had encountered this same dual grouping, almost identical, with only minor variations of numbers and postures. The ceasing of work on the railroad had thrown many bread earners out of work, and there was unease in lovely Walpole because of this.

I felt Sylvia stiffen next to me as we passed them by; for a moment their attention focused on us, and I remembered Dr. Burroughs's words—that women unescorted by men were vulnerable.

"Rubbish," I said aloud. That made Sylvia laugh, and the moment passed.

The omnibus from the train depot was a little early that afternoon, and Sylvia and I arrived in the square just as my family was alighting from the coach.

I stood and gazed upon them for a moment, delighting in the sight of Abba, with her sensible brown dress and sewing basket dangling from her arm, for she never sat without a piece of mending or darning in her lap; Lizzie, shy and looking a little confused at the commotion, her beautiful long white pianist's hands fluttering pale in the sun as she retied her bonnet; May, the youngest of Abba's "Golden Brood," our pet, dressed in a pink frilled frock and with her bangs curled on her broad forehead; Anna, a grown woman with a hesitant smile and lovely eyes; and Father. Father, with his sharp, noble features, his long, elegant figure, his patched and mended clothes, his air of constant distraction comingling with nobility of the highest degree.

Anna saw me first, gave a little gasp, and opened her arms. I threw myself into them. Soon we were all hugging and exchanging kisses, Father going so far as to kiss Sylvia on the forehead, thinking for a second that she was one of his own. It was a busy market afternoon, and many people in the square tut-tutted at our public affection, but no amount of disapproval could dampen an Alcott reunion.

"Have you many trunks?" I asked. "Uncle Benjamin said he would send his cart for them."

"I don't see it," said Abba, looking around in a worried manner. "There is no cart. And there are more trunks than we can possibly carry."

"He might have forgotten," I said. "He is increasingly forgetful." Now worried myself, I looked at the pile of Alcott trunks, worn and battered things but also heavy with our worldly possessions, and knew there was no way we could transport them to the cottage ourselves. Father alone had four heavy trunks of books and papers.

"Say, you can't leave those boxes here, in the way," said a man's voice. I turned and saw a very tall and gangly man, a veritable Ichabod Crane, with the arrogant eyes and bobbing Adam's apple of Washington Irving's schoolteacher, glaring at us. Sheriff Bowman, Walpole's single officer of the law.

Father extended his hand. "I am Bronson Alcott," he said hopefully.

"Still can't leave them things in the way," said Sheriff Bowman.

"Leave them here," said a different man's voice from behind me. Mr. Tupper came out of Tupper's General Store and gave me a half smile. He had red hair and hazel eyes and a ginger-colored walrus mustache above his lip. His white apron was stained pale green with pickle juice. "Didn't mean to startle you, Miss Alcott," he said. "Passengers can leave packages here for pickup later. Charge is a nickel a day for storage."

I had met Mr. Tupper already on several occasions; he ran the Whig store, and my cousin Eliza Wells had given me stern orders to shop there, not at the Democrat store, or I would make trouble for her family. Walpole was very firm on those lines and more divided in politics than any other issue.

Though he, like other Whigs, was an antislaver, I had no fondness for Mr. Tupper; he overpriced his goods and was often rude. Political morality is well and good, but one must uphold principles in mundane matters as well. Charity begins at home.

However, we had no choice but to accept his offer for trunk storage, though the charge was excessive. I gave him a nickel from my bag, and Mr. Tupper and his boy began carrying our trunks off the sidewalk and into his store.

"Do put it down gently," I called to him as he disappeared through the door of Tupper's General Store with a trunk May had packed for me as well. I had traveled to Walpole without my skirt hoop. Comfortable reader, if you wonder why I did such a thing you have obviously never sat for long periods of travel in a hoop skirt, which is somewhat like a clothy balloon but not tied at the ankles, thankfully. May, however, had been so mortified by my lack of stylishness she had packed the hoop into its case and brought it.

"The case is old and fragile . . ." I called to the store's interior.

Too late. There was a loud thud.

Obviously Mr. Tupper had never had to deal with crinolines and hoop skirts which, once wrongly bent, are never the same again.

HALF AN HOUR later we had returned to the cottage that Sylvia and I had prepared. I held my breath and pushed open the door. Abba entered first, then Anna, Lizzie, May, and Father.

They looked around in curious amazement at their new home.

Suddenly I saw the cottage, and my own work in it, through Abba's eyes. The windows were still streaky; the curtains in the dining room were lopsided. I had chosen the wrong rug to lay between the blue silk settees.

But Abba turned to me with glistening eyes and enfolded me in her embrace once again.

"You have made us a castle," she said. "It is perfect and beautiful."

I remembered the reading I had given Sylvia earlier in the day, about the ideal true woman. I realized then that I had been describing Abba.

"What is that house next door, Louy?" asked May, curious. "Have they girls my age? Do they have afternoon parties?"

"I have not met the people," I told her. "They seem to be away."

"It is a big house," said May, impressed. "And look, there is lace at every window. They must be very wealthy. I do hope we'll be friends."

Not too friendly, I thought. I had so much writing I wished to accomplish, and overly friendly neighbors can be such a distraction.

"We are going to have a lovely summer," I told my family. "All calmness and quiet."

CHAPTER TWO

Mother—or Femme Fatale

IN THE MORNING, I rose before everyone else and dressed quietly in a castoff pair of Father's old trousers, a sweater such as the kind worn by fishermen, and a boy's cap with my hair tucked up in it.

I slipped out the kitchen door and made my way through our back garden, which grew only weeds and stones because the house had been uninhabited for the past year. I opened the creaking gate and followed a path I remembered from my childhood visits.

The milk cart made its slow, horse-clopping way down High Street, at my back, but little else moved except the fluttering, chirping birds. Walpole was only half-awake, and the air was fresh and clean, my step buoyant.

The ravine was just minutes away from our cottage. Mist rose up from the ground as if the earth itself were breathing, and a pretty babbling brook dashed down the ravine, whose sides were fringed with pines and carpeted with delicate ferns and moss. I loved this place, and decided instantly that my story of ideal womanhood, about strong Kate and handsome Mr. Windsor, would have a ravine in it.

I took a deep breath, executed some knee bends, and stretched my arms overhead in preparation.

This was what my Boston circle did not know about me: I was as fast on foot as any long-legged boy, and I had the stamina of an athlete. In Concord, as a child, I won all the footraces and never needed to take a leading start, as the other girls were given. "What a shame she's a girl," Emerson had commented once to Father, after seeing me run. Father, characteristically preoccupied with thoughts of a lecture he was to give, had answered, "She is? Ah, yes. Though I protest, dear Waldo, that it is never a shame to have daughters, though I admit they are somewhat expensive to clothe. Lace and embroidery, you know." And then, with the occasional flash of preternatural brilliance that often startled his hearers, he had said, "At least she will never wear a uniform and march behind a military band." That was years before we realized that the North and South problem would lead to war.

In the Walpole ravine I ran till my legs ached, till my lungs burned, till the sun was higher in the sky by an hour or more.

And then, panting, I sat on the ground and stared up at the beautiful blue sky. Abba had been right: Time in the country was just what I needed. Peace and quiet.

When I returned to our cottage, Cousin Eliza, the generous woman who had helped outfit the house loaned us by her father, Benjamin, was in the kitchen, unpacking a basket.

She screamed when she saw me, and reached for the broom.

"Eliza," I said hurriedly, taking off my cap and shaking out my hair, "it's me, Louisa."

"Oh." She gasped, hand over her heart. "I thought you were one of those Irish scoundrels come to rob the silver. Why are you dressed like that?"

It seemed pointless to address her first remark and point out that an Alcott household never contained silver. "My exercise clothing," I explained. "I'll change and be right down to help."

Ten minutes later, now dressed in my workday brown linen dress with ink-stained cuffs, I was helping her set the table for breakfast.

Eliza was a woman who had all the virtues except beauty, or so I had heard townsfolk gossip, though I found her large eyes and warm smile to more than overcome for a weak chin and a figure much challenged by the strains of procreation; she was also much pitied by those townsfolk because she had a difficult household of four rambunctious children and a hard-luck husband, Frank, whose ventures for profit almost always failed, and so they were dependent on her father, in whose home they all lived.

"How is Cousin Frank?" I asked, wiping a spoon on my apron. Sylvie had washed them last, and she had not quite mastered that simple chore.

Eliza clucked her tongue. "Frank was fixing the back porch and banged his thumb with the hammer this morning. I suspect he's at home with his hand in an ice bucket. You did give me a fright," she said, laughing. "They brought them Irish in to work on the railroad, and there's been trouble in town ever since, what with the railroad work stopped." She set out the coffee cups. "The Dutch begun the railroad here in Walpole, but the board voted to replace them because the Irish would work cheaper. There's been Saturday-night fist-fights ever since."

Finished with setting the table, Eliza reached up to pull the linen window shade down. She had to stand on tiptoe to do it, so I helped. Our dining room window was directly opposite a neighbor's window, and I saw two people sitting there, a man and a woman.

"Our neighbors have returned," I said. "Do you know them, Eliza?"

"That's Mrs. Tupper and her invalid brother," she said in a cold voice. "She's a newcomer. Last year she married Mr. Tupper's son—you know, the family that has the general store in the square. I heard they were in Boston, to the health clinic. You'll meet Ida. Everyone does. Last month I saw her sitting in the garden with Frank. Her head was on his shoulder. Ah, men are silly." Eliza clucked her tongue and drew the curtains shut with such vigor I thought they might come down. "There's a son as well," she said.

Abba came downstairs first, still yawning and stretching, and almost bumped into a wall because she had thought she was still in her Beacon Hill house, where the rooms were arranged differently. Anna came down with circles under her eyes, for she hadn't slept well. "How loud the frogs are!" she said. "They make my ears buzz."

Lizzie soon followed, humming a tune, and May came down with curling papers in her hair. Minutes later Sylvia and Father made their way to the breakfast table, where Eliza had spread out rolls and butter and boiled eggs.

We chattered all at once and arrived at an agreement to have tea together at the Willis house that afternoon. Eliza rose—somewhat reluctantly, we all observed—after her second cup of coffee and returned home to her brood and to polish her silver teapot.

"I suspect she has troubles at home," Abba commented, watching her niece disappear around the corner.

It was a hectic day of unpacking the trunks that had been delivered by Mr. Tupper for an added charge of a dime, and when teatime came we were all glad for a break. I led the way to Eliza's house, marching in front and occasionally pointing out local landmarks such as the tin shop, the inn, and the tavern. Mostly, though, as I walked I composed my story in my head, hearing a conversation between Kate and Mr. Windsor that was heavy with secret longing.

By the time we arrived at the house on the north side of Main Street I suppose my face might have looked a little startling to Eliza when she opened the door to me. She held a pot in her hands, a stew she had been simmering for supper later.

"Oh, Louisa, whatever is wrong?" she exclaimed, reminding me that when I composed in my head I often made strange faces, or so I have been told. "Has there been an accident in the village?"

"I'm sorry, Eliza. I seem to be always taking you by surprise. I was simply thinking of a story," I explained.

"I see. Just a moment, dear friends," Eliza said, fleeing down the hall. I heard her in the parlor, slamming drawers, drawing curtains, throwing balls and dolls into a box to stuff into the cupboard—doing those very things that Abba and I do when company arrives and the parlor is not quite ready.

We were left standing in the hall.

"Look," said Anna, smiling. "Oh, it is just as I remember it from our childhood visits. There is the mangy moose head for Uncle Benjamin's hats, and that grisly umbrella stand." She pointed at the object, made from an elephant foot, in which Uncle kept the collection of walking sticks I had been so fond of as a child, carved ebonies each topped with a gilt pagan deity configured as a handle, a set of four brought from Egypt.

Anna and I had dueled with them as children, and I had always chosen the one with the little goddess on the handle. Hathor, Uncle Benjamin had said her name was, and Anna had chosen Ra, the round sun deity. No child had been allowed to play with the Anubis-handled cane, for he, with his long, pointed jackal snout, had been deemed too dangerous. "You'll put someone's eye out with that thing," Uncle had always warned. Anubis was still there, the gilding of his figure less tarnished and worn than the others, for even Uncle did not like to use that cane.

I touched Hathor for luck and followed Anna's exploration. The blue-and-white portrait plates of George and Martha Washington, painted in China so that those familiar faces seemed somewhat Oriental; the teak plantation chair now used to hold fire logs; a cabinet of tiny wooden wine cups from the Japans; and other assorted items acquired over a lifetime of foreign exchange and travel. It was eclectic and marvelous, and I felt a thrill of excitement, for Uncle Benjamin always told the most wonderful stories of shipwrecks and pirates and opium dens. Largely, I suspect, they were invented, for his career in shipping had been marked by prodigious good luck, and he himself was a somewhat timid soul who preferred his library to seafaring.

"Come in," Eliza said a moment later, balancing a baby on her hip. The stew had been forgotten somewhere; I discovered the pot later on the parlor carpet.

Uncle Benjamin, a tall, gray-haired man adorned with an ancient embroidered silk shawl, red Turkish fez, and battered tapestry slippers that were his at-home wear, appeared behind Eliza. Under his silk shawl he still wore the full pleated trousers and puffed-sleeved coat popular in his youth. He cut a strange and charming figure.

"Abba!" he exclaimed. "Dear Abba! And Bronson!"

There followed a good five minutes of hugs and how-are-yous, and then Eliza tried to steer us all down the hall.

"Father," she shouted. "We were just about to have tea. Will you join us?"

"Tea? Yes, yes," Uncle Benjamin shouted back. And so we went into the parlor.

It was somewhat dusty and shabby, not for lack of caring or even money, but for lack of time and energy. Reader, even if they are not mentioned in these pages, when Eliza appears imagine her always with a child attached to her leg or clinging to her hand. A sweet bun had been ground into the carpet; potted violets on the windowsill wilted for lack of water.

"Frank is in the back, fixing the chicken coop," Eliza said. "A fox got in last night." She sighed.

"Is his thumb better?" I asked.

"Yes. But he seems to have a dampness in the lungs today.

Grippe, I'm afraid. All the children have had it. One comes down, and the others just have to have it as well." Eliza sighed again.

"She complains too much," said her father. "Sit down, sit down. I'll have Mrs. Fisher bring us our tea. Louisa, are you better contented now that your family is here?"

"Much better," I said. We all sat, somewhat gingerly, for Father had found a rag doll under his chair cushion and we wondered if we might find something sharper under our own. Conversation lagged, because a child had thrown a ball through the open parlor window and it had landed on another child's head, who now set to wailing and had to be put down for a nap.

"Back in a minute," said Eliza, carrying one child and tugging at another.

Uncle Benjamin and I smiled at each other. He was a rascal, no doubt. He thought I was one, too, for as a child I had climbed all the trees in his garden and lost one of his fishing poles in the Connecticut River.

Sitting there in the parlor, with the deer heads and hunting trophies and Chinese porcelains and Turkish carpets, I remembered the fun that Anna and I had had years before, when we were young enough to play at dress-up, and Uncle Benjamin let us rummage through the trunks in the attic.

Eliza returned with her housekeeper, Mrs. Fisher, and the two of them set out the tea things with a great clattering of plates and cups.

As Eliza poured the tea, I examined the objects on a small table under the window, a magnifying lens and, beneath it, a small flake of stone with an impression in it of a small, rounded snail, so old it had petrified.

"Are these yours, Uncle Benjamin?" I asked. "Have you taken up a new hobby?"

"No, they belong to Clarence, Ida's son. He is careless, and leaves objects all about," Uncle Benjamin said. "He brought them over to show Eliza and never fetched them back home."

The front door chimed, and Eliza stiffened. Footsteps came down the hall.

I looked up and saw a woman—a female, I would call her in one of my "blood and thunder" stories—unknown to myself; she was not unknown to Uncle Benjamin or Eliza.

"Come in, come in," he said. "My Boston relations are here and we are having tea." His face had brightened suspiciously upon her arrival.

"What meticulous timing," Eliza said. She turned and gave me an unhappy look. "Louisa, I told you you would soon be meeting Ida Tupper."

Mrs. Tupper, with a great swaying of her pink sprigged hooped skirt and bobbing of her feathered bonnet, entered the parlor.

"Ah!" she exclaimed gaily. "You are the family now inhabiting the house next to me! Benjamin told me you were coming. Isn't he an old sweetie, letting you have that house free of cost!"

Father cringed. His noble nose flared. Philosophers are almost always above such things, but he disliked being reminded that the Alcotts were often at the mercy of others' charity.

"I am Louisa Alcott," I said, quickly offering my hand to end that particular conversational lead. "This is my mother,

Mrs. Alcott, and Father, my sisters Anna, Lizzie, and May. And our good friend Miss Sylvia Shattuck." Each person nodded, obviously fascinated by this vision of femalehood.

Ida Tupper was buxom and of smallish height, but her elaborately coiffured blond hair and richly feathered hat made her a foot taller. Her womanly figure was exaggerated by her wide crinoline skirt and an expensive fox stole around her sloped shoulders. Father, the vegetarian, stared in heartbreaking dismay at the poor creature's still-attached head, with the black-bead eyes.

A large ruby ring flashed on Mrs. Tupper's right hand, and a three-stone diamond ring glittered on the other. Her smile put her face in conflict. She pretended sophistication; she seemed more of a child playing at dress-up, since there was a simplicity to her that bordered on silliness.

"Let me kiss you, my child," she said, doing just that instead of contenting herself with the offered handshake, and then she retreated a step and gazed at me.

I gazed back, trying to memorize her face and gestures so they could be added to my notebook. Here was the perfect foil for my sincere and sensible Kate Loring. Here was my Miss Amelia—all flounces and coquettishness and not an ounce of common sense, at least in comparison to Abba.

"Your naughty uncle said naught of your arrival, but then how could he? I have been out of town, you see. Down to Boston and Worcester to take my brother to see another specialist, while I saw my dressmakers. There are no decent dressmakers in Walpole, you know, just that poor Lilli Nooteboom, the Dutch girl, with her old-fashioned patterns." She paused to breathe, then began again. "You are to call me Ida, not Mrs. Tupper!" said this woman I had met the moment before.

Abba gasped. In addition to being married to the philosopher of Concord, she herself was descended from one of the oldest families in New England. Such precipitous familiarity did not suit her.

Benjamin winked at me from under his red Turkish cap. "Don't rush the child; she'll take fright," he said.

"We are a family who values manners," said Cousin Eliza coldly, now herself spying the long-lost pot of stew and trying to push it under the settee with her toe.

"Thank you," I said, "but perhaps Uncle is right, Mrs. Tupper. I'm sure we'll be great friends once we've had a chance to actually get to know each other."

"I do hope so," cooed Mrs. Tupper, sitting next to me on the settee. "I heard from dear Eliza that you are theatrical? Will you be performing in Walpole? There is a group of young people and such who put on the occasional play here."

"I had thought I might, but I have been so very busy, preparing the house and . . ." I stopped. I had been about to say, "writing," but I did not like to discuss my work with strangers. There is no better way to take the wind out of a story than to discuss it before it is written. ". . . and finishing my seaming," I said. Even Ida Tupper should understand the task of seaming linens.

"Well, I do hope you and the other young people will provide some summer entertainment. It can be so humdrum in Walpole, can't it, Benjamin? I get quite fed up to the gills with quiet days and quieter nights. I suspect it is because I spend so much time caring for an invalid, and because my dear husband, Jonah, is gone from me for so long. It is unfair, that is what it is. Unfair." Ida Tupper pulled a lace handkerchief from her little netted purse and sniffed. "Oh, I miss him sorely. Ain't it so, Benjamin? Many's the afternoon that that kind man sitting over there"—she waved her handkerchief in Uncle's direction—"that generous soul, gave me his shoulder to weep upon."

"Tea?" asked Eliza frostily. "Your cup is empty."

"Thank you. It took ever so long for Benjamin to use my first name without adding the last. How are you today, Benjamin? Did you sleep well last night?" Ida Tupper asked, drying her eyes and forcing a brave smile onto her face.

Benjamin blushed a color no less intense than that of his red Turkish cap. I recalled Abba saying he hadn't called his wife by her first name until they had been married a year. I doubt he had ever referred to her sleeping habits. Uncle was keeping fast company.

CHAPTER THREE

The Mortal Ravine

"Mrs. Tupper, is your husband still run off, then?" asked Eliza sweetly, arranging a pillow behind Benjamin's back.

A run-off husband! Oh, where was my notebook?

"Oh, you are such a tease! Yes, he is still traveling. And where is yours, Eliza?" countered Mrs. Tupper.

"Mending the chicken coop, I believe, or perhaps now he is repairing the roof. At least I have a vague sense of his whereabouts, more than some wives," Eliza said with a wickedness I had never before heard in her voice.

"Now, Eliza," said Benjamin.

Mrs. Fisher came in just then with the tea tray. She saw Mrs. Tupper, gave her a sour look under knitted brows, clattered the tray onto the table, and left without a word.

Eliza stared unhappily at the service. Mrs. Fisher had used the best china, the transparent hand-painted kind that is meant to sit in a glass case and look pretty because it is really much too delicate to use. I knew exactly what my cousin was thinking, and I, too, would have been more at ease with a thick mug. But housekeepers can be vain about such matters; when company arrives, even just poor relations, they feel they must trot out the good stuff.

"My husband is a commercial traveler," explained Mrs. Tupper with a bright smile in my direction. She helped herself to a plate and a piece of seedcake, and that gesture revealed much about our neighbor. Well-bred women wait to be served by the hostess. "Poor Jonah works ever so hard, because he knows I do like the nice things in life. Don't you, Louisa? Like the nice things. Poor man. He does love me so, and I him, of course. I think a woman without a husband to guide her is lost, don't you?" She crooked her pinkie over her teacup and smiled.

Eliza and Abba exchanged glances. Anna peered devoutly into her teacup, trying not to smile. May and Lizzie stared openmouthed at this vision of femininity.

Sylvia, sitting opposite me on a footstool, since all the chairs had been quickly claimed, calmly stirred her tea, then gave me a knowing look. We had both left Boston to escape this kind of thing, her eyes said. And then she said aloud, "From the frying pan to the fire."

"What was that?" asked Mrs. Tupper in her high, chirping voice.

"I said, 'This year, the mountains look higher,'" answered Sylvia calmly. "Don't you think? I must read my Confucius and see what he thought of mountains."

Mrs. Tupper squinted out the window, puzzled.

"I understand your household includes your brother and son. They don't take tea?" I asked.

Her bright smile momentarily dimmed. "Clarence, my son, is out of town at the moment. He has many interests. And my brother is a complete invalid, poor man. He has the fever again today, and must stay indoors with a compress. You know how weak he is, Benjamin." She pouted. "And my father-in-law, Mr. Tupper, avoids us, I think. That is, he never calls on us, nor does he escort me to Sunday service, as one might expect. I might call him mean-spirited, if I were inclined to gossip, but one never speaks ill of the dead, or of the family; that is my belief. Mean-spirited. I would never say that. I am quite afraid of him." She giggled and fluttered her spangled fan.

Father had had enough of this aimless style of conversation. He decided it was time to quiz Sylvia, one of his favorite pastimes.

"Sylvia, you have not revealed this latest reason for fleeing your home," he said, sternly stirring his tea and accepting a plate of cake from Eliza. Sylvia, the family once approximated, usually ran away from home twice a year. Now that she was grown, it still counted as running away in society's eyes, since she left without a husband, which she disdained to acquire, or a father, who had gone to his heavenly reward (or elsewhere) many years before.

"Mother has said I must never darken her doorstep again," Sylvia said. "She has thrown me out of the familial hearth. Cast me away from the ancestral home."

"That nonsensical speech means you and your mother have quarreled," said Abba. "How you young people love your dramas. Could you be a little less hyperbolic and a little more specific about what has happened?"

"It is because of your conversion to the Romish faith," guessed Father.

"Catholicism?" Sylvia looked confused. "Oh, that was months and months ago. Now I am reading Confucius. The Oriental. 'Men of intelligence are free from doubts, moral men from anxiety, and men of courage from fear.' Isn't that charming?"

"I'm not certain that charm demonstrates progress in your logic," said Father. "I will have to reread him to decide. Benjamin, do you have a volume of Oriental philosophy?" and without waiting for an answer, Father wandered out of the parlor. We heard his footsteps move down the hall, toward Uncle's crammed library.

"Your mother is a little high-strung, but she would not cast you out for reading Confucius," Abba said gently. Cousin Eliza was enchanted. She had the same look in her eyes I remembered from when her father told us pirate stories.

"No. I have turned down another marriage proposal," Sylvia admitted.

Sylvia was one of the Boston Belles, possessing a soft blond beauty that, combined with her family's fortune, had produced several marriage proposals already. To her mother's dismay, Sylvia also possessed a distinct dislike of children, especially babes-in-arms, and had what Father called a wandering intellect. She passed through phases, having at various times dedicated her life to portrait painting, the violin, French poets, Aristotle, Roman Catholicism, and now Confucianism. She had little time for beaux and no time for a husband.

"Tell them whose heart has been broken," I prompted.

Sylvia grinned wickedly. "That awful little Jimmy Steinway. Three lumps, please. You remember him, Louy? The short boy with the large red nose?"

"Steinway? As in the piano family?" spoke up Ida Tupper, wide-eyed with interest.

"An offshoot," said Sylvia. "Practically a weed. The Kansas City Steinways. Oh, Mother was so distressed when I refused him. 'Who else will have you?' she screamed, and then fainted. So I have been banished till I come to my senses. Is that date bread? I'm famished."

"It is date bread, with fresh clotted cream. It seems to me, Sylvia, you are already at your senses," I said, passing her a plate with a large slice on it. "From what I recall of Jimmy Steinway, he would not make you a good husband. He gambles excessively, drinks even more, and once when I asked him if he had read Goethe he said, 'Is he that German fellow who has the cobbler's shop on Brattle Street? Next time you see him, ask if he can mend morocco leather.'"

"The Steinways," repeated Ida Tupper in a calculating voice. Even an offshoot of that well-known family was probably very wealthy. I could read her thoughts. Money married money. Sylvia, despite her scorched gown and mill girl's appetite, was wealthy, and Ida Tupper had a son.

The tea hour was not an extended one, as Eliza was obviously weary from her household duties, so we returned to our cottage and disbanded to our various activities—Sylvia to meditate on the sayings of Confucius as found in a little bound translation, Lizzie to her piano, Anna to her correspondence, May to her paint box, Abba to her kitchen, and Father . . . he took a glance at the bare earth in the side yard, found a pair of overalls and boots in the pantry closet, and promptly began digging untidy rows, pleased to have space for a vegetable patch.

Now this patch had somewhat mystified me, when Uncle first showed me the cottage that he was allowing us to inhabit. It had been dug recently, as evidenced by uneven mounds of bare black earth, yet nothing had been planted, and Uncle Benjamin could not say who had dug it.

Father saw no mystery but only good fertile ground. "We will have fresh vegetables again," he announced.

Abba and I exchanged worried glances. As skillful as Father was in eating vegetables, he had little talent for growing them; indeed, those summers when we had counted on the produce from his garden to sustain us we had come close to starvation.

But Abba was a loving and supportive wife, one who was truly "able and willing to face storm as well as sunshine and share life's burdens as they come," as I had described in my story "The Lady and the Woman."

"Shall I help you dig, Bronson?" she asked. "Louy, you go to your writing shed. You shall read us some pages later tonight."

AT FIVE O'CLOCK, we had gathered again in the dining room for a supper of water and bread and cheese, when there was a knock upon the front door.

I opened it to find Mrs. Fisher, Eliza's helper, standing there with a steaming casserole in her hands.

"Mrs. Wells sends it with compliments," she said. "She felt badly that the tea party was not a success."

Abba, who had followed behind me, took the casserole. "Tell Eliza, please, that we had a lovely time, and are most grateful for the hot dish. Will you join us, Mrs. Fisher?"

Mrs. Fisher's eyes opened wide, then narrowed with suspicion. Abba had a habit of ignoring class rules and was as liable to invite a maid to share her table as a Boston Brahmin.

"Have to get back to the house," Mrs. Fisher said. "One of the tykes emptied a bottle of ink into the carpet. But thank you for the invitation."

She turned to leave, then thought better. "It were that Mrs. Tupper that spoiled the party," she said. "She spoils most things."

"You are not fond of Mrs. Tupper?" I asked.

"It's not my place to gossip," said the stalwart Hampshirian. "But she's a newcomer. Only been in Walpole two years and still has outlandish ways. Insists the ladies' Methodist fund-raising committee have a spring bazaar, not an autumn one. That kind of nonsense."

"I see," I said solemnly. "Well, I look forward to meeting her son, Clarence Tupper." I didn't, but this seemed a probable way to obtain information about him. It was.

"Clarence is not the sociable type," the housekeeper readily supplied. "Not 'less he's been drinking, and then he'll give you a chase. Bad as the Dodge boys."

"Dodge boys?"

"Them that looted and robbed up Manchester way. Twenty years ago it was, the year we had the blizzard in June, but Manchester folk still remember how those boys would get drunk and chase the town girls and then . . . well, you can guess. Some say they was involved in worse than that, robbery and all sorts of no-good things." She stopped and took a deep, righteous breath. "I'll say no more. And he is Mr. Hampton, not Tupper. Mrs. Tupper has been widowed and remarried. I leave you to your supper." She wrung her hands and turned to leave.

THE NEXT MORNING, after my solitary run in the ravine, Sylvia and I walked down elm-shaded Main Street to the town square to purchase provisions, including seed packets for Father's new venture. It was a lovely morning, full of birdsong and bright colors from the exuberant flower beds.

"It is already July," said Sylvia, walking beside me. "Isn't it a little late to be putting in a garden?"

"It is," I agreed. "But who will tell Father so? He has faith in nature."

Our first visit was to Tupper's General Store, to purchase sugar and cornmeal. We passed again the two rows of idling laborers who glared at us and whispered things I did not care to hear. Sylvia blushed but held her head high.

"Did your trunks arrive safely?" Mr. Tupper asked when we entered. "I sent them over myself in a cart." He was breathing heavily, as if he had just finished a great exertion. Sweat dripped from his brow, and his mustache was dark with it. His shoes left muddy trails in the sawdust on the floor.

"Safely enough," I said, "though one trunk had a battered corner." I did not add that my skirt hoop would never again achieve a perfect circle. Such bitterness is pointless.

"So you are the daughter of Bronson Alcott, the philosopher?" Mr. Tupper asked, reaching under the long wooden counter for the box of darning wools. "You did not mention it. I knew you only as a relative of that scoundrel Ben Willis."

Reader, as well-known and beloved as Father was through his writings and educational philosophies, I never found it useful to announce myself to the world as the daughter of a famous man. People must take me for myself. I was not, am not, the type to enter a general store and say, "My father is renowned."

"I am his daughter," I admitted now. "Are you interested in philosophy?"

He paused from his work of sorting out black wools from white, and gave me a hard look, declining to answer my question, although I had answered his. When he took my shopping list I noticed the unusually large gold signet ring he wore on his right hand.

"Do you want a package of six needles or a single?" he asked gruffly.

"Single. Why do you call Uncle Benjamin a scoundrel?" I asked.

"Walpole would be better off without such eccentrics."

By eccentricity, I assumed he referred to Uncle's penchant for strange attire and tall tales of piracy on the seas. Or did he refer to something more sinister?

"We all have our little quirks," I answered, feeling defensive.

Mr. Tupper seemed different today. When the Alcotts had left their trunks and packages with him, he had been frowning, obviously ill at ease, nervous, in the way men of business are when they cannot make a difficult decision. Today he was self-assured, even impertinent. He had the air of a man who has acted rather than hesitated.

I left him to complete Abba's list as I looked over his shelves and tables. Sylvia had already found a display of calicoes and was unrolling a length of green against her skirt to judge the color.

The store was pleasantly arranged, with a rack of readymade day dresses in one corner, a large display of straw hats, and a shelf of books that could be purchased or rented (Reader, of course I checked for my own, *Flower Fables*. It was not there.), as well as the usual barrels of pickles, sacks of grain, farm tools, and a locked cabinet of patent medicines.

"Here for a long visit?" Mr. Tupper asked, as he measured out a tablespoon of spinach seed.

"I don't know how long," I said truthfully.

"Well, there are some that come and never leave," he said, sounding displeased. He referred again, I was certain, to Uncle Benjamin, who had moved his family to Walpole ten years before.

A daguerreotype of a young man framed in gilt hung on the wall over a display of bolts of sprigged muslin. He was square-faced with large eyes and a merry smile and a chin that suggested he would do just as he pleased. His right hand rested in his lap; he wore the same style of ring as the store owner.

"My son," said Mr. Tupper, following my eyes. "He married against my wishes. Haven't seen hide nor hair of him in half a year. Ida says he's traveling."

I peered more closely. Ida's husband had to be a full decade younger than she was, if not more.

"Ayeah. She changed him, all right. Doesn't write anymore, just sends picture cards once in a while," the shopkeeper said. "Not like him at all, to waste money on picture cards when a penny letter would do. I just pray he hasn't come to harm."

"What harm—" I started to ask, but was interrupted by the loud tinkling of the bell as the door swung open. Mr. Tupper gave me my basket, took my quarter, and directed his attention to the new customers.

"Well," said Sylvia, when we were back outside. "He is not friendly."

"No," I agreed. "I am curious to know the cause of his dislike of Uncle Benjamin, as well as the extent of it. It is not wise to have open enemies in a small town."

"Any town," said Sylvia. "Let's go back home, Louy. I'm sure I can find a passage in Confucius pertinent to this situation."

She was only half jesting, and her eyes were merry, but before I could answer, I saw her face change from laughter to grimness; she looked at something over my shoulder.

I turned around, knowing already that whatever had so changed her expression was something to dread.

Coming down the Walpole sidewalk was a group of men carrying a litter, and on that litter was a body covered with a sheet. Rusty, coagulated blood blotted the sheet.

"What has happened?" A man with rolled-up sleeves ran out of his cobbler's shop, a huge needle in one hand and the unstitched leather sole still in his other. He waited next to us on the sidewalk, peering nervously at the approaching men with their litter.

"Ernst Nooteboom," called one of the men. "Found him dead in the ravine."

All movement stopped. Gossiping housewives, skipping

children, apprentices with brooms, shopgirls carrying trays of tea, even the leaves on the elms seemed to cease their trembling—the entire square froze in disbelief. The two separate rows of tobacco-chewing unemployed laborers grew still. Unexpected death has that effect.

A woman stepped away from her group of friends. She had fair skin and two long blond braids trailing down her back. A shopping basket hung over her arm. She moved slowly, not wishing to arrive at the side of that broken body but knowing she must. When she pulled the covering off the dead man's face, six eggs spilled from her basket and broke on the cobbles. No one paid any attention to them.

"Ernst?" said the woman gently, as if trying to wake a child from a deep sleep. When he did not respond, she screamed. She shook him so hard the litter carriers had trouble maintaining their awful burden. Finally she collapsed to the ground, wailing, and her friends circled around her once again, not to exchange gossip or recipes, but to comfort, as women do, making a cordon of their arms as though they could fend off further disaster.

I looked back at the cobbler. "She be Lilli Nooteboom, his sister," he said. He still held the shoe he had been stitching, and the huge needle with its cord was suspended in air, frozen in time by the coldness of death.

Lilli Nooteboom would not be comforted by the women. She raged against the men carrying her dead brother, weeping and gasping, tearing at her hair, shaking her fists at the sky. "Where did you find him?" she sobbed.

"Bottom of the cliffs, Miss Nooteboom. Seems he fell," said the man closest to her. He avoided her gaze.

"No," she said, now somehow calming herself. "He did not fall. My brother climbed in the Alps; he was a summer guide. He had sure footing, my brother. Never does he fall." Her voice was accented with deep Dutch "R"s and the upending inflection.

"Don't know nothing about that, miss," he replied, still afraid to look into her eyes.

"I do know about that," insisted Miss Nooteboom. "He does not fall. Something else has happened to him. Oh, I told him we should not come." And she began to weep anew, then once again controlled herself.

Her blue eyes were like ice, sharp and cold. "Something else has happened," she insisted. She looked at the row of laborers in their tweed caps and white tunics.

"Well, will we carry him home?" asked one litter bearer, shifting his weight a little in discomfort. The body under the sheet was not small; it must have been a strain even for four men to carry him all the way from the ravine.

"Eh. Home, to the dining room," said the dead man's sister in a strangled voice. "I will put a clean sheet on the table and prepare him. And then I will be speaking to the sheriff." She led the way, looking straight ahead with those piercing blue eyes.

The processional passed Sylvia and me, where we stood on the edge of the sidewalk in front of Tupper's General Store. The sheet wasn't quite long enough to cover the dead man's feet. I had a good look at them.

The leather soles of his shoes were worn smooth and had not been crisscrossed with the incised Xs with which walkers and climbers increase boot traction. No sensible person would walk on a cliff in shoes like those on the feet of Ernst Noote-boom; certainly no hiking guide would take such a risk.

"It were an accident," said a man behind me. I looked back and saw Mr. Tupper standing there.

"Beg pardon?" I asked.

"Mr. Nooteboom. He fell."

"So they said," I answered. Mr. Tupper seemed plainly distressed by something; I could see it in the trembling of his hand. "An accident," he repeated.

The procession disappeared around a corner and the day slowly returned to its previous condition: Birds sang in the ancient oaks and elms, children played at stick and hoop, the idling laborers grumped and talked among themselves. Groups of women stood in closed circles, whispering. Now, instead of recipes, they talked of Ernst and Lilli Nooteboom, I was certain.

CHAPTER FOUR

Knitting Lessons and a Wake

Sylvia and I returned home to find Ida Tupper sitting in the kitchen with Abba.

"Look," she said with great glee. "Abba is teaching me to knit!" She held up a tangled skein of wool and a needle with two lopsided, uneven rows of knit one, purl two. Ida wore pink-striped linen that day and skirts with enough yardage for two or three of my workday gowns. She looked youngish in a strange way, as middle-aged women who deny their maturity often do when adorned in insistently youthful style. "I thought I would come keep your mother company. We musn't let her get bored here in the country."

Abba, looking patient but tired, was too kind to point out to her new neighbor that there was dinner to prepare and rows of vegetable seeds to be planted and so had let herself be coerced into yet another task. Judging from the unevenness of Mrs. Tupper's knitting stitches, it was an impossible task.

"I've never attempted a sock before," said that woman

gaily. "Mother insisted I learn crewel embroidery and china painting instead, you know—what ladies do. I learned a bit of hat trimming as well, what Parisian ladies occupy themselves with. Trimmed that one." Ida pointed to a confectionery of white starched lace and peacock feathers now resting on the table near her elbow. "Jonah bought it for me before he left," she said. "Oh, it is ever so expensive, I'm sure. You'll not find another like it in Walpole. I asked Lilli Nooteboom if she could make a dress to match and she was just speechless, poor thing. She has no talent for dressmaking, really she hasn't."

"Ah," I said.

"Louisa, you look pale," said Abba, putting down her needles. "And Sylvia, you are trembling. What is the matter?"

I pumped water into the sink from the kettle, and stuck more wood into the stove to blaze up the fire.

"Lilli Nooteboom is the matter," I said. "Her brother has fallen from a cliff, it seems."

"Ernst?" Ida Tupper looked up from her lopsided knitting. It seemed she was on a first-name basis with a great many people.

"Ernst," she said again, wonder in her voice, and a touch of fear. "I do hope he will recover without a limp; it is so awful when a man limps. Such a nice young man. So very tall, and that funny accent. His sister, of course, is another story. So cold, so formal. She purposely shut a door once in my face; I would swear she did it on purpose."

"Ernst Nooteboom is dead," said Sylvia.

I had wished to announce the mortality a little more gently, but Sylvia was in her straightforward phase.

Ida Tupper dropped her knitting. "Dead? I never thought . . . What a catastrophe." Her voice trailed off, and I feared she would swoon. She did not. Instead she rose from the wobbly kitchen chair and went to the window. It was the side of the house that faced her own; she stared into her own front parlor.

"Oh, dear." Ida turned back to us. Tears seeped from her eyes. "And I was just saying horrid things about that poor girl. I sympathize with her, I really do. It is awful to lose a loved one. I know, I know."

We all sat for a moment in silence and brooded, as people do when a death has been announced. Mrs. Tupper dabbed at her eyes.

"Don't cry," said Abba, going over to her and patting her hand. "I'm sure the town will do what it can for Lilli Nooteboom. There will be a raffle and a dinner to raise money for her, once the viewing and funeral are over."

"Yes," said Ida Tupper. "Tonight I will go through my trunks and find what I can give her myself. You are right, Abba. We must all be very brave."

It seemed to me that Lilli Nooteboom was the one who must be brave, and the thought of short, buxom Ida Tupper's castoff dresses on tall, thin Lilli Nooteboom was almost enough to make me smile.

Father came in just then for his cup of tea, and to discover what delayed the arrival of his seed packets. He found the four of us sitting at the kitchen table.

"You look like someone has died," he said.

"Someone has." I took off my plain straw bonnet and placed it on the table next to Ida's confection. "Ernst Nooteboom, one of the Dutch workers. He fell into the ravine."

Father folded his arms over his white work shirt and squinted. He had been so delighted to have a vegetable patch again that he had taken to dressing in farm clothes and coming to tea with his suspenders drooping. If anything, such informal attire made his thin, aesthetic face look even nobler.

"I hope it was not worse than an accident," he said. "I mean, this has nothing to do with the ill will between the Irish and the Dutch laborers, I'm sure."

I was not. I thought of Ernst Nooteboom's smooth-soled shoes, his sister's conviction that he could not have fallen because he was too practiced at climbing, and this young man's death acquired a sinister quality. *Well, climbers do sometimes fall*, I thought. But the thought nagged rather than reassured.

"Tomorrow we shall call on Lilli Nooteboom and pay our respects," said Abba.

LILLI NOOTEBOOM, WE learned from Eliza, lived in rooms in Mrs. Roder's boardinghouse, the big gray house at the east end of Westminster Street. The following afternoon the entire Alcott family, including Sylvia, donned their formal calling clothes, left the little cottage, and turned in the direction of that street. Anna and Abba talked quietly about household matters; Father and Lizzie murmured occasionally about family friends—dear Mr. Henry Thoreau had sent a letter from Concord, where he was working as a gardener and continuing his study of Greek. But the conversations were muffled and we walked largely in silence, a reminder of the serious purpose of our visit.

Soon the more densely placed houses and stores of Walpole thinned into irregular lots, affording a view of the Connecticut River and, just before that, the huge scar in the earth where the ground had been dug and leveled for the railroad tracks. When in employment, Ernst Nooteboom must have been able to make it from his door to his work site in less than two minutes. A practical man, I thought, willing to give up the amenities of living close to the village square in order to save time. Practical men do not hike in town shoes.

Mrs. Roder opened the door to my knocking and greeted us with a stormy expression and a broom in her arms.

"Thought you were those ruffians," she explained, placing the broom back in the corner and smoothing her apron. Her explanation did not flatter what we had considered to be our best attire. The landlady was an elderly woman, tall and strong and formidable-looking. New England stock.

"Ruffians?" asked Father, interested.

"The Irish railroad workers. They make trouble here some nights, because some of the Dutch live with me," she said somewhat apologetically, deducing now from Father's voice that he was more in the order of a gentleman. "Threw eggs at the house last week. Sad waste of good food, don't you think? They will be sorry when the law has to deal with them. Mr. Nooteboom bloodied one of their noses, after the eggs. Oh, that poor young man!"

I wiped my feet carefully before stepping off the rag rug before the door. Mrs. Roder's hall was sparkling clean. "May we pay our respects to Miss Nooteboom? I understand she lives here."

"She does. You may. Front room. It was the only room had a table long enough for that poor young man." Mrs.

Roder shook her head, pointed out the exact doorway, and went back to her chores in the pantry. The Alcott tribe moved in the assigned direction.

The sun had not yet set, but that room was almost as dark as night. Three layers of curtains had been tightly closed and only a single candle burned. Lilli Nooteboom knelt at the side of the table, a black shadow of a woman in a dark room. When my eyes adjusted I saw the spray of wildflowers lovingly spread over her brother's chest, and the crucifix holding them in place. The room was cold; pails of ice had been placed under the table to preserve the body until the burial.

Lilli started at our steps and looked over her shoulder at us.

Father, Sylvia, and my sisters took chairs that lined a wall, and sat with bowed heads. Abba and I knelt on either side of Lilli Nooteboom and offered prayers. Lilli began to sob. When Abba put her arm about her shoulders, the young woman, feeling the warmth and strength emanating from Abba, leaned her head there and wept freely. Abba had that effect on people: Here, you thought, was a personage you could trust completely.

I turned my attention to her brother, on the table. I hadn't seen Ernst Nooteboom's face before. Now I saw the strength of his jaw, his wide-set eyes and long, straight nose, and how his pale hair fell straight back from the broad forehead. He had been a fine-looking young man. *Such a man should not die so young,* I thought, *not before he has lived his share of years.*

Also evident on that fine face was a deep gash on the side of his head, and his right leg had an unnatural angle to it; bruises showed on the hands and torn fingertips; he had tried to gain a purchase to break that mortal fall. Had his fingers left marks on an attacker? He was a stranger, but like his sister I could not believe that his fall had been an accident.

We prayed together, silently, and I stayed on my knees until Lilli herself stood.

"We have not been introduced," I said then, "but we wanted to offer our sympathy."

"Thank you. So few people have come." Lilli extended her hand and swayed unsteadily from grief and the lack of sleep that often accompanies it.

"She needs air. Take her outside, Louy," Abba said. "We will stay with Mr. Nooteboom."

I took Lilli's arm and led her to the side porch, where a pretty flower bed of crimson poppies glowed defiantly against the brown earth. Lilli gulped big drafts of air, and color returned to her drained face.

"Have you been in Walpole long?" I asked, after she had wiped her eyes and blown her nose.

"Three years," said Lilli, leaning against a column for support. "Our mother and father sends us here, to make our way. I have six brothers and sisters at home." A tear splashed down her cheek, and Lilli dabbed her eyes again with her crumpled handkerchief.

"Will you go home now?" I asked gently.

"Home? No. I cannot. I am sent. I stay. Ernst would wish me to stay. We had plans. He is gone. I make plans now." She stood straight again, defiant.

I didn't think I had ever heard a braver speech. Lilli pointed past the flowers, past Mrs. Roder's lawn and picket fence, to the gash of the empty railroad bed.

"See?" she said. "That part where the trees have not been felled. That part where the railroad must pass by. That is Ernst's and mine. We buy as soon as we come and Ernst guesses the direction the track will take. We eat bread and milk, wear only one dress and one suit, save everything. Now, is mine." She gazed at the patch of mud with pride. "No, I don't leave," she said. "I stay and earn money so I can send home. And I will get an American husband, become American lady."

There was a moment of silence as we both stared into the distance, trying to see the unseeable future.

"May I ask a question, Miss Nooteboom?"

"Yes?" She looked at me with a little frown creasing the pale skin between the white-blond eyebrows.

"Did your brother often go climbing in his town shoes?"

"Never! Never would he do such a thing. I told you, we save every penny, are very careful of our wardrobe. Town shoes are not for such wearing." In her anger, she pounded a little fist against the porch railing

"How do you explain what happened, his falling from the cliff?"

"It is as I told the sheriff, when I go to his office this morning," Lilli said. "Ernst came to where I was working in Mrs. Simon's nursery—I sew the clothes for her children—and he told me he had a meeting with a man who wanted to talk about his lot. Our lot." Her gaze wandered again to the distant patch of mud that was all she owned in this world. "Ernst told me he would not sell. Ever. My children would grow up in the house we built there. The town would grow in that direction, to follow the train, and we would build a big house, big enough for an inn, and behind it a pen to fatten cattle before shipping to Boston markets. Ernst was a clever man." Her eyes glowed.

"Did your brother say where the meeting was, and with whom?"

"Not where. But yes, whom. Mr. Tupper. Always Mr. Tupper wants to talk, to meet, to buy our lot. I think in a few days, when he thinks is a good time, he will come to me with the offer, as well. And like Ernst, I will say to him no."

Lilli frowned and clenched her fingers, folded now in her lap. "There is something else," she said. "Ernst's pocket watch. Gold, from Grandpapa, and with a leather fob till we could match a gold one with it. All Ernst had of value, and he wore it always. It is gone."

"Do you remember when you last saw it?"

"I think the day he went out, the day they say he fell. Yes, he was wearing it that day. But not when they carried him home."

I put my hand over Lilli's in comfort.

"Now, Miss Alcott, I thank you for calling," she said. "But I go back to Ernst. Will you come to the funeral?"

"Of course."

RETURNING TO OUR cottage required that we walk back down Main Street, past Tupper's General Store. I remembered how the day before, Mr. Tupper had insisted repeatedly that Ernst's fall had been an accident.

"I have an errand," I said to Abba and the rest of the family. "You go ahead, and I'll be home in a few minutes." Sylvia gave me a questioning glance. I cleared my throat and she quickly decided she, too, had an errand to run. Friends often have these codes; Sylvia and I had perfected ours.

Mr. Tupper was in his shop, arranging a new shipment of cotton sheeting on a table. He looked up as we stepped in and his doorbell rang overhead. He looked wary. His ginger-colored hair was tousled, his eyes clouded and red.

"Miss Alcott and friend again," he said without enthusiasm. "May I help you?"

"I have been to see Lilli Nooteboom," I said.

He flinched, as if something heavy had fallen.

"A tragedy," he said. "If you will excuse me, I have work to see to."

"Miss Nooteboom said that her brother had an appointment with you the day of his death." I stared Tupper squarely in the face, unwilling to let him avoid my gaze, to escape my questions.

He shifted from foot to foot and twisted his hands into his paint-spattered work apron.

"That's what she told Sheriff Bowman, as well," he muttered. "I've already had a visit from him."

"Yes, Miss Nooteboom mentioned an officer of the law."

Mr. Tupper, already flushed, turned even redder. His eyes bulged somewhat with an emotion I took to be anger, and he twisted his hands into his apron, as if seeking self-control over them. I took a step backward. "Little busybody," he muttered, and I wasn't certain whether he referred to Lilli or me, until he followed it with: "And did she tell you that she and her brother were famous for their quarrels? That she had threatened to elope and he had locked her in her room for two days?"

No, she hadn't told me that.

"Did you meet with Mr. Nooteboom that day?" I asked, deciding the subtle approach had outlived its usefulness.

"I did not. How is this any business of yours?" He glared at the floor, which meant, of course, that he was lying.

"If there is an inquiry you will be asked to explain your whereabouts," I said.

"I can. I'm a busy man. It's my word against hers." The bell chimed and a woman towing two clamoring youngsters entered. He rushed over to wait on her with an alacrity I had not before observed in his attitude to customers.

He was absolutely right, of course. Her word against his.

MY MIND WAS awhirl with thoughts when we finally returned home, and I knew there would be no room in my imagination for the phrases and sentiments I needed to pursue my story about true womanhood; I decided to go for a solitary walk, instead.

My feet, of their own will, led me along the path to the bottom of the ravine. The image of Ernst Nooteboom and those rusty stains on a white shroud rose before me.

Curious, I walked the perimeter of the ravine, looking. After a half hour I found it—a spot where the ancient flat stones had been jarred loose by an impact, and marred by a rusty splatter of blood. The place where Ernst Nooteboom had died. The ravine no longer seemed quite so beautiful. I lifted my eyes from that dread disassembly of stained stones and tried to find evidence of his fall in the side of the ravine. It was there, a trail of broken ferns and smoothed dirt where a body had alternately fallen through air and tumbled down cliffside. I marked the spot in my memory, planning to explore the top of the cliff for the origins of Ernst Nooteboom's fall. Tomorrow, I told myself. It was close to suppertime, and Abba would need help.

CHAPTER FIVE

A Woodland Encounter

WAKING UP FROM a dream in which Ernst Nooteboom was carried past on his pall and the bottom of his shoes shone as smooth as glass, I rose even earlier than usual and took the mountain path up the ravine.

The path was wet and treacherous, and the bubbling brook was a frothy brown from night rains. It was a long, difficult hike over tempestuous terrain, and I was puffing and muddied from several falls by the time I reached the top.

How close the sky seemed at that place, though. The pines were tall and looked as old as Eden. Birds sang with a wilder note, and the world of teapots and parlors and the rules of etiquette seemed very far away.

The search for the place from which I estimated Ernst Nooteboom had fallen to his death took an hour, and when I found it I had to lie flat on the ground to peer over the cliff, down past the stony gray wall where pale green ferns clung, to the place where a rusty bloodstain marked a death.

There was no indication that a man, or two men, had been here two days before, and that a mortal accident had occurred. No indication except . . . and there it was, fluttering in the breeze, caught on a bramble. A piece of paper.

I rose cautiously to my feet and moved away from the edge of the ravine, toward that single inkling of man's intrusion into this wilderness.

When it was in my hand I sighed. A shopping list, pencil on brown paper. Eggs. White silk thread. A half pound of potatoes.

It could mean nothing, but it did seem to be the same paper with which Mr. Tupper wrapped his parcels.

The forest grew thicker just before this spot, with clumps of trees so dense they were like green curtains. I walked for another ten minutes or so and was soon swallowed by the shade of the ancient trees. I could have been in a fairy tale. Chipmunks darted through the leaves, unafraid, and squirrels chattered from the boughs. A doe and her fawn froze before me for a lovely moment before bounding away. Mankind and its institutions seemed far away. In fact, I seemed closer to the elf land of my childhood imaginings.

Then and there was born my next book, *Christmas Elves*, a children's collection I could time for profitable Christmas sales. I would begin it even as I was finishing my short story "The Lady and the Woman." It would be a far cry from the "blood and thunders" I published anonymously. How wondrous is the imagination, that it can beget faithless husbands, mad brides, and benign fairies, all from the same material of life!

As I walked, I became totally absorbed in this next writing project, thinking of names and plots and settings, almost unaware of the beautiful forest around me, when I heard a man's voice singing at the top of his lungs, and his song was not a church hymn. In fact, the lyrics would have made a sailor blush.

Curious, I walked toward that voice, mindless that I was alone and approaching a stranger who, judging from the diction of his chosen lyrics, drank stronger stuff than coffee at breakfast.

There was a smoldering campfire, a leaning tent, a rope clothesline with leaf-littered blankets and crumpled shirts airing on it, tin pots glinting in the sun. The pristine forest had acquired a tenement. I crouched behind a tree, spying.

The camping baritone was tall and thin, with slightly rounded shoulders and a scarecrow look to him. He was about twenty-five years of age, I estimated, with black hair and green eyes. He could have been of pleasant appearance, had he been groomed and sober. Instead his suspenders dangled about his knees and his white shirttail flooded over his waist. His trousers were grimy with dirt; his dark hair stood on end, and seeds and bristles punctuated his side whiskers. His face was red from drink.

Common sense told me to turn and leave. Curiosity bade me stay. Was he a tramp, out living rough like this? His soiled clothes appeared to be newly and expensively made, with velvet trim and brass buttons.

I watched from behind the tree, fascinated. After a minute he ceased his bawdy song and crouched before his fire. He commenced to run his fingers through his already severely disarranged hair, and I thought I heard sobs.

"Poor old sod," he muttered. "Poor old thing. I never thought that's where . . ."

I couldn't quite catch the last part of that mumbled sentence. I leaned forward, and a twig broke under my foot.

He was not as inebriated as I had first surmised.

"Who's there?" he shouted, rising to his feet. "Stand and show yourself!" He grabbed his gnarled black walking stick and brandished it in my direction.

I stepped out from behind my tree.

"I do beg your pardon," I said, smiling in what I hoped was the soothing and nonthreatening manner appropriate for addressing a madman. "I was out for a walk and . . ."

His crazed glare stopped the words in my mouth. He stared as though I were a ghost or woodland elf.

I remembered I was dressed in boy's clothing, and that in the humid warmth of the morning I had rolled up the sleeves of my sweater and my trouser legs, and both arms and legs were now bare before this stranger. Worse, a bough had removed my cap, and my hair tumbled down my back. My hair was chestnut-colored, and there was a considerable quantity of it.

"Are you a fairy?" he asked in slurred amazement.

"That I am not," I said, pulling down my sweater sleeves and knotting up my hair. "I am Miss Louisa Alcott, a visitor here in Walpole."

"Why are you dressed like that?" he asked suspiciously. "Are you in disguise? Are you here to cause more harm? Did she send for you?" He tilted his body to look at me, and I feared he would tilt himself right over into a fall. Yet I dared not approach to steady him.

"I run," I said, puzzled by his barrage of questions and determined to memorize them exactly as he had said them, since there seemed to be some purport in his phrases that needed sorting out. Instead of answering those strange questions, I stalled with one of my own: "Why are you camped in the woods?"

He sat down now, and put his chin in his hands.

"To discover fossils. And to get away from them," he said. I understood from his voice that he fled some group of people, not petrified remains. He looked up wildly. "I can say no more." He began to weep! "Go away," he sobbed, raising his fists.

I fled. Gentle reader, be assured I did not flee so quickly that I did not first ascertain one fact: This camp spot was not far from the edge of the cliff from which Mr. Nooteboom pitched to his death. I had come by a longer path, but ended up very close to that same place.

I DID NOT speak of this encounter to Abba or Father or Sylvia. Something stayed my tongue. I believe I wished to make sense of that strange encounter, to discover its meaning, and so I let it simmer in my imagination. I returned home to discover Abba singing happily in the kitchen, and enjoyed such a flush of creative energy that I went straight to my writing shed and began my elf stories, though strange worries about the death of Ernst Nooteboom fluttered through my thoughts. I spent most of the day writing, mindless of all else. Abba, my inspiration, left a tray outside my door and kept all others away.

"May I read it, once it is done?" she asked with maternal eagerness.

"I ask no greater honor than to place it in your hands," I said. In my younger days, Abba read everything I wrote. Well, almost everything. There was the issue of those lurid "blood and thunders" that I wrote for the money they brought. They were not Louisa May Alcott's work but the sins of some personage known as Anonymous and sometimes Flora Fairfield.

I emerged from my shed feeling slightly feverish, and when Abba announced we were to visit Eliza the next afternoon I almost decided to stay alone at home to rest.

Something bade me go, some instinct for discovery. It had occurred to me that Walpole was missing several young men: Ernst, who had died; Jonah Tupper, who was traveling; and Ida's son, Clarence, who likewise was said to be traveling. Such a strange coincidence!

At Eliza's the next day, I asked Ida—for of course Ida, in all her flounced glory, was in attendance—if she had heard from her traveling husband.

She trembled and sighed.

"It is unfair," she declared, gazing sadly out the window, "the things a wife must put up with. Don't you find marriage to be frightfully unfair, Abba?"

Abba, who had finished an entire sock in the length of time it took Ida to cast on one ragged row, shook her head.

"Not at all," said that staunch mother. "I can't imagine life without my family about me."

"But that's exactly what I mean!" wailed Ida. "Jonah is gone ever so long. I do worry."

At that precise moment Eliza and Mrs. Fisher came in with a tray of glasses and lemonade, followed by Uncle Benjamin. The day was breezeless and humid, and we were prostrated by a heat that pressed heavily upon us with invisible hands. It took a great force of will, I recall, simply to fan oneself.

"He's a rascal, that young husband of yours," Uncle said, giving Ida a little peck on the cheek.

"Isn't Benjamin an old sweetie?" Ida cooed, and gave a coquettish twist to her fan by using it to hide her face, except for her eyes and brows. Eliza coughed gently and caught Abba's eye.

Benjamin, dressed in his famous red cap and embroidered slippers and cape, eased himself onto the settee opposite Abba. These two were great friends, despite the long periods between visits, despite Benjamin's eccentricities. He had married her beloved sister and there was a connection between them that had grown even stronger after that sister's death. They shared memories no one else had, and there is no bond tighter than that.

"Here, old sweetie," teased Eliza, handing her father a glass of lemonade. We all settled back into our chairs and listened for a while to the drone of insects, wishing with all our hearts for a breeze to stir the curtains and lift the heat. How I longed for the simple tunics Abba had dressed us in as children, so that I might be free of the layers of muslin, the chemise, drawers, crinoline, bodice, skirts, etc., etc., that encumbered a woman in the name of modesty in those days. I always suspected they were simply trying to weigh us down to prevent a mass escape of females.

From somewhere upstairs, a child began to wail, and then there was the rhythmic sound of a rubber ball being bounced against a wall.

Eliza ignored both and sipped her iced lemonade. "I paid my respects to Lilli Nooteboom this morning," she said. "Such a tragedy."

"I feel quite faint," said Ida. She took a silver bottle from her reticule. "Medicine," she said. She poured a capful into her lemonade, and the Saturday-night smell of gin filled the room. Abba's right eyebrow cocked up.

Mrs. Fisher, the housekeeper, came in carrying a plate of sliced melon and making a show of how hard she was working. The glance she gave Ida Tupper was not warm.

"It is a sad event when a young woman has an ocean between herself and home and her brother dies, leaving her alone in a foreign country," said Uncle Benjamin, oblivious to the unvoiced female judgments that made the heavy atmosphere even heavier. "Careless of young Nooteboom to fall like that. Mrs. Tupper, may I have a spoonful of that medicine of yours?"

Eliza opened her mouth to say something, but then shut it firmly. Abba frowned. It was no secret that Uncle Benjamin was fond of what he termed "something stronger than water."

"Oh, dear," said Ida, making a face like a child who has smashed a plate, cute and guilty at the same time. "My medicine has introduced a note of discord."

"Nonsense," said Uncle. He held out his cup, and Ida poured.

"As I was saying, we visited poor Lilli Nooteboom," Eliza began again. "Now she is alone. Although solitude would not be such an awful thing. No children, no husband or parents . . ." Her voice trailed off and her eyes grew dreamy.

"Miss Nooteboom is a young person of an argumentative nature," said Uncle Benjamin, shaking his head. "She's not made many friends in Walpole. A tragedy for her, though. Now she'll have to stay in rented rooms instead of living in that house he had talked about building for them. A tragedy."

"Fate is mysterious, isn't it, Louisa?" Eliza asked, breaking out of her reverie. "Perhaps Mr. Nooteboom was meant to live in the lowlands, and height destroyed him. I'm sure there is a metaphor in there somewhere."

Uncle laughed. "'Not all is contained in your philosophies,'" he said. "That is from *Hamlet*, is it not?"

"But Louisa," Eliza said, "the strangest thing. As we were leaving Mrs. Roder's hall, that old Dr. Burroughs was entering. I hadn't thought he and Miss Nooteboom were on speaking terms, since there had been some quarrel between Ernst and the doctor."

"I believe I heard thunder in the distance," said Father, who had been drinking his lemonade in preoccupied silence.

We all sat up straighter, somewhat startled, thinking that he was speaking symbolically, as he was sometimes inclined to do.

"Thunder," he repeated. "Excellent. I put in the spinach today, and another row of potatoes. Rain is just what they need."

"Did Dr. Burroughs indicate the purpose of his visit?" I asked, feeling livelier. A breeze had started rippling the curtains and sliding papers back and forth on Uncle Benjamin's corner desk. He rose and weighted them down with books and letter openers and a little statue of a sphinx.

"He said he wished to see the corpse," Eliza said. "I would have felt more comfortable if he had said, 'view the deceased,' but he did not; he said, 'see the corpse,' and it sounded a little gruesome."

"He was a medical examiner," I explained. "He has an interest in . . ." I paused. I had almost said, "corpses." "An interest in mortal wounds," I finished.

"Well, little Lilli Nooteboom did not seem pleased to receive him," said Uncle Benjamin.

"No?" asked Abba somewhat distractedly; she had left linens hanging on the line to dry, and now it certainly looked like a storm.

"They were having words," said Eliza. "More lemonade?"

"That was thunder," Abba said. "We must try to make it home before the rain starts."

I agreed wholeheartedly, since a wet costume would mean a whole day of washing, drying, and ironing those twenty pounds of muslin that constituted accepted female attire. (Wearing Amelia Bloomer's new short skirts and trousers was still liable to get a woman arrested for indecency.) However, a thought had formed in that part of my brain in which I was keeping mental notes and jottings about the death of Ernst Nooteboom.

"What words?" I asked urgently, as the Alcott tribe rose as one and moved to the hallway.

"Why, last summer when Dr. Burroughs was visiting he exchanged angry letters with Ernst Nooteboom, and the two never made it up," Eliza said, rooting around in the cluttered hall table for Abba's straw hat. "Ernst had been ill with a high fever. Dr. Burroughs wished to inspect him to make sure it was not yellow fever. He is an old busybody, isn't he? At any rate, Ernst refused to see him. The old man was sorely wounded, thought it an affront to his reputation."

Uncle Benjamin clucked his tongue and straightened his Turkish cap, which had tilted somewhat. "You don't know what an epidemic of fever is like. Dr. Burroughs remembers the last one. He thought Ernst owed it to this community to prove he carried no mortally communicable illness."

Big drops of rain splattered heavily on the slate walk; the sky had turned a sickly green.

"Oh, dear," said Ida, frowning up at the glowering clouds. "I have my parasol, but neglected to bring my walking stick, and the paths will be slippery."

Without so much as a by-your-leave she helped herself to a cane from Uncle's elephant-foot stand.

"Good day, all," she called over her shoulder, her pink-striped skirts flashing.

THE NEXT DAY the Alcotts attended the funeral of Ernst Nooteboom. There were few mourners there, since many of the Dutch workers had already moved on to other places, while the railroad company finished its negotiations for the final line. Mrs. Roder had taken time from her chores to attend, and a few of the town's older citizens were there, as funerals sometimes pass as a form of entertainment, or perhaps preparation.

Uncle Benjamin and Cousin Eliza attended, and Ida Tupper had also arrived, dressed in black silk and lace and with a black silk corsage on her shoulder that flounced all the way up to her little pointed chin. She wept copiously and murmured, "Poor Ernst," several times.

To my surprise, Dr. Peterson Burroughs attended, dressed in his black suit and looking sterner than usual, as if he did not approve of the young dying.

"Foolish boy, foolish boy," he kept muttering. Lilli studied him from behind her handkerchief with barely concealed fear.

"I understand you tried to administer to Mr. Nooteboom last summer, during a fever," I whispered to the doctor, who had chosen a place at my side, as we circled the final resting place of that poor young man.

"He would not permit me to see him," Dr. Burroughs whispered back with some agitation. "He had never seen an epidemic of yellow fever. He endangered us all." Was the good doctor capable of carrying a grudge all the way to the graveside?

The minister looked in our direction and we ceased whispering.

The Walpole churchyard was an ancient ground filled with stone memorials of leaning angels and stone tablets of funeral poems. I made notes in my head about one particular stone angel that drooped and wept in exaggerated Gothic fashion, suitable for description in a "blood and thunder" story.

Lilli, dressed in her black mourning, looked almost like a spirit, so pale was she. She wept quietly as the minister intoned the brief service, and Abba and I held her hands throughout it for comfort.

"He did not fall," were her last words to me, when the

brief service was over and black dirt was shoveled over the wooden coffin.

But who would wish to murder the young Dutchman? Who would push him over a cliff to his death?

Someone he knew was the immediate answer, for he went to that spot willingly; he hadn't been dragged or carried. Someone he knew who had power over him of some sort, for he went to that dangerous, wild place in his town shoes. Or someone he trusted, and did not fear, until it was too late.

I wished I had spent more time with that inebriated camper, although my own sense of self-preservation had discouraged lingering at the time. It was such a small walk from that campsite to the cliff's edge.

CHAPTER SIX

The Strange Encounter
Explained

WHEN, THE NEXT day, Father found an old row of raggedy rhubarb at the edge of his weedy vegetable patch, Abba decided she would preserve the stems with sugar for next winter.

"Excellent tonic," Father said with approval. "Cleans the body. Nature does provide, doesn't it, Abba?" he asked happily.

"It should provide the jars as well as the rhubarb," said Abba. "Louy, will you walk into the town square and buy a dozen jars?"

I had finished my morning run and not yet begun my afternoon writing, so I agreed readily enough. I had woken up with a strange thought that morning. In small towns, and even in the individual neighborhoods of larger cities, shopkeepers often attend funerals when the deceased was a customer. The Nooteooms shopped at Tupper's, yet he hadn't been there. Perhaps he feared Lilli's accusations, feared that others would believe her.

"Madam, I am here to do your bidding," I said to Abba with a bow. "A dozen jars, purchased from Tupper's. And half a pound of wax for sealing, I assume."

Sylvia accompanied me, and Lizzie came along as well. She seemed to be growing even shyer, and the family had decided we should try to "bring her along" a little more.

"I don't see why you need me to come shopping with you," said Lizzie, who had been reading a sheet of music and practicing the fingering of it on the scrubbed kitchen table. While May, the youngest, was our spoiled child, Lizzie was our angel, quiet, gentle, never complaining—until one required her to don a party frock and go to some home where gavottes would be played and young men would ask for a dance, or to some afternoon party where other young women would wish to talk of hair fashions and skirt trimmings. Lizzie was more like Abba than any other of the "Golden Brood," believing that "society" was purposeful only when the stronger were helping the weaker, and that all else was frivolous and often just plain silly.

"It's silly to comb your hair up and put on a better frock just to do the marketing," she complained.

"I know, my dearest," I said. "But come just the same. Keep us company. We may need you to help carry things."

That settled it, of course. If she might be of use, all dissent from Lizzie ceased.

Walpole was enjoying a golden summer day, with red and purple flowers glowing in tidy brown beds and green trees overhead all aflutter. With each passing summer day the village seemed to grow even more beautiful. Yet a crime had occurred, I was certain, and I felt an undercurrent of menace.

I believed Lilli Nooteboom: Her brother had not fallen, but had been pushed.

Our first stop was at the post office, to send off Anna's correspondence—a dozen envelopes thick with pages of her elegant handwriting, going off to friends in Boston, Concord, Syracuse—and Father's own thick correspondence to Ralph Emerson. Our second stop was at Tupper's General Store.

It was not crowded that morning. Indeed, except for one other, we were the only customers. That other was Lilli Nooteboom.

She stood there, her face stormy, her ungloved hands clenched. She wore dusty black mourning. The two of them, Lilli and Tupper, were staring each other down in the center of the store, leaning forward but not touching, as if some macabre dance were about to begin. The bell chimed as we entered, but they seemed not to hear it.

"I know," she said, glaring at him, her white face, surrounded by all that black mourning, looking like the full moon in a midnight sky. "I know what you have done, and you will pay for it."

He stared back, his hands opening and closing into fists.

"I know," she accused, then ran out, brushing past us.

Mr. Tupper rearranged his features into their more habitual expression, something between a smile and a sneer, and took my list and basket. His glowering posture, those severely forced-back shoulders, the chin jutting into the air, even the way his ginger whiskers seemed to bristle, discouraged me from making inquiries about that confrontation between himself and Miss Nooteboom. People in the state of mind that seemed to engulf the shopkeeper usually do not talk at all, or when they do talk, express half-truths and obfuscations. Or he might just tell me it was none of my business.

Our purchases were quickly made and even more quickly paid for—ten more cents out of the thirty-two dollars I had to my name—and we left without a word other than "Good day." Tupper gave us a withering glance, which reminded me of another errand.

"We also need some greens for supper," I said to Sylvia and Lizzie when we were back in the sunlight. "Abba is making a fish chowder with river trout."

Next door, at the greengrocer's—which was frequented by Whigs and Democrats alike, since Walpole had just the one greengrocer on the square—the store was busy with shoppers and animated conversation, much of which seemed to be about Ernst Nooteboom and his sister. "Looking to buy that acreage near the river," I heard one man say. "Add to the lot he already had."

"Tupper wanted it for his son," another whispered.

I hovered over a bin of strawberries and selected a basket for our dessert. Eliza had a strawberry patch, but her brood had dispatched the fruits almost before they were ripe. Another dime gone from my steadily lightening purse. How soon, I wondered, before I sold another story? Would the *Saturday Evening Gazette* purchase "The Lady and the Woman"? And could I finish my tale of woodland elves in time for Christmas? That was a lovely thought—another book in the Boston Corner Book Shop, perhaps right next to Father's and a shelf or two above Emerson's, a case over from Hawthorne's; poor Henry Thoreau, down there alone on the right in the Ts. If I finished *Christmas Elves* in time for that holiday, think of the celebration the Alcotts could have!

"Louy?" asked Sylvia. "You seemed to disappear there for a moment."

"Ah. A lovely daydream struck me," I said.

Just as we were leaving the store, Dr. Peterson Burroughs entered, towing two unhappy-looking grandchildren who just about reached his knees. "A penny each," the doctor said sternly.

"Mama let us have two pennies each on Tuesday, after our castor oil," the older of the two spoke up, looking up at her grandfather with huge, round black eyes.

"She is a spendthrift," said the gentleman. He spied me and tipped his old-fashioned derby hat. The other men of Walpole wore the new light straw boaters to keep the sun off their heads, and much fun they were, too, those wispy hats that tended to fly off and leap about the streets; it was a pleasure to see men chase their hats like children chasing their hoops. But Dr. Burroughs wore his beaver hat in winter and his derby in summer, and that was that, I assumed.

"Ah, Miss Alcott. You have recovered from the sad occupation of yesterday? Not feeling liverish? Funerals are not good for young women, not good." His smile was vulpine.

"I would rather they were unnecessary, especially when the deceased dies before his reasonably expected length of years, but one goes to these rituals to support friends in mourning," I said.

He looked at me from under his knitted brows. "I, too, felt it my duty. Yes, my duty. A man must do his duty, even when it is unpleasant."

His emphasis on *duty* left me somewhat queasy; it was a word used often by politicians to justify the unjustifiable, as in, "It is our duty to return fugitive slaves to their owners." What had Dr. Burroughs meant by it?

BACK AT THE Alcott cottage, I unpacked my shopping basket at the kitchen table. Abba looked unhappy.

"Eliza and Benjamin are here examining Father's vegetable patch," she said. "And Mrs. Tupper and her son are in the parlor. He seems to have returned from wherever he has been. It's not quite clear. Well. Best to get tea over with. Prepare yourselves." Abba handed me the teapot to carry in, while she and Sylvia cut and buttered more bread for the tray.

I saw him before I entered the room, his dark hair and sunburned face peeking through the fringes of the parted doorway curtain. It was the strange young man I had encountered at the forest campsite. He was better groomed, of course, with a clean shirt and stock, dark jacket, and his dark hair brushed back from his bronzed forehead. His back and shoulders seemed not quite so rounded, and he carried himself with self-assurance. His green-and-gray needlepoint waistcoat set off his green eyes very smartly. He would have caused quite a stir in what Sylvia and I termed the "meat market" afternoon socials of Boston, where mothers displayed their marriageable daughters.

I paused. It happened, in that pause, that I overheard a bit of conversation. Is it my fault if people will continue private discourse even after they hear a tread at the threshold?

"You should never have married him," muttered this young man, making fists that he held at his sides.

"You've seen his postal cards; you know as well as I, there's been no harm," Ida Tupper whimpered.

"That is not good enough. Tell me the—"

But just then Sylvia came into the hall with the clattering tea tray, and Ida Tupper and this young man stepped apart from each other and assumed neutral expressions.

"Louisa, my dear," said Ida Tupper with forced good cheer. "Come in, come in." She invited me into Abba's parlor as if it were her own. "Meet my son, Mr. Hampton."

Clarence Hampton and I stared at each other in amazement.

"The running fairy," he said.

I thought it wiser not to exclaim, "My weeping tramp!"

"You have met?" Mrs. Tupper asked, her voice high with surprise and a little distrust. I have often remarked that tone of voice in mothers who have sons of a marriageable age when those sons are smiling in a friendly manner at a young single woman without fortune or prospects of one—a woman such as myself.

"We have, ever so briefly," I admitted. "Please have a chair, Mr. Hampton, and don't stand about so formally." He sat. Mrs. Tupper looked pale and trembled slightly; she seemed afraid of Mr. Hampton, whose teeth were clenched and whose eyes flashed angrily whenever he looked at his mother.

Sylvia gave me a knowing glance and sat next to me on the faded settee. She looked longingly out the window to where Benjamin and Eliza were admiring Father's vegetable patch.

"Please meet my friend, Miss Sylvia Shattuck," I said.

Sylvia gave Clarence Hampton a forced smile, which he returned with a curt nod. He seemed in an unsociable mood. Had he come to tea simply to quarrel with his mother?

"Clarence has been on a trip, haven't you, dear?" said Mrs. Tupper. She had dressed in dark blue that day, with skirts so fully crinolined they puffed and billowed like high seas on a stormy day. Her hair had been pulled back into a snood decorated with glass pearls, and she had rubbed rouge into her lips and a little stove black into her brows. She looked pretty, in a bold sort of way.

"Just as you say, Mother," said he of the flashing green eyes and clenched jaw.

"His avocations often take him afield," she continued, fussing with the knitting in her lap. She had taken to carrying it about constantly, but never seemed to make much progress with it. "Like his stepfather. It is my misfortune to surround myself with men who must wander. Except for my dearest brother, of course, who is completely housebound." She sighed heavily, and I'm sure would have shed a tear if I gave her my full attention. I did not.

"Are you also a man of business?" I asked her son.

"I am an amateur scientist," said Clarence Hampton. "An undergroundologist." He did not look at me when he spoke; I could tell he remembered our earlier meeting and was ashamed of it. He had been drunk; he had cursed and wept. Why?

"Ah," I exclaimed now with interest. "The new science of geology."

"Some call it that, though the name will not hold. No, it

will be hereafter referred to as undergroundology," Mr. Hampton asserted with masculine confidence, and finally raised his eyes to meet my glance.

I had a tart retort on the tip of my tongue for Mr. Hampton, my own impression that most people will not prefer a science with six syllables to one with four, but at that moment Uncle Benjamin ambled in, wearing his red fez cap and tapestry slippers, as usual. He had added an embroidered robe—Arabic, I think it was—to his ensemble, and he looked, for all the world, as if he belonged to some eccentric gentleman's club and was costumed for the Fourth of July parade.

"Benjamin, Benjamin." Mrs. Tupper sighed, shaking her head so that the pearled snood swung with disapproval.

"My dear?" Uncle asked, genuinely puzzled by Ida's criticism. "Louy, pour me some tea, if you will."

"Were you speaking of geo . . . of undergroundology when I first entered and brought your conversation to a close?" I asked Ida Tupper.

She began trembling once again. Her son laughed most oddly.

"Yes, in a way," he admitted. "Shall I tell them, Mother?" He rose and stationed himself before the fireplace, as if to begin a lecture.

"Do behave, and if you can't, then leave us," said Ida Tupper.

He gave her a look that . . . well, if any of my family had given me such a look I would have turned to salt.

"It seems we are not to speak of it now," said Clarence Hampton, sitting down again.

85

Uncle Benjamin came into the parlor with his spyglass jutting from his pocket.

"They are disrupting the raven population," he said. "Down where they ceased laying the train tracks and left the earth gashed, there was an old rookery down there, and now the birds are showing up everywhere."

"I hope they don't roost in the chimney or the attic," said Ida Tupper. "Clarence, you must go up there with boards and nails and make sure there are no holes."

Clarence nodded and stared out the window. Sylvia passed him the plate of biscuits, and he took one without even looking at her. Eliza's housekeeper had said he was fast, but he seemed oddly immune to my friend's appeal. His obvious indifference seemed even stranger, since his mother knew of Sylvia's wealth and certainly had passed that information on to her son.

Abba came in carrying a second pot of hot water for the teapot and announcing that her rhubarb had just come to a simmer and must be stirred, so she could not join us. She left as quickly as she had entered, with a briskness of step that bespoke dallying.

"Rhubarb preserves," said Ida Tupper. "It's ever so long since I've had them. Wonderful blood tonic. I wonder if they are carried in town? I was doing my shopping this morning, and stopped in to pay my respects to my father-in-law, though he never returns the courtesy. I could have asked about rhubarb." She barely took a breath between such disparate topics as ravens and roosts and relatives. "He has made a bid on Lilli Nooteboom's lot. Do you think she will sell, Benjamin?"

"I hear the Dutch are stubborn," answered Uncle. "Ida,

you mustn't think of financial matters; it will bring on the migraine."

"You are right, Benjamin," she answered meekly. "I have a husband and son and brother to think about such matters for me. I think women who understand money are so masculine."

Clarence Hampton made that odd laugh once again.

"Mrs. Tupper, how is your brother's health today?" I asked, wishing I could redirect the conversation to the science of geology and knowing she would not allow it. Etiquette was quite strict on what was permitted for discussion in the parlor and what was not. Talk of the new science, like politics, like finance, was reserved for other areas of domestic life, for that magic hour when the men rose from the table and went to the porch or to the den with their brandy and cigars. Oh, how I envied them that hour.

"Poor, poor man. He is not better, Louisa, thank you for asking. He is much in need of nursing. In fact, I should be going now. It is time for his afternoon bowl of broth, and he will take it from no hands but my own." She rose with much fussing and smoothing of skirts and patting of curls into place. "Come along, Clarence, since you are not in a social mood."

Clarence woke as if from a dream. His gaze lingered on Sylvia in belated acknowledgment of her. He rose and took her hand, placing a kiss on the fingertips. Sylvia blushed.

I saw mother and son to the door.

"Forgive me if I seem indiscreet, but it seemed to me you were in a moment of discord when I arrived in the parlor," I said to them. "Is there a matter in which I may be of assistance?"

Mr. Hampton gave me a long, steady look. The fire in his eyes calmed; his face grew composed, almost masklike. "I had just told Mother I had entered an arrangement to collect fossils for private collectors," he said. "She disapproves."

"Hardly the work for a gentleman," she added. "All that digging. He will ruin his hands."

"Oh, families are just horrid!" Sylvia exclaimed when I returned to the parlor. "How mean of Confucius to say that filial piety is the root of humanness." She stomped from the room.

Uncle Benjamin stared after her, amazed. "What a strange girl. Have I offended her?"

I gave him a quick hug. "Not you," I said. "She has developed an aversion, I think, to teatime, since it often seems to produce bachelors along with the tea tray."

"Well, she'd be better off not thinking of Clarence Hampton in that way." Benjamin stood and tapped his walking stick on the floor for emphasis.

"Why do you say that, Uncle?" I asked.

"He's even stranger than Miss Sylvia, a real handful, coming and going at all hours, mucking about on the mountain digging for fossils instead of taking up a real career. Amateur scientist. I never. But his mother won't say a word against him, even when he sulks all day. I suspect he's jealous. That young man cannot abide it when his mum caters to another. She's warned me. He had tantrums as a tot."

So Clarence was one of those men who required all their mother's attention? How had he felt when his mother had married? What were the relations between Clarence and his absent stepfather?

"I've seen a tintype of Mr. Jonah Tupper, Ida's husband," I said. "He seems young."

"He is," Uncle Benjamin said. "A callow youth. Ida and Jonah met at the Fourth of July celebration last year. She and her brother had taken a house for the summer, for the country air, she said. Well. Jonah and Ida are young. They eloped. Louy, promise you'll never elope. It shames the family."

"I promise," I said, refraining from pointing out that Ida, the "young" bride, already had a grown son at the time of her elopement.

I sipped my tea. It had gone cold. I drank it anyway.

"Ida made a bad choice," Benjamin continued. "Young Tupper turned out to be a scoundrel, up and left. Wouldn't be surprised if he has a girlfriend or two in other counties. My dear, I shouldn't be speaking of such matters with you. Abba would be furious with me. You are much too young."

"I am grown and I have heard sadder stories in Boston."

"Young Jonah packed his valise and travel samples in November, and hasn't set foot in Walpole since. Have you ever seen the samples they make for bells? Tiny, dollhouse size, but the sound is . . ." Uncle rambled on, and I followed my own train of thoughts.

"Did Clarence and his stepfather get along?" I asked. Uncle stopped in midsentence. He had still been speaking of bells.

"No. Clarence seems to get along only with pretty young women." Uncle Benjamin sighed. "He's helpful for chores and mending the steps and such—that is, when he's down from the mountain—but a moodier young man I've never known. He kicks cats, and you know what I think of men who kick cats.

You've met Clarence, my dear," Uncle said, "and if you have an ounce of sense you'll keep clear, and your friend will, as well."

"We will stay clear, thank you," I said.

"Clear of what?" asked Father, who came in just then, mindless of time and wondering when tea would be put out.

CHAPTER SEVEN

Confrontation in the Forest

PROMISES ARE DIFFICULT to keep, though I broke my pledge to Uncle to "steer clear" in a form neither of us anticipated. Curiosity about Mr. Hampton's campsite, and its proximity to that place from which Ernst Nooteboom had fallen, led to another unexpected encounter with Clarence Hampton.

Friday of that week I finished my morning run in the ravine with considerable energy still left. I thought often of Mr. Nooteboom and regretted his untimely demise in such a beautiful place. But it was beautiful, and if one avoided places where death had occurred . . . well, there would be few places we could inhabit in this world.

The evening before, Ida Tupper had come over for another knitting lesson from Abba, and had said something about being lonely because Clarence had taken the barge up to Charleston for some supplies not available in Walpole. She expected him to be gone several days, for he would probably do some fossil digging there, as well.

I used the opportunity of his absence to hike up the ravine to his camp. I hid behind thick trees for several moments, watching for signs of occupation and activity. There were none. The stone-ringed campfire was black and damp-looking; the blankets that would have been airing in the sun, the pots, all the detritus of human activity were out of sight, probably stored inside the brown oil tent while their owner was away. I came out from behind my tree and approached the tent.

Boldly I pulled the flap and, on my knees, peered inside. I remembered my childhood yearning to be a boy as I studied that tidy interior, with the brightly striped camp blankets folded over a thin mattress made of straw, the shining pots hanging from a chain, clanging in the slightest breeze, the lantern next to the mattress, and the pile of books there, waiting to be read. How lovely to sleep in the open, undisturbed except by the call of the owl or the nightingale!

Reluctantly I let the flap drop and backed out of it on my knees, a strong sense of trespass making my cheeks feel hot.

I walked around the tent, which was solidly anchored some twenty yards from the edge of the cliff, where a thicket of bushes and trees obscured the view. Still, it did not seem possible that Ernst Nooteboom could fall (or be pushed?) from there and not have that fall be witnessed by Mr. Hampton, if Mr. Hampton were in his camp that morning.

Had he been? His mother had said he was out of town.

I paced, hands behind my back, studying the ground and finding nothing unexpected, only footprints going back and forth from tent to campfire, footprints coming and going from the path that led to this secluded place. There were no signs of violence, nothing on which my imagination could concentrate or focus. If only I knew what to look for!

I sat under an ancient oak, enjoying its filtered light, the cool feel of the air that swirled under its thick canopy of leaves. My eyes closed of their own accord.

A hand clamped roughly onto my shoulder and pulled me to my feet.

"What are you doing here, Miss Alcott?" Clarence Hampton, his face just inches from mine, was furious. His green eyes glinted dangerously. He shook me with such vigor that my head snapped back and his fingers tore into my arms.

For a moment I felt true fear. If I screamed I would be heard by nobody. Only the chattering squirrels and chirping birds were close enough to heed my cries. Then common sense prevailed, and surfacing up came the courage and outrage required for self-preservation.

"Mr. Hampton, unhand me," I said calmly. And to make my point, I brought up both my arms at once and broke his hold on me. It was a street trick I had learned from a Boston urchin who had tried to pinch my reticule. (Instead, the child let me buy him a raisin bun and sugar water in exchange for conversation and a few demonstrations of his singular talents.)

Mr. Hampton and I stood, separated only by inches, glaring and trembling, he in anger and I in outrage. A gentleman does not put his hands on a lady in that manner. And then, of course, it occurred to me: Clarence Hampton was not a gentleman. He dressed well and spoke well, but those are easily acquired arts. His origins were elsewhere. His mother, Ida Tupper, was evidence, for she was no lady.

He was the first to drop his eyes, finding as an excuse the

need to straighten his hat, which had been knocked askew. Oh, reader, how deep is the heart! I felt pity for him!

"Forgive me," he said with a complete lack of repentance. "You took me by surprise. It is not wise for a woman to be here alone. This can be a dangerous place."

"So I have heard." I straightened my own tilted cap.

He reached up and tucked a lock of loosened hair back under it. "I rather prefer this morning attire to your afternoon tea frock," he said gently. "But tell me, Miss Louisa, what are you doing here?" He carried a string of trout over his shoulder, and his trousers were damp at the ankles. He had been fishing, not taking the barge to Charleston. I made a note to pay little attention to anything Mrs. Tupper said.

There was no response I could make that would not aggravate the situation. If I lied, he would see it was a lie. If I admitted to a curiosity about the matter of Ernst Nooteboom's death so close to his campsite, that would hardly soothe the situation. So I said only, "Sorry to have intruded." I walked away, feeling his eyes bore into my back. It was difficult to walk slowly and calmly, rather than break into a run.

"Miss Louisa!" he called, his voice having resumed its cynical tones. "Miss Louisa, I really mean you no harm. But you would be safer to avoid this place."

It could have been a well-meant warning about the dangers of trekking alone so far from town. It could have been a threat.

THAT SECOND ENCOUNTER with Ida Tupper's son only increased my curiosity about her household, and I decided it was time to pay a call on her brother, the invalid. Courtesy required it of me, after all. We were neighbors.

"Let me guess," said Sylvia, when I asked her to accompany me that afternoon. "To meet Mrs. Tupper's brother."

"Excellent. And how do you come to that knowledge?"

Sylvia grinned. "Because it is the place I least wish to visit."

The Tupper house, immediately next door to our cottage, was whitewashed, with a huge front porch and stained-glass windows. It was large, very large, I thought, for a family of four: Ida, Jonah, and her son and brother, especially considering that the son and husband seemed rarely at home. Ida, judging from her stylish afternoon gowns, exotically feathered hats, and habit of name-dropping ("I had tea with Mrs. Bellows, my dear, such an old sweetie. She has promised to introduce me to the governor, when next he is in Walpole!"), had great expectations.

I pulled the doorbell. It took a very long time for the housekeeper to answer. She was a young girl—very young for the position, it seemed to me, and somewhat simple of mind. Abba would not have approved of such an arrangement; the child still belonged with her mother.

"Yes, miss?" she said with a curtsy, holding the door only partly open and gazing up at me with huge eyes. "The missus ain't at home."

"Is Mr. . . ." I faltered. "I am here to see Ida Tupper's brother," I said, realizing I did not know his name.

" 'Cor," cooed the little housekeeper, making her eyes even larger. "No one comes to see 'im!"

"Well, it would seem we are here to rectify that oversight. Announce us, please, my dear. And, miss, what is his name?"

I thought her brown eyes would fall out, so large had they become. "Mr. Wattles, miss. Mr. Jonathon Wattles. Wait here."

With much turning and looking over her shoulder, the little housekeeper made her slow way down the long hall and disappeared through a door at the end of it. I heard mumbling and exclamations; a thud that indicated a piece of furniture had been knocked into or even turned over, much rustling of paper and scraping of chairs on floors.

A full ten minutes later the child housekeeper came back out and signaled that we were to come down the hall and enter. She curtsied again and closed the door after we had entered that room.

It smelled as all invalids' rooms smell, of lavender and mint compresses and the more stringent scent of a body that has not had enough fresh air and sunshine. The curtains were even more tightly drawn than in the waking room at Mrs. Roder's boardinghouse. I could barely see. When my eyes adjusted I made out, in the darkest corner, a chaise and a figure on it, wrapped in blankets despite the warmth of the afternoon.

"Forgive the dreary atmosphere," said an old man's quavering voice, "but the light hurts my eyes." He coughed, and a spasm seemed to shake the breath out of him. "I am afraid a mistake has been made. My nephew, Mr. Hampton, is not at home, nor is his mother. Annie should have told you."

"I have come to make your acquaintance, sir," I said. "I have the house opposite and wanted to make myself known to you, as your new neighbor."

"How kind!" He beamed. "I never have company. Come

sit by me, my dear. You are my new neighbor? Ida has mentioned you."

"I hope my visit does not inconvenience you. Yes, I am Miss Louisa Alcott of Boston, visiting for the summer with Mr. Benjamin Willis and his family. This is my good friend Sylvia Shattuck." I approached and sat on a chair opposite. It was an old-fashioned ladder-back chair such as the kind used in waiting rooms and offices, designed not for comfort but to keep visits short.

"No inconvenience at all," he said, and another cough shook his body. He was silver-haired and elderly, with a beautifully groomed white beard flowing over his chest. Ida's mother must have borne sister and brother with many years between them, but that was not uncommon.

"Shall I ring for tea?" the gentleman asked.

"Don't bother. I see you are trying to rest. I know you have recently returned from a journey to Boston, and must be greatly fatigued. But I brought a gift, since we are neighbors." I smiled, and my smile was returned, though his was a tight, close-lipped smile.

"Rhubarb preserves." He accepted the jar with reluctance. "Generous of you, very generous. My digestion does not allow such delicacies, but I'm sure Ida will enjoy it on her evening toast. Be a dear and put it on the table there. I will give it to her when she returns." He coughed. "Don't be afraid, child. Come closer," he said to Sylvia, who had hung back. Sylvia took two steps closer.

"Do you play?" I asked, spying a large cabinet piano in the corner.

His laugh had a dreary ring to it. "I used to. Now my hands

are useless." He brought one out briefly from under the blanket and it had a clawlike quality to it. "Rheumatism." He sighed.

"I am sorry. It must pain you."

"Especially when it rains. But I must not complain. I have my sister. She plays for me, and reads to me until her voice gives out." His smile was resigned. "My nephew attempts to amuse me with his fossils."

"You must happily anticipate Mr. Jonah Tupper's return, to provide you with companionship," I said.

"I must," he agreed with a pronounced lack of enthusiasm. He seemed disinclined to pursue a conversation. Many invalids, when left alone too often, lose the art of conversation. He yawned.

I stood. "Well, I'll not tire you further. Good day, Mr. Wattles."

"Good day, my dear. Call anytime." His voice was friendly, but I doubted his sincerity. He seemed content with his tightly closed curtains, that dark, airless room, and I wondered how gay Ida Tupper suffered through her long evenings at home. How eager she must be for the return of her young husband, even if her brother was not.

I VENTURED TO ask Mrs. Tupper about her husband the next afternoon, when she arrived for another knitting lesson with Abba.

Ida put down her knitting needles and brought a piece of paper out of her reticule. She quickly returned the paper before I could get a look at it, as if it were too precious to give into other hands.

"Yes, I have had a message from my precious Jonah," she said happily. "Mr. Tupper is somewhere in Michigan, and has taken several large orders for church bells. We shall be able to purchase a new carriage next spring."

"Have you need of a carrriage? Walpole seems a very walkable place," Abba said.

"Oh, yes," said Ida Tupper. "No lady goes without a carriage. Our position will require it, and Jonah is so very good at his work of selling bells. When I write to him I always say, 'Dearest Jonah, when you enter the Pearly Gates, as you are certain to do, virtuous as you are, you will hear your own bells ringing.'" Ida Tupper picked up her knitting needles and beamed, pleased with her witticism.

"If you know only that he is somewhere in Michigan, how do you get such messages delivered?" I couldn't help but ask. Really, even the simplest of minds must have a hint of logic to it. Her smile evaporated.

"Why, Clarence mails the correspondence and keeps track of such things," said that trusting mother, frowning with confusion. "I will ask him. But now it is time for my walk." She rose with a self-conscious smoothing of her pink taffeta skirts. "We musn't turn into an invalid like my brother, Mr. Wattles. Do you wish to take the air, Benjamin?"

Cousin Eliza's eyebrows shot up. She was also in the kitchen, helping Anna put up a patch of dilly beans, and Benjamin was there as well, for he had finally found a volume of Confucius in his library and had brought it over for Father.

Uncle Benjamin rose, gave me a hug, and then picked up his cane. "Got to keep the old legs limber," he said. "Will your brother be joining us, Mrs. Tupper? The air would do him good."

"Perhaps we should send Louisa over to minister to him," suggested Eliza.

"I think not," Mrs. Tupper said quickly. "He needs peace and quiet. The slightest sound gives him torment."

"Well," said Uncle Benjamin, and he gave his arm to Mrs. Tupper.

"Have a nice walk," I said.

When she looked back at me, her smile was triumphant.

"I do not like this situation," said Eliza after they had left. She shook her head. "Father out walking with Mrs. Tupper."

"There is no real situation," said Abba in her consoling "there, there" voice. "All men like a bit of attention."

"I think tomorrow I will ask Uncle Benjamin to walk with me," I said. "I have had little opportunity to speak with him this summer. I had forgotten how busy life in the country can be."

Eliza shot me a grateful glance.

ABBA COOKED US a fish chowder that night. "Mr. Hampton sent over the trout," she said. "Wasn't that thoughtful?"

Very. I couldn't help but wonder if he was bribing me into silence, not to reveal our confrontation in the forest. Well, I wouldn't—not for him but because it would worry Abba.

CHAPTER EIGHT

A Game of Croquet

THE NEXT DAY was mild and dry—perfect walking weather, perfect weather for taking aside a beloved elderly uncle and having a heart-to-heart. He had warned me to steer clear of Mr. Hampton; now I must try respectfully to warn him of the possible misinterpretations that could be placed upon his friendship with Ida Tupper.

We began with talk of other matters, and I asked him if he knew aught of Dr. Peterson Burroughs, for that aged medical examiner continued to intrigue me.

"He's going to make a bid on Lilli's land, when she auctions it off," said Benjamin, tapping his walking stick. He carried the Egyptian ebony with the silver Hathor handle. We were walking by the river, scouting for the deep pools where the trout liked to swirl and jump. I wondered at which of these places Mr. Hampton had been fishing the day before.

"Does he wish, at his advanced age, to build another house?" I asked.

"Not Dr. Burroughs. He's an antiprogressive. He wants the land so no one else can build on it. Such a purchase would delay the completion of the railroad for a long, long time, I think," Uncle Benjamin said. "I wish I had known them," he continued, stepping cautiously over a mud puddle.

"Known what?"

"The good old days that Burroughs keeps talking about." Uncle laughed.

"I wonder to what extent Dr. Burroughs would go to stall that progress he so hates," I mused.

"Don't worry your head about it," said Benjamin, obviously of that school that equates the feminine nature with an inability to do sums.

The path was muddy, and I hitched my skirts up to my knees, revealing patches and a few new holes in my stockings. Such open revelation of the condition of one's stockings was reprehensible, certainly, but preferable to spending the rest of the day scouring mud off the hem of my dress.

It was a lovely day, filled with sun and birdsong and, now, Uncle Benjamin's companionship. We linked arms and walked in silence for some moments when a wider path allowed this affectionate display.

We turned a corner in the muddy path and the river widened, revealing a semicircle cut into the bank where sun glittered on shallow water. This little arena was filled with minnows darting this way and that; I crouched down for a better look, oblivious now to the damage to my dress. There is something about the way the sun shines on darting fish that entrances me, as if the water has taken prisoner a gliding moonbeam; as a child in Concord I spent many hours with a muddied, crouching Henry Thoreau, mesmerized by the sight.

"There is something else we should discuss, however briefly is up to you," I began cautiously, remembering there was a purpose to this walk.

Because his knees had stiffened with age he could not sit beside me at the river's edge, and so there was no chance of eye contact, which was just as well. "Mrs. Tupper seems to spend much of her time in your company."

"And Eliza's," he said. He tried to crouch, and his knees made the most alarming noises. "She is lonely."

"Yes, but it seems to me that Mrs. Tupper plays the coquette with you, you know."

"Indeed!" Benjamin snorted. He looked pleased. I could see how a man of his years could be flattered. "Indeed." He grinned and sat, with some effort, on a log. His knees again creaked as loudly as a rusty gate. "Well, I am old enough to be her father."

That was even more alarming than his noisy knees. When men protest of a paternal age in that manner they are often obscuring contradictory desires.

"She is alone too much," he continued. "Her husband has gone off, and that son of hers . . . well, I wouldn't count on him for anything. Are we to leave her on her own? You've met her, Louy. You see that she is uncomplicated, almost innocent, like a young girl. If I don't keep an eye on her, she may come to grief." He poked his cane in the water and stirred up a swirl of mud.

"Then you have set about to preserve Mrs. Tupper's virtue," I said. "You are a romantic." *A hopeless romantic,* I could have added.

AFTER OUR WALK, Uncle Benjamin turned down the path to his house with a decidedly jaunty step. I went in the other direction, to the county clerk's office. So much talk about land values and speculation prompted me to look at the local deeds and maps. The clerk made it plain by his loud slamming of the wooden bureau drawers that I, an outsider, should have little interest in local land ownership, but I spent an interesting hour checking boundary lines. Mr. Tupper had recently purchased many acres on the north town line. Lilli Nooteboom's acreage along the river was completely fenced in by his own. I knew that in the country adjoining acreage was a reason to marry; was it also a reason to murder? Below the Nooteboom and Tupper acres—completely overwhelmed by them, in fact—was a little plot marked *Burroughs.* The doctor owned land that had, until this decade, faced onto miles of virgin wilderness. Now his land, to say nothing of his view, faced the development instincts of a new generation.

Uncle Benjamin owned two lots, one containing the house now inhabited by the Alcotts, and the house in which he lived with his daughter, Eliza, and son-in-law and grandchildren. Both lots were well within the old town limits.

AT BREAKFAST THE next morning, Anna buttered her bread with great concentration as I described my ramble with Uncle Benjamin.

"Uncle is lonely, even living in the midst of Eliza's pack," she said. The Alcott family, as usual, was up at dawn, and Abba's "Golden Brood," the Alcott girls, gathered around the table, eating, Abba said with joy, like farmhands. Father was already in his study, and Abba was at the open window, inhaling deeply and admiring the mountains.

Soon she will marry, I thought, watching Anna. She had no beau that we knew of, and Anna wasn't the kind to keep secrets. But the previous winter spent working as a governess in Syracuse had changed her; being away from her family had imbued her with both independence and sadness, for solitude had not suited her. I thought soon she would want her own family, so she might never be alone again.

And what would become of me? Marriage was far from my thoughts. I was more concerned with writing, and always in the back of my mind was that character, Jo, the tomboy whose story I had yet to discover.

Anna looked up from her toast, smiled, and commented, "I have news as well. They seem to take two things very seriously in Walpole: politics and gardening."

I looked at her expectantly over my morning paper, an edition posted from Manchester. I had just opened the page to the theater section. Gentle reader, I was still at the stage of my life in which I considered a career on the stage and spent hours thinking how I might perform four times a week, rehearse twice a day, tour most of the month, and still write my stories. I had not yet found that plan. It seemed to require an extra afternoon for every day, and an extra day for every week.

"Dearest Anna, the basis for your observation?" I asked.

"Well, yesterday when you were walking with Uncle Benjamin I decided to walk to the square and buy some stationery. I purchased it at Hubert's, the Democratic store, rather than at Tupper's, the Whig store. I have heard the prices are lower there."

"A fatal error," I teased, referring to her choice, not the prices.

"It was!" Anna blushed. "When I came out of the store, one of Eliza's friends saw me and said, 'You're as bad as Lilli Nooteboom. She and her brother shopped here. See what happened to them.' And then she walked past and stuck her nose in the air." Anna was amazed.

"I should have warned you," I said. "When I first arrived, Eliza was very pointed in her instructions that I was to shop only at Tupper's. 'It's like this,' Eliza told me. 'The Whigs want the railroad to finish coming through as soon as possible, even if it means some people have to sell their land or even houses cheap to make way. The Democrats rant about losing family rights and being sold out to the merchants and industrialists. But industry is the future, isn't it?' And so Walpole takes this matter of where one shops very seriously."

"Surely not seriously enough to push one over a cliff, for that's what this woman seemed to hint at," said Anna, shaking her head.

"No," I said with great uncertainty. "It could not have come to that." Could it? Execution for shopping on the wrong side of the street? Yet Mr. Nooteboom had thereby slighted hot-tempered Mr. Tupper, who was a Whig, and it was Mr. Tupper whom Lilli had accused.

"Oh, Louy, you are supposed to be having a rest," said Anna, who guessed the direction of my thoughts.

"And what of the gardening?" I asked, to distract her. "You've learned they also take that quite seriously."

"Well, the townspeople have started to come by Father's garden in the afternoon to offer advice and make comments," she said.

"All of which Father ignores," I said.

"Of course," said Anna. "Besides, it hardly seems he needs advice. His seedlings are growing quite nicely."

"See for yourself." Abba rose and went to the window. She pointed to the raggedy rows of determined little sprouts already reaching to the sun.

"Good soil," said Abba with a smile.

"It must be miraculous soil," I said. "I wonder what was planted there last year?"

"Probably nothing, since the cottage was vacant," said Abba.

"But when I first began setting up our household, that side patch had been dug up," I said.

"Louy, don't turn everything into a mystery," said Abba, humming a little tune.

I stayed at the window for a long while, looking at that patch of ground between our house and Ida Tupper's. My imagination, the one that creates bodies in moonlit gardens and widows in Cuba and love-weary damsels who leap from bridges, my "blood and thunder" imagination added a strange new scent of sickly-sweet rot wafting in from the window overlooking the vegetable patch.

It called to mind something that Dr. Peterson Burroughs

had said on our train journey north to Walpole; that it was first the smell that led him to the place wherein the murderer, Webster, had hidden the left thigh of George Parkman.

I took my coffee cup to the sink and folded up the paper. A notice on page four, which I hadn't finished reading, caught my eye. A Peter Dodge had been buried recently in Manchester, *mourned by few*, and *survived or not, as their where-abouts are unknown, by two brothers*, as the paper bluntly stated. I would have to remember to tell Eliza's housekeeper, Mrs. Fisher, that one of the villains of her childhood had been laid to rest.

ANNA SET UP a croquet set, borrowed from Ida Tupper, in our back lawn, explaining that the new game was a great favorite among her friends in Syracuse and we should learn it as well. Reader, as you know by now the Alcotts were not part of the new moneyed leisure class and had little time for games. But it was summer, and both the Alcott and May names (from Abba's side) were well respected in the East; Anna was deter-mined we should "keep up."

Eliza left the children at home with Frank, who was re-framing a doorway, and joined us, and it was good to see that weary woman grow merry with sport and the light conversa-tion that accompanies a carefree summer afternoon.

"Now, knock your ball through the wicket and push mine out of the way," Anna instructed Lizzie.

"But that seems so rude!" Lizzie protested.

"Indeed, it does," agreed Eliza, swinging her mallet to relax her wrists more, as previously instructed by Anna.

"I'll do it," said May with gusto, racing forward to accomplish the required move.

"But it was my turn!" wailed Lizzie.

Anna pushed her straw hat lower over her forehead to keep the sun out of her eyes. She laughed and laid her mallet on the green grass. "You must play by the rules, darlings, or the game makes no sense at all."

"Even then, it hardly makes sense," said I.

Sylvia, watching from the sidelines, declared in a superior voice, "I have seen greater activity and athletic accomplishment at the meeting of a stamp-collecting club."

"Then you come play," Eliza said. "You can have my mallet."

"No. Confucius did not approve of competitive play."

"You made that up," I accused somewhat testily, for I had planned to spend the afternoon visiting again with Lilli Nooteboom (and, hopefully, learning more about the situation between Ernst and Mr. Tupper) but had been gently coerced into this game instead.

Sylvia took from her pocket the little volume she carried at all times and leisurely thumbed through it. "Ah!" she exclaimed. 'A wise man is proud but not vain; he is sociable, but belongs to no party.' Nor does he play at games with sticks and balls."

"That says nothing at all about playing croquet," pointed out Lizzie.

"Get out of the way, Lizzie; I'm going to knock your ball out-of-bounds." May grinned wickedly.

"Here, here, not like that," said a male voice from behind the hedge. There was a squeaking and straining sound, and the invalid, Mr. Wattles, appeared in his wheeled chair.

"Let me help you," said Anna, rushing forward to greet him. She pushed his chair closer to our group.

"You, young lady, struck a dead ball." Mr. Wattles's fine white beard shook in protest.

"I what?" Lizzie asked.

"Your sister's ball had made the point and is therefore dead to all direct shots. You did not have the right to roque her ball."

Lizzie put down her mallet and tugged at her bonnet strings in confusion.

"You seem to know the game, Mr. Wattles," I said. "Perhaps your guidance would serve us better than Anna's memory of the rules."

"Do join us," said Anna, "and I will bring you a cool drink."

He must have been spying on us from behind the hedge. How long had he been watching us? Loneliness, I assumed, had driven him from his invalid's couch into the afternoon air. Despite the warmth of the day, he had a lap rug over his legs and was gloved. The pain and stiffness of rheumatism often drove people to such desperate measures.

"You must hold the mallet like this," he said, taking my mallet and demonstrating the proper grip. "Tuck the thumbs under. They musn't stick up or you will have no strength to the shot."

Out of his sickroom, in the fresh air, Mr. Wattles seemed a much cheerier companion. Even his complexion seemed much improved, with patches of pink in his face and on the tip of his nose, and his brown eyes shining. His face was barely lined, only one stern wrinkle between his brows and a solitary one marching across the white forehead.

Anna came up with a tray of lemonade and offered him a glass.

"I am so pleased you have ventured out," I told him. "I have longed to increase our acquaintance."

He smiled, and there was sadness in the smile. "Most days I can do nothing but sleep," he said. "Or try to sleep. Sometimes the pain disallows even that. I fear I was less than hospitable during your first kind visit to an old man, and wished to make it up."

"Oh, I'm sure you are not so very old," said Lizzie, who had kind words for everyone. "If you have a piano I would be pleased to play some cheerful music for you. Perhaps it would lift your spirits."

"A grand idea, a grand idea," said Mr. Wattles. "But not today. Today you must play your game of croquet and I will explain the rules as I recall them. Ida is shopping, and she would be pleased to know I was in the fresh air."

I warmed to him, and wondered how uncle and nephew got along; was Clarence appreciative of having his mother's brother live with them?

"I think that was a point, Lizzie. Well done," said Anna, dividing her attention between Mr. Wattles and the ongoing game.

"It was. Excellent, young woman." Mr. Wattles beamed. "Remember to keep your thumbs tucked. And you, Miss Louisa, you are employed?" he asked.

"In many ways. I take in sewing, and in Boston I have a school for children. I also sold a book last year, and hope to sell more." I frowned. I was facing the sun, and May's ball was between mine and the next wicket. Should I try for a complicated "roque croquet" by sending her ball flying while mine raced for the metal arch? I tried; I missed.

"Next time, my dear, you'll make it," Eliza cheered.

"I have read your book, *Flower Fables*," Mr. Wattles said.

"I am very flattered. It was but a work for children," I said. I tried to be modest, but I still felt such a thrill whenever anyone said, "I have read your book," that I'm sure it showed in my expression.

"The child is father to the man," said Mr. Wattles. A fly buzzed about; he waved it off with his handkerchief. "It is important that children have edifying literature."

"I hope it amuses as well," I said. "It is difficult to edify children who are so bored they will not read the book." And then that name, Jo March, popped into my thoughts again. She often did, since she had first entered my imagination the year before. Jo March would be a character who would not bore children, I decided.

"But didn't you have another activity last year?" asked Mr. Wattles. The fly continued to buzz at his head; he waved at it and his cuff link caught on the wavy mass of his white beard. He gingerly untangled it.

"Another activity?" I paused.

"I read in the papers. You must not be modest, my dear. You helped discover a murderer."

I hesitated before answering, having a strong dislike of employing the topic of my friend's death and the incidents that followed it as small talk on a bright summer afternoon. "Constable Cobban had the case," I finally said. "My involvement was slight."

"Tut, tut," said Mr. Wattles, clucking his tongue. "Such

desire to stay out of the limelight is very attractive in a young woman. Her choice of friends can be equally attractive. Or questionable."

"Your meaning, sir?"

"You have struck up an acquaintance with Lilli Nooteboom, have you not? Ah, my dear, don't look surprised. Even invalids follow the events in a small town. I advise against this friendship; she is sly and untrustworthy."

"That is a hard charge against her," I said. "I have not found her so."

"I don't like to speak ill of the working class," said Mr. Wattles. "But I will just say she is no longer allowed into our home. When she delivers Ida's orders, she stays on the front porch, and is paid there."

"AND THEN," EXCLAIMED May over soup that evening in our pale blue dining room, "then Clarence Hampton burst through the bushes at us! I quite screamed with fright! He looked like a madman!"

"Pass the bread to your father, dear," said Abba. "And we must have a talk about your reading habits. You seem to have acquired a touch of melodrama. Surely he was not at all like a madman."

"He had been drinking," Anna affirmed quietly. "And he was furious with Mr. Wattles for being out of the house on such a hot day. He wheeled his chair so quickly back through the hedge I thought there might be damage."

"To the hedge?" asked Father. "It is vegetal and therefore regenerative."

"No," said Anna even more quietly. "Damage to frail Mr. Wattles."

"Do you think Mr. Hampton is always drunk, or just most of the time?" May asked.

"I have met him thrice," Sylvia said, giving in to the gossip. "Once in Mr. Alcott's vegetable patch when we quarreled over undergroundology, once in town when I posted a letter, and at tea. Thrice I smelled gin. Judging from the looks Clarence Hampton gets in town, I would say many families have noticed his weakness. He seems distinctly unpopular."

"If looks could kill, I suspect Mr. Hampton would be dead many times over," May said. "Is the cream really gone, Louy? Could I have more? I hate fish soup without cream."

"You came across him in Father's vegetable patch?" I asked Sylvia.

"He was poking around," she said. "I mean literally, poking a stick here and there."

"Now that is uncalled-for, pestering my chard," said Father, riled by this blatant cruelty to vegetables.

"Perhaps I should have a word with Mrs. Tupper," said Abba. "I do not like to stick my nose in where it does not belong, but that young man needs a firmer hand. I would be quite, quite upset if he should spoil your father's vegetable garden. By the way, Louy, a letter has come for you."

CHAPTER NINE

An Old Friend Appears

THE LETTER WAS from Fanny Kemble.

The great actress was an old friend of the family, since she was as intelligent as she was beautiful and enjoyed the company of what she called "thinkers." She had a Madonna-like face, and her voice was absolutely thrilling. How to describe it? Somewhere between birdsong and thunder, low, yet womanly. The year before, she had been in Rome, visiting with the Brownings. Upon her return to America her father had died and thrown Fanny into deep mourning. Some said that Mr. Kemble's death had been a kindness, for old age was bearing harshly on him and he was so deaf he could not hear his daughter's beautiful voice. "How sad," Anna had remarked, "to no longer hear birdsong and children's laughter."

"Is she in Boston? It is unfortunate we will miss her. What play?" Anna asked. She lifted the emptied soup tureen from the table and looked over my shoulder at the letter I was still reading.

"Queen Gertrude, from *Hamlet, Prince of Denmark*," I said. "Do you remember, Anna, last year when she visited and performed that soliloquy in our parlor?" I stood and imitated the pose Fanny Kemble had used, leaning forward as if about to lose my balance above the grave of poor drowned Ophelia.

"'Farewell! I hoped thou shouldst have been my Hamlet's wife; I thought thy bride-bed to have deck'd, sweet maid, and not have strew'd thy grave.'" I moaned, trying to match Fanny's thrilling tones.

Anna shivered. "Such a cruel play," she said. "So much bloodshed in it."

"She asks if she might visit us," I reported with great enthusiasm. "She has never seen Walpole, New Hampshire, and is desirous of country air." I wished that I had pursued my original plan of seeking an affiliation with the amateur troupe of Walpole so that I might discuss a play or two with Fanny and seek her advice, but I had been so busy. Time, in the country, somehow seems to pass even more quickly than in a busy city.

"Tell her yes, to come to us," Anna said, "but first help me with the washing up. Abba, you are to sit in your chair and rest."

"I admit to an ache in my feet," Abba said, and Lizzie and May rushed to find extra pillows for her chair and footstool. Father went to check on his chard and see that it had come to no harm, and his shadow fell long on the dark ground, spotlighted by one of those long, lovely summer dusks when the sun seems to linger like a child unwilling to go to bed.

While washing the soup spoons and shaking out the napkins I found myself thinking about Ernst Nooteboom, and wondering what had become of the long-absent Mr. Jonah Tupper, and why Mrs. Tupper's son, Clarence, had such a fondness for obliterating himself with gin. Perhaps, like Hamlet, he had a disturbed conscience. Hamlet, who had lost a father and hated his stepfather.

THE NEXT DAY Abba prepared peach pies for Eliza's household, and we all went over with her to visit. Ida Tupper and her son, though uninvited, joined us for tea. Clarence seemed ill at ease; perhaps he wished to apologize for his rudeness during our croquet party but did not know how. He paced in the parlor till Uncle muttered that he should come or go but not wear out his rug in indecision.

"I'll leave, sir," said Clarence, wounded. But before he could reach the door, Mrs. Fisher appeared and announced a caller for the "old gent." This took us all by surprise, for in the weeks in which I had been with Uncle Benjamin, not a single townperson had called on him.

"He has a valise with him," the gaunt housekeeper said unhappily. "I think he means to stay."

"The name of this wanderer?" asked Father, puzzled. "I believe the family to be complete. Abba, dear, are we missing a child?"

"Indeed we are not," said Mother, equally puzzled.

"Not a child, but a friend," said a low voice from a dusty, bedraggled figure now standing in the archway between parlor and hall.

I ran to him just as he ran to greet me, so when we literally ran into each other our embrace was a little more impactive than either of us intended. Llew squeezed me in a big bear hug, sweeping me off my feet and around in circles. Because of my height, only Llew, even taller than I, ever successfully completed this maneuver once I reached adulthood.

Reader, lest you think either I or my family encourage such familiarity among casual friends, let me tell you at the outset that Frederick Llewellyn Hovey Willis was not just any young man, or a mere Sunday visitor. He came closest to being a brother to me, being an orphan and having spent so much time in the bosom of my family that Father all but considered him a son. We had missed him greatly, since the year before he had left Boston and removed to Michigan to study medicine.

"How's the whistling coming?" Llew asked, putting me down again. "Or are you too much of a grown lady now?"

I pursed my mouth and whistled a full verse of "Yankee Doodle Dandy."

"Better than ever," he said. "Sir." He turned to Father and extended his hand. To Abba, the woman who years before had discovered the child Llew alone and injured on the Boston–Still River stagecoach, and had brought him home for a hot meal, he gave a hug even more forceful than the one he had given me.

"Is this my caller?" asked Uncle Benjamin somewhat petulantly. "I never saw him before."

"Mrs. Fisher confused the greeting," I told him. "This is a friend of Father's."

"Your neighbor's maid said I might find you here," Llew said.

This was Llew: curly black hair, brown skin, big black

eyes, handsome nose, fine teeth, small hands and feet, tall, very polite for a boy, and altogether jolly. Suddenly I felt a great desire to include Llew in one of my stories as a kind of modern hero. I remembered that other character who had been wandering in my thoughts for over a year, Jo March, with the long legs and boyish habits and impoverished family. Jo and Llew would make an interesting match in a story—as friends, of course. I would call him Laurie. Laurie Lawrence, and he would live next door to the March family and be their benefactor, just as mine had been his.

To compensate for his being orphaned—for the poverty his mother and father suffered before dying, poverty rendered more bitter since his grandparents had been wealthy but would not help because they had disapproved of the marriage—to compensate for all that, I would render Laurie fabulously wealthy in my story.

I had three characters—Jo and Laurie and Abba, who, of course, would be the heart of the novel. Marmie. Wasn't that what she had called her own mother? Now I needed a plot, other characters, a title. They would come in time.

"How long can you stay?" I asked Llew.

"A fortnight or longer," he answered. "I am on holiday from my studies, and since you are in the mountains, I thought I would spend time with my new avocation."

Ida Tupper leaned closer to Llew, looking at him over her pink feathered fan—I had realized some time ago that she was nearsighted—and gave him an appraising glance. Clarence Hampton, I observed, watched his mother with narrowed, speculative eyes. He wore a brightly checkered waistcoat that day, new, it seemed, and expensively made, like all his wardrobe. Did selling fossils really pay that well? Or was Jonah Tupper supporting a grown stepson as well as his wife? If so, that would only increase the problems in a household that seemed already quite problematic. There was another possibility. Ernst Nooteboom's missing gold watch could easily have been sold to a less-than-reputable jeweler outside of Walpole. A good gold watch would fetch enough for a year's wardrobe.

"Llew, I'm so pleased to see you!" Sylvia exclaimed. "When you leave Walpole, let us travel together. I'll return on the train with you so I don't have to travel in the women's car. All those wailing infants, you know. No wonder men pack escortless females into those cattle cars. The racket!"

"I'll see you all the way up to your mansion door," agreed Llew willingly. "But I just arrived. Let's not talk of departure!"

At the word *mansion* Ida Tupper sat up straighter.

"Llew, my boy," said Father, ignoring Sylvia, for she and he did not see eye-to-eye on many issues, female emancipation from the roles of wife and mother being one of them. "You have a new avocation?"

"I do, indeed. Geology, sir. It is all the rage in Clearwater, and there are more tavern brawls over the theories of Cuvier and Lyell than over actresses. Not that I brawl, of course," he added, turning bright red.

"Undergroundology," said Clarence Hampton, ceasing his pacing and sitting in a chair close to the tea table.

"Beg pardon?" said Llew.

"The new science will retain the name of undergroundology," Mr. Hampton asserted, as he had earlier with me.

"Clarence, dear, how can you discuss something as boring as science when there is a lovely young lady present?" Mrs. Tupper said. Her hand was over Sylvia's in a gesture she intended as motherly but that served only to frighten my friend, who was staring at me, wide-eyed with dismay.

"You know the science, sir?" Llew asked, stepping away from Abba, who still had her arm about his waist, and moving closer to where Clarence sat.

"I do. It is my avocation as well."

"And you follow the theories of Lyell, of course," Llew said.

"I do not, sir. I am a Cuvierian," Clarence replied hotly.

"I would have guessed you to be of English and German ancestry," Father said, scratching his chin.

"Did you?" said Uncle Benjamin. "And all this time I thought his people were Swiss." And Father and Uncle promptly began a separate conversation between themselves about the merits of various nations.

"A Cuvierian," said Llew, frowning and taking a chair. "Then you believe in the Doctrine of Catastrophes?"

"Clarence, darling, wouldn't you like to take Miss Sylvia for a walk in the garden?" asked Mrs. Tupper.

"The Doctrine of Catastrophes?" I asked, interested in this new phrase and ignoring—so Sylvia might as well—Mrs. Tupper's suggestion.

Sylvia wrenched her hand from its determined captor and moved closer to the armrest on her side of the settee. "The Doctrine of Catastrophes sounds like one of my mother's moods," she offered, reaching for another piece of date cake.

"Only a fool and an atheist would follow Lyell," Clarence said.

We realized the two young men were responding only to each other, and other talk in the room ceased. All eyes turned to the two young men.

Llew again turned a bright red, this time with anger rather than embarrassment, and his fingers twitched. I knew the signs. I also knew that calling Llew an atheist was not a way to earn his friendship. Before deciding on medical studies, he had attended Harvard Divinity.

"What is this doctrine?" I asked.

Llew answered me. "The Doctrine of Catastrophes, Louisa, is a ridiculous theory that states that the mountains and gorges and rivers were formed by immediate divine intervention rather than the slower processes of nature, and that mass extinctions occurred overnight. George Cuvier was a misguided Frenchman who thought that science should be used to buoy our belief in the Bible."

"And Charles Lyell was a drunken Scot who maintained that the world is no more than a mechanical toy. An atheist," Mr. Hampton said in a loud and hostile tone. I wondered if we might perhaps have a brawl in Uncle's parlor. The two young men were leaning toward each other, separated by a nose length, all but growling.

"Gentlemen," said Abba. Her voice was sweet and lovely, but could also be quite authoritative. "As much as I value intellectual discourse, I object to your tones. Be courteous."

Llew and Clarence put distance between themselves, making self-conscious motions of straightening cravats and crossing legs, all the while glaring at each other over rattling teacups.

"By the by," Ida said as she rose to leave. She looked at

me. "I have had a letter from Mr. Tupper, Louisa. He is in Detroit, and has taken an order for a bell there. Actually, not a letter. A telegram, wasn't it, Clarence? You brought it in yourself. What was the name of that parish? Oh, my memory is so bad!"

"I am pleased that you have had word from him. Is your husband well?" I asked.

She smiled. "Very. I will pass along your regards when I write to him."

"What a very strange family," said Llew when they had left.

"The brother is equally strange," I said. "A confirmed invalid who never leaves the house, except to give instructions in croquet, it seems. Llew, dear," I added, carrying the tea things into the pantry for washing up, "have you friends in Detroit? Is it so very far from Clearwater, where you have been living?"

"Have you a mind to visit in the autumn when I return? Nothing would give me greater pleasure," he said, though I could see conflict in his face: desire to spend more time with his "sister" and also the worry that goes through the bachelor mind when it discovers a feminine visitor is to intrude on his masculine quarters. Desire won, and he smiled with delight, and took my hands in his.

"I have something more immediate in mind." I took back my hands so that they could be better used rinsing out the teapot. "Could your friends discover what church or chapel in Detroit is currently being constructed or renovated? Which might require a new bell?"

Llew's smile turned to a lopsided grin. "I had forgotten how you love a mystery," he said. "Remember when we tried to act out 'The Murders in the Rue Morgue'? You always cast me as the orangutan."

"Because you were the strongest and needed to carry us about after you murdered us," Anna said, laughing.

"I could send a telegram or two," Llew said.

WE, ALL THE Alcotts and our two adopted siblings, Llew and Sylvia, sat under the stars that night.

The evening was mild and clear and smelled of new grass and other growing things. We lay on our backs on stable blankets and gazed upward. Nights in Walpole were very dark compared to Boston. The country sky was brilliant with pinpoints of light, and every once in a while, like a small streaking miracle, a shooting star would cross the heavens.

"That is Orion," said Father, pointing up, his noble profile looking chiseled against the evening sky. "That ancient constellation has looked down upon many mastodons—when they were fierce animals, not bones and fossils. Perhaps there are no more mastodons simply because mankind killed them all in their erroneous desire to eat flesh," he mused. We had been talking about geology and the search for fossils, and the mastodon skeleton that had been found in New Jersey.

"Much as the sperm whale will soon be harpooned to extinction because of our need for lamp oil," he continued, sighing deeply. "Why use lamps when you can sit under the stars?"

"They are useful for reading by," commented ever-practical Abba, who, even prone full-length on the ground, was busy at her knitting. The clacking of her needles sounded in time with the chirping crickets. "And for mending by. Go to bed, May. It is well past your bedtime."

"Perhaps I will find my own mastodon. Good night, darlings," said May, and her pretty blond head with its curls and snub nose disappeared into the cottage. The heavy wooden door slammed hard behind her.

"You work too hard, Abba," said Father. "Must you spend so much time mending? And what could be read in books or journals that is not already contained in the heavens?"

I agreed that Mother worked much too hard, but Father, in his limited masculine thinking, did not reflect that if Abba did not perpetually mend his wardrobe, he would soon be in a state more natural than even he would condone.

As for reading lamps, I did not agree with him on that point at all. The stars were lovely, but even lovelier was curling up in my reading chair with a volume of Goethe or Shakespeare. And I couldn't help but reflect on a certain insincerity in his words, since he sat up late each night rereading Hesiod's *Works and Days* for agricultural information, although he refused all advice, even Hesiod's, and determined that the creator would provide all that the little seedlings needed. Nor did he believe in staking beans or planting lettuce in tidy rows. (I refrained from pointing out that if women took the same attitude to linen as he did to vegetables we would all be wearing stalks of hemp rather than shirts and shifts.)

Walpolians were as bemused by his gardening methods as his family, and I often caught Abba watching him in his patch and shaking her head in loving amusement.

"There is much we know of medicine that is not contained

in the sky," said Llew shyly, commenting on Father's critique of Abba's habit of journal reading. Llew had been silent during most of our stargazing, for he did not like to contradict Father, but he was also an honest boy who spoke his mind. "But speaking of extinction, what was that bit about Mr. Tupper at the end of Mrs. Tupper's visit? There seemed to be an undertone to that small talk."

"Mr. Tupper seems not in evidence," I said, "and has not been in evidence for many months now."

"Ah." He understood, now, the importance of those telegrams he had already sent off.

"It does seem a strange way to run a marriage," spoke up Anna in the darkness. She sat directly in the middle of our gathering, leaning against Abba, with a plaid lap robe over her knees to keep the dew from her dress.

"Travelers often are away for months at a time," said Father somewhat defensively. He himself traveled often, to give his conversations and lectures.

"When you travel, you write long letters every day, and this young man prefers infrequent picture cards and telegrams," replied Abba, and though she spoke with some heat her knitting needles never paused. "When we were courting and you traveled, you wrote twice, sometimes thrice a day."

Father cleared his throat. "I was writing to the most noble of women," he said. "How could I forget that honor?"

"Perhaps the ill will between stepfather and son has encouraged the young husband to stay away," suggested Llew.

"Why do you say that?" I asked, looking away from Orion and turning in Llew's direction. I felt the same, but wanted to hear Llew's reasoning.

"Did you see the look in his eyes when his mother mentioned her husband, and this telegram about bell orders? He's a shifty-eyed fellow. I don't like him." Llew leaned up on his elbows. "And I smelled gin on his breath. I can't imagine he made for a comfortable home life between his mother and stepfather."

At that moment, next door a door creaked open and a light appeared on the path in front of our cottage, a lamp carried by Ida Tupper's maid. As she approached, the stars overhead dimmed from the intrusion of harpooned-sperm-whale oil, and Father rose to his feet, muttering.

"Mrs. Tupper has sent a message," the girl announced. "I am to deliver it immediately. It won't wait for breakfast." Obviously Ida Tupper thought it very important. She had sent the child out in the night with her curling papers in her hair.

"Well, we'd better read it, then," said Abba, rising somewhat stiffly from her place on the blankets and accepting the note. "But you go home, child, to your rest." The little maid giggled and ran off. There, too, was evidence of something amiss in the household; a wise mother should not employ a child so young, so pretty, when her bachelor son is at home, and that son has a reputation.

"The young people are invited to a picnic," Abba said, reading. "There is no mention of a chaperon. It seems Mrs. Tupper herself will not attend."

"Abba, Anna is already twenty-four," I said. "I am twenty-two."

She looked at us somewhat wistfully. "Of course." She sighed. "I forget sometimes how grown-up my 'Golden Brood' has become."

"When is it?" Llew and Lizzie asked simultaneously.

"In three days, if the sun shines. Mrs. Tupper writes she will pack a hamper for you, and hire a mule to carry it. She asks if Miss Sylvia Shattuck prefers her chicken fried or boiled. Clarence is to bring his banjo and songbook."

"Banjo?" said Sylvia. "Oh, my." We laughed.

"Did someone mention frying a chicken?" asked Father, who was still studying the night sky. "How very unkind. And a mule. These young people have strong backs of their own."

"Indicate that the mule will not be required; you can each carry a hamper. I agree with your father on that." Abba folded the note and gave it to me.

Mrs. Tupper's intrusive note ended the magical night under the stars. We began to rise, yawning and stretching, and made our way back into the house, to our beds. I found a wooden cot in the kitchen pantry, dusted it off, and spread fresh linen and blankets over it for Llew, who was to bunk down in the little parlor.

"Like when I was a child and pretended I was camping in your parlor," he said happily as I helped him arrange the blankets over the cot. "Perhaps we should hang a sheet over this for my tent, and tell ghost stories?"

I hugged him close. Llew, my childhood friend, my brother of choice. *Laurie*, I thought. *He is my Llew, but he is Jo's Laurie.*

"It is too late for ghost stories," I said. "Look at you; you can barely keep your eyes open." A shock of dark hair had fallen over his half-closed eyes.

"It has been a long day," he admitted, pushing back the hair.

"Sleep now," I said, giving him a sisterly kiss on the forehead. He looked as if he would say something, but changed his mind.

Upstairs, Sylvia and I sat up quite late, whispering as Anna breathed slowly, already deep in sleep.

"From the frying pan to the fire?" Sylvia said, pulling the blankets up to her chin, for the night had grown chill. "I left Boston to get away from Mother's persistent attempts at matchmaking, and here I am being matchmade by your Mrs. Tupper, I think."

"You are rich, my dear, and her son is unwed."

Anna stirred and mumbled in her sleep. I reached over and tucked her blankets in tighter.

"He seems an unsuitable choice for a husband. All that gin." Sylvia yawned. "I'm going to sleep now, Louy. See you in the morning." Her eyes closed and she began to snore, ever so gently.

I lay awake, thinking of what Sylvia had said. Clarence had the reputation of being "fast," of being a flirt with the girls and a bit of a heartbreaker. Yet his behavior toward lovely Sylvia had indicated complete indifference. Why? Was it part of the general derangement I had noticed in him?

When my questions about Clarence began to fade under the softening of awareness that announces sleep is not far behind, I realized I was dizzy with joy. I couldn't remember the last time I had had all my loved ones, at one time, under the same roof. I smiled to myself and watched out the open window until Orion, that steadfast hunter, moved to a different part of the sky.

Once, I thought I saw a figure moving in Father's vegetable patch, but realized it was a shadow cast by the moon.

CHAPTER TEN

The Bell Foundry

IDA TUPPER MISSED her next knitting lesson, and her maid acquired much leisure time, which she spent in Uncle Benjamin's kitchen, gossiping with Mrs. Fisher, which was how we learned that Ida was off to Manchester for shopping.

"I hope there will be no extravagant foolishness over this picnic." Abba sighed. "May is at such an impressionable age, and if she comes home with a taste for caviar and sherbet packed in ice I will not be pleased."

"Caviar is fish eggs," Lizzie protested, making a hideous face.

We had all gathered as usual in the cottage kitchen for morning porridge, Father with his nose in a book, Abba with flour on her nose from rolling biscuits, May with her pet mole peeking out of her pocket, Lizzie with her curls loose on her shoulders and with a sheet of music stuck in her waistband, and Anna, dear Anna, dreamy-eyed and in a serene world of her own.

Llew came to the table in his shirtsleeves and dressing gown, his dark hair rumpled from sleep and his cheeks rosy. He looked young and boyish and not at all like the studious medical student. Sylvia sat next to him, for they were already close friends united by a common bond: the Alcotts, whom they loved and who loved them.

Sylvia looked a little strange, for she had pulled her blond ringlets into a stern bun at the base of her neck, and her morning gown had long bell sleeves and that strange, prim little collar. "It is Mandarin style," she announced, when Abba asked if the new costume was Parisian. "Confucius was a Mandarin."

Father looked up from his book. "Philosophy isn't adopted with a change of wardrobe. It goes deeper," he warned.

"Oh, I know," Sylvia said brightly. "I have decided to change my diet as well. No coffee, thank you, Abba. Tea, if you please. With no cream or sugar."

Father sighed and returned to his reading, absentmindedly sticking his butter knife into his coffee cup and his spoon into the butter bowl.

"I, myself, am eager to try caviar," offered May, reverting to our previous conversation.

"Then you had better find employment," Abba said. "Our budget barely allows hen's eggs."

After breakfast, Sylvia sat in the garden, meditating, and I spent several hours in my writing shed, working on my elf stories. When I wearied of elves and edifying endings, I returned to work on "The Lady and the Woman," always keeping Abba as my inspiration.

"You have given your idol a heart, but no head. An affectionate or accomplished idiot is not my ideal of a woman," I let Kate tell Mr. Windsor. I had much of the dialogue, but was still uncertain of the setting for this story. My tendency was to place them in Rome or other places of the sophisticated world to which I had traveled only in my imagination—so that, dear reader, at least my imagination could travel!—but this story, because it was inspired by Abba, should be set closer to home. Where?

LATER, WHEN THE sun was past its zenith and the heat began to dissipate somewhat, Sylvia and I took a walk to the river. First we stopped in front of Father's vegetable patch and pondered.

"It is a wonder," Sylvia said. "Look, the Brussels sprouts must be an inch tall already. I did not know your father had a green thumb."

"That's the wonder," I said, crouching down and peering at the little green plants. "He does not have a green thumb. This must be wondrous fine soil." I stood again rather quickly, since a passerby was also gawking at Father's garden, and it would not do for a lady to be seen crouching in the dirt like a child. Anna and Lizzie and May wished to be well thought of in town. (I had already promised never to whistle in public.)

"A fine patch," said the straw-hatted gentleman. "I'll get his secret yet."

"I assure you there is no secret but that the soil here is very fine," I said.

He gave me a wink. "Of course," he agreed. "Of course." He walked on.

"I believe there is a mystery right here in the vegetable patch," commented Sylvia.

"I wish the patch were on the other side of the house," I admitted, "not the side facing the house of the missing Jonah Tupper. I have an uncomfortable feeling."

We also stopped at Tupper's General Store to get some mending yarn for Abba. The store was empty of customers. Across the street, I saw some known town Republicans entering Hubert's, along with the Democrats.

"Business seems to have fallen off," I couldn't help but comment to the counter girl.

"It's because of Ernst," she whispered. "Lilli is telling everyone that Mr. Tupper was there when Ernst fell. That Mr. Tupper pushed—"

"Cease your useless chatter!" said Mr. Tupper, storming through the double doors of his back room. "Ah. It's Benjamin Willis's niece from Boston. Still here with us?"

"Might Sylvia and I again look at your box of sheet music?" I asked. He took the box out from under the counter and pushed it at me.

"Take your time," he said, meaning just the opposite.

Sylvia, who read music with an amateurish but reliable expertise, hummed some of the songs for me. I rather liked a black spiritual called "Jacob's Ladder," as the music was exciting and the lyrics contained many hidden references to the Underground Railroad. In Boston, the Alcott family was a secret part of that organization, helping fugitive slaves flee north to Canada and freedom.

Sylvia, much more a romantic than myself despite her habit of turning down marriage proposals, insisted that

Lizzie would prefer "Darling Nelly Gray," a love song. I agreed without pointing out that Nelly Gray was a black female slave sold away from her home.

When our purchases were complete and Abba's little marketing basket was full, I thanked Mr. Tupper for his assistance (he had done nothing) and added a cordial, "Uncle Benjamin sends his regards." That was a lie, but I wanted to get to the bottom of the apparent hostility he felt for my uncle.

He glared even harder, his hazel eyes turning icy and narrow. "No, Mr. Willis don't send his regards, any more than I send him mine," Mr. Tupper said. "There's ill will 'tween us. You can tell him I said I'd just as soon dance on his grave as tip my hat to him."

Sylvia and I, speechless with amazement, went back out into the daylight, only to see Lilli leaving Mr. Hubert's general store with a shopping basket over her arm.

"Lilli!" I called, and waved my free arm.

She looked up and crossed over to where we stood. "Morning, Miss Louisa. And Sylvia." She looked down at her black skirts, her black shoes, waved a hand in its black lace mitten. "I needed to walk, to get out of my room."

"Of course," I said. "Even in mourning one should take care of one's own health. There is a bench under the tree just over there. Shall we sit for a while?" I took her arm and we walked to the shaded bench, away from the dust of the street.

"Is your uncle, Benjamin Willis, in good health?" she asked. "He sent me such a kind letter of sympathy." She paused and took a deep breath. "It is good to have relatives near you. I wish . . ." Her voice trailed off.

"Have you second thoughts about staying in Walpole?" I asked.

Sylvia opened a bag of cinnamon candies and passed it.

"No," said Lilli, taking a cinnamon ball. "No. I stay."

A squirrel chattered overhead in the elm tree and studied us, the intruders, with its little black eyes. Lilli had said, "I stay," with such vehemence, and last week she had mentioned acquiring an American husband as one of her goals. Was there a secret beau? Oh, these horrible rules of conduct that forbade intimate questions for such a long time!

"Well," Lilli said after a long while, "I return to my room. There is a living to earn and linen waiting to be hemmed." She rose from the bench.

"Lilli, before you go, can you tell me something?"

"I will try," she said, "if it is something I know."

"Is there a reason for Mr. Tupper's antipathy"—she frowned in confusion—"for his extreme dislike of my uncle?"

"Ah!" she exclaimed with a knowing nod. "That I do know. It was your uncle, Mr. Willis, who introduced Mr. Tupper's son, Jonah, to Ida, who was soon Ida Tupper."

"That would explain it," I agreed.

Lilli said farewell and turned east. Mrs. Roder's boardinghouse was in the opposite direction. She was taking the long way back, it seemed.

"I HAVE HAD a telegram," Llew said with great excitement when we returned home. "My friend Charles asked his friend Alwyn, who is studying for the ministry in Detroit. He says a new Catholic parish, the Immaculate Conception, might be needing a bell for its new church. The priest in charge is Father O'Connor." Llew looked pleased with himself, for he knew his acquired information was valuable.

"Are you tired, Sylvia?" I asked.

"No. What do you have in mind?" asked my friend.

"Another walk. To send a telegram to the parish of the Immaculate Conception, and then a visit to the bell foundry. I have always wanted to see a bell cast. Haven't you?"

Sylvia's eyes twinkled.

"Indeed I have," she said.

"I would enjoy the exercise," Llew said regretfully. "But I am having a devil of a time memorizing the symptoms of breakbone fever and malaria. Which produces albuminous urine?" He scratched his head. "I'll go back to my studies."

Another telegram was quickly dispatched to Father O'Connor, asking if he had additional thoughts or suggestions about the bell. Another dime came out of my purse. I sighed.

O'Rourke's Foundry on the southern outskirts of town, as might be deduced from the name, was owned and managed by one Michael O'Rourke, a stocky Irishman with carrot-red hair and thick boiled-wool overalls decorated with myriad little black burns, where sparks had leaped at him. Mr. O'Rourke showed us about his premises with great enthusiasm, having, as he pointed out, few visitors, and fewer of those being of the female persuasion.

The redbrick foundry was smallish, as such establishments go, he admitted, with a single storage room where the bronze bricks and used bronze fittings, purchased from the ragman, were kept; one furnace room with a huge oven, in front of which was a large box on wheels in which the sand mold was held and the molten metal was poured; a tiny, untidy office; and a many-windowed finishing room, where the bells were engraved and polished.

"But we make the best bells in the East," O'Rourke boasted.

Three men sat before bells of various sizes in the finishing room, working with engravers and chisels. I admired the delicate vines and bellflowers of one, the neatly engraved Latin script of another. We paused longest in the pouring room, where he was preparing the mold for a new bell. I could hear the strange bubbling of boiling metal in the cauldron, and the air was heavy with heat.

"Nice weather today!" he shouted above the roar of the furnace and the clang of the finishers and the bells being tested. "That's important. Changeable weather can ruin a bell. Sometimes they bring in the schoolroom children for an outing, but I hate that day, for fear one of the little 'uns will topple against the furnace or fall into the mold!"

"Have any ever?" Sylvia shouted back. "Fallen in, that is?"

"Not in my time! T'ank the holy angels! How long till pouring?" O'Rourke shouted to another man in even thicker overalls who was inspecting the boxed mold wheeled to the side of the cauldron.

The laborer held up one finger, indicating, I believe, a single hour. Sweat flowed down his face in rivulets.

I tugged at Mr. O'Rourke's sleeve and pointed to the door, sensing that he might have a moment of freedom.

We sat under an umbrella, for no trees grew close to the

O'Rourke Foundry. Sylvia complained about the lack of shade.

"Ever seen the Czar Kolokol?" O'Rourke asked somewhat testily.

"I have not been to Saint Petersburg," Sylvia replied. "Nor do I think the czar would receive me. I could not even get admittance to Miss Jenny Lind's dressing room when she was in Boston."

O'Rourke chuckled. "Czar Kolokol is a bell." He rolled down the suspenders of his overalls and unbuttoned his shirt collar to let off some of the heat that had accumulated in his work suit. "The largest bell ever cast, some two hundred and twenty tons. And never been rung. A bell that's never been rung is worse than a pretty girl that never—"

I interrupted quickly. "Tell us why it never rang, Mr. O'Rourke."

"It cracked during the fire of 1737. Bells are funny that way. They need heat to be created, but once born, they dread fire much as people do. So no trees near my little workshop, little misses. One lightning strike and the work of a year or two is up in flames."

"Have you been here long, Mr. O'Rourke?" I asked, thinking it time to bring our conversation closer to my original purpose for the visit.

"Fifteen years. Came over from Belfast. My church there had a bell cast in the ninth century, and still rung true as daylight. Lovely sound, lovely." His rugged, square face softened, and his eyes closed at the memory, as if he were hearing that bell.

"Then you know the town well," I said.

"Well?" His eyes flew open and he laughed. "I'm a new-comer by New England standards, miss. As is that uncle of yours."

"You know Uncle Benjamin?" I asked, startled.

"Well as any man in Walpole," he said. "A great man with some fine tales to tell, and not stingy with the pouring of port after dinner. But he keeps strange company these days." O'Rourke blushed a bright red.

"You mean Mrs. Tupper," I guessed.

"Certain I do. And she a married lady and all."

"It is a friendship, no more," I defended my uncle.

"Well," said O'Rourke, scratching at his whiskers with a thoughtful squint, "there be them that t'ink themselves above the moral imperative."

"Uncle Benjamin thinks no such thing," I insisted.

" 'Twasn't your uncle I meant," O'Rourke said. " 'Twas herself. Your uncle is not Mrs. Tupper's only gentleman com-panion."

He rose from his wooden stool, went to the leaky rain bar-rel, and brought up from it a tin cup of water, of which he drank half and poured the rest over his florid face and flamelike hair.

"Her brother lives with her, as well as her son, Mr. Hamp-ton," I said.

O'Rourke shook his head, and heavy drops of water splashed around him. "I've met the brother at Sunday meet-ing. He attends once a month or so. He is stooped and bearded and strapped into that wheeled chair, and the son is thinner than . . ." He paused.

"Thinner than whom?" I asked, perplexed.

"I have seen another man come out of that house,"

O'Rourke said, running his sooty hands through his red hair. "This is kitchen gossip, though. I'm no better than a woman."

"Please," I said, ignoring his harsh criticism of women's penchant for discussing others, "this might be important. What did you see?"

"Well, 'twas the other week. The day Ernst Nooteboom fell, in fact. I was coming in early to the foundry and I passed by Mrs. Tupper's house. A man was coming out the side door. He weren't the milkman."

"Did you see his face?"

"It were barely dawn and he wore a brimmed hat." O'Rourke ran his hands over his wet face, streaking the soot that had accumulated on his cheeks. "His face I weren't able to see. But he was heavy-built. Dressed like a city fellow. I'm not the only one to have seen him. Mr. Fortbra saw a stranger fishing one day, about dawn, dressed in those city clothes. Mrs. Amherst saw a man crossing through her backyard at dawn, heading toward the ravine."

"My goodness," said Sylvia. "This town does acquire detail. Am I spoken of in such a manner?" Sylvia, as one of Boston's Belles and an heiress of considerable fortune, had a reasonable distaste for being the subject of gossip.

"You really want to know?" asked O'Rourke, squinting even more deeply so that his eyes almost disappeared.

"I do," said Sylvia staunchly.

"There's bets on whether the wedding will be a June or December one."

"Wedding?" she asked faintly.

"You and young Mr. Hampton. His family likes to marry upward."

Sylvia fanned herself briskly. "Well, Mr. O'Rourke, if you wish to profit from such bad taste, I recommend putting money on the fact that there will be no such wedding. I never."

"It is your fatal beauty," I teased.

"It is my shares in the Cheshire Railroad, and you know it. Tell me more about bells, Mr. O'Rourke," Sylvia said. "But not wedding bells."

His blue eyes, which had before sparkled with gossip, now grew luminous. "They have souls," he whispered. "Each one different. I've known evil bells and bells that could heal, and bells that refused to sing, though no engineer could figure out why. There's a bell in County Cork that rings by itself every year on October thirty-first, and it can't be stopped even when cloth is wrapped on the clapper."

"Really?" asked Sylvia, wide-eyed.

"And I've heard that you have a new order," I said, leading the conversation to my purpose.

"I do. And how did you know that, lass?"

"From the commercial traveler's wife herself, Mrs. Tupper."

O'Rourke scratched his whiskers again and ran his fingers through his hair so that it stood up, looking even more flamelike. "Strange thing, that order. Do not usually happen in such a manner. See, a bell is a very specific thing; the weight, shape, tone, decoration—all that is usually decided after much correspondence. I've known some ministers put more thought into their church bell than the choice of wife. When you think about it, a bell does last much longer than a wife."

"What was strange about this order?" I asked. His conversation, I had marked, had a meandering style that needed stern guidance.

"No previous correspondence, no putting out of feelers or asking of questions. Just the order for a bell, sent by telegram, no less, half ton, brass, middle tone, and no decoration other than an inscription. No decoration! Think of that. You'd think the order had been placed by someone who knew nothing at all of bells and cared even less than they know."

"Strange," I agreed. "And the order was sent in by Mr. Tupper?"

"It seems so. It referred to Mr. Tupper's commission, which was to be held by me till further notice. But the deposit was to be paid by a draft drawn from a Walpole bank, not a Michigan bank." O'Rourke squinted and leaned closer to me. "The bank account was Mr. Clarence Hampton's. Why is he buying a bell for a church his family don't attend?"

To make it appear that Jonah Tupper was in Michigan, I thought.

Sylvia and I rose to leave. Mr. O'Rourke stood and pulled his overall suspenders back up to his shoulders. Soon a new bell would be poured; another of his "souls" would enter the world.

I had one last question. "You said Mr. Tupper's order included an inscription for the bell," I said. "Would you tell me that inscription, Mr. O'Rourke?"

"I would. It was the strangest part of this affair, for it was not a Latin tag but a French one. Most unusual. Had to ask the schoolteacher to tell me its meaning. It was *"Abondance déclarée.'"*

"I have heard Mother shout that," said Sylvia, "while playing at whist."

O'Rourke turned white, then red with anger. "That beat all," he muttered. "I'm a gaming man myself, but a frivolity like that on one of my bells? I've a mind to refuse the order."

"It is more than a gaming term for cardplayers," I said. "In some common parlance it describes a state of ambition that has become greed. A desire to win all."

"That beat all," O'Rourke said again.

CHAPTER ELEVEN

A Rough-and-Tumble Picnic

THE DAY OF the picnic dawned fair, with not a cloud in the sky. I awoke to the country smell of pine and wildflowers mixed with the pungency of flapjacks and coffee from the downstairs kitchen, and so stretched and sighed in my bed with great pleasure. And then I remembered the picnic, and my contentment disappeared. I would much rather arrange my own activities (including a good four-hour shift in my writing shed) than surrender my day to the machinations of Ida Tupper's son.

Poor Sylvia was even less inclined to go. "He'll be bringing me plates of pâté and buttered rolls all afternoon. He'll ask me to go for walks with him," she complained from under the bed quilt, refusing to rise.

"I might let it slip that you are secretly affianced and therefore he can never hope for a return of his affection," I said. My qualms and concerns about the nature of Clarence Hampton made me willing to prevaricate rather than risk an entanglement of any sort between that mysterious man and my best friend.

"Sylvia is engaged?" asked Anna, coming into the bedroom just then, her arms full of fresh towels and chemises carried up from the laundry room behind the kitchen. "Who is the fellow? Do I know him? Why weren't we invited to the betrothal supper?" She tapped her foot impatiently.

"Truly, she is not." I laughed. "It is a ploy."

"An extreme one," said Anna thoughtfully. "What if that lie gets back to Boston and Sylvia's mother?"

Sylvia stared back at me for a long moment. "It would serve Mother right."

"But, Sylvia, didn't Confucius require his followers to respect their elderly parents?" I said, looking up at the ceiling to avoid her gaze.

"Louy, don't do that," Sylvia protested. "You play me along like a trout. Yes, I have been fishing once or twice. You play me along and humor me, then turn it all around so I don't know if I'm coming or going."

"Well, today you are going, so get dressed," I told her. "If the rumor spreads too far, we will find a way to make it up to your mother."

WHEN CLARENCE ARRIVED at ten with his buggy and two-horse team, we four Alcott girls, along with Sylvia and Llew, climbed up.

Clarence looked almost cheerful that morning. He tried to smile, producing a kind of grimace that reminded me of falsely brave men entering a surgeon's office to have a bad tooth pulled. He wore an expensive plaid suit and well-polished boots, but seemed to have made an attempt at playing the country squire by donning a straw hat.

Llew was dressed in farmer's overalls and well-worn boots, for he intended to use this time well, by digging for fossils after lunch. He was like Father in his insistence that life was best lived for work, not pleasure. He sat next to Clarence on the driver's board, and we five girls filled the two benches in back. There was little legroom because the hamper from Ida Tupper was large enough to contain a body or two. Why, I asked myself, was I thinking of bodies?

Abba, her face rosy from kitchen duties, was at the front steps to see us off. Father waved from his vegetable patch. The potato plants were already a hand tall.

"To the mountain?" Clarence asked us over his shoulder. "Or to the river?"

Sylvia and I exchanged glances and studied our boots. "The mountain, please," I said, hiding my smile. A lake, for the Alcott girls and Sylvia, meant swimming, but since my family had believed in progressive education even for daughters, swimming meant donning a chemise and little else. And that would not do in the company of Llew and Clarence. "Remember Walden Pond?" Sylvia grinned. I nodded.

Clarence snapped his whip over the horses' heads, and we jolted off.

"Perhaps we can visit your campsite," I called from the back of the buggy, holding on to my sun hat.

Clarence did not answer, but his shoulders flinched as if I had struck him.

The drive lasted well over two hours, since we stopped

often to pick wildflowers, which we stuck in the horses' hal-
ters and our own hats, and we delayed for half an hour in
wild berry brambles, hunting and picking the first ripe ones
till we could eat no more. At one moment I found myself picking next to Mr. Hampton.

"Mr. Hampton," I whispered loudly, a true stage whisper,
seeking his attention.

He looked up from the spiderweb he had been examining, for in the middle of the web sat a spider black and round
as a ripe berry. "Yes, Miss Louisa?"

"I offer you information of a private nature, and ask your
pledge not to repeat it. Not even to your mother," I whispered
urgently.

He leaned closer.

I couldn't restrain my slight recoil. Though we never
mentioned it, I still remembered the feel of his angry hands on
my shoulders, shaking me.

"Miss Sylvia is secretly affianced," I said. "She cannot
announce it yet, but would have you know of her attachment
to another."

Unfortunately at the moment Sylvia, only some yards
away from us, lost her footing and fell laughing into the arms
of Llew.

"She does not seem affianced," said Clarence, knitting his
brows. "I could predict a stage career for her successful playing of an unattached young woman," he said. "As it happens,
you need not fear I will impose myself. After twenty-three
years with Mother, I prefer women of a more sincere nature.
I have put up with more than my share of brief enthusiasms
and crocodile tears."

I started to speak in Sylvia's defense, to argue that she was, at heart, a serious and intelligent young person, but since I had achieved the desired effect of discouraging Clarence, though not in quite the way I had planned, I let him have the last word in that conversation.

We returned to the buggy, our lips and fingers stained purple, and Llew and Clarence began a heated and protracted conversation over geologic theory. If they had been small boys they would have already been pushing and shoving at each other. But they were men and fought with words instead of little fists.

The sun shone; butterflies flitted past. Part of our trail led along the river and a section of ravine, and I composed in my head for my story of Kate and Mr. Windsor, noting the "rocky way, following the babbling brook that dashed foaming down the deep ravine, whose sides were ringed with pines and carpeted with delicate ferns and moss."

The spot Clarence Hampton had chosen for our picnic was a green meadow of wildflowers protected between two stands of old pine, and beyond the nearest stand was a rock cliff that dropped forty feet down. A small stream gurgled merrily through the meadow, and a grouping of sheep scattered here and there rendered the scene idyllic.

"It is private land, but I've asked permission of the landholder," Clarence assured us. "People in these whereabouts take their property rights very seriously. There is a path that trails halfway down to the bottom of the ravine, if you will risk it." He himself took a book from his pack and sat down to read under a huge oak.

The womenfolk, as Llew had termed us, began the task of

spreading blankets and setting out plates of chicken and boiled eggs and preserved fruits and sultana cakes, no easy task, since we were all wearing our crinolines and full skirts and to tip those at any angle was to invite the wind to toss the whole kit over our heads—a most embarrassing situation, as I'm sure you can imagine. So carefully we leaned and turned and put out the picnic, ravenous after the long ride despite the berries. When the dishes were arranged we sat cross-legged under our full circled skirts, looking like exotic Buddhas balanced on muslin print lily pads.

Llew and Clarence (who shut his book with an audible sigh) built a small fire so that we might have tea or coffee if we wished, quarreling over the proper way to circle the pit with stones and the correct method of laying the branches and kindling, each insisting his way was more efficient.

We ate splendidly and far too much, and then napped. Before sleeping I composed in my head, recording the details of our journey, for I had decided that the story of Kate Loring and Mr. Windsor would be set in just such a journey up a mountain, beside a babbling brook:

"This stream reminds me of your style of woman, Miss Kate," said Mr. Windsor, as, leaning on the rude railing of the bridge, he glanced to Kate, who stood erect, on a projecting crag, with folded arms, and the red light streaming full upon her thoughtful face and gleaming eyes.

WE AWOKE TO the sounds of screaming.

I sat up first, pushing away the straw hat I had placed over my face to keep it from sunburn. But the sun was strong and had dazzled my eyes through the hat, and at first I could see nothing but round explosions of brilliant light. When the dazzle passed I looked in the direction of the scream, the cliff's edge, and saw a man, flat on the ground, reaching his hand over the cliff. Another man held his feet to keep him from going over, and three young women—the source of the screaming—swirled in panic about them.

"She's fallen over the cliff!" yelled the man holding the ankles of the other man, for by then I had screamed myself, raising the alarm among my own group, and was running toward the cliff edge to give assistance.

"Helen!" one of the terrified young women yelled. "Hang on, Helen!"

"I am," came a calm voice from beyond the rim of the chasm. "Don't carry on so, Myrtle. You'll set my teeth on edge."

"Well, you're the one who fell over," said the creature I guessed was Myrtle, who, dressed in pink gingham with several bows in her hair, pouted.

"Can you reach her?" I asked, kneeling next to the first man in the human ladder. I looked over the edge to see how far Helen had fallen, terrified of beholding some bloodied, bone-broken vision, a feminine version of Ernst Nooteboom, although the voice coming up over that cliff edge had argued against such a vision.

I looked over, and a perky face with a snub nose smiled up at me, just inches away.

"You must be Miss Louisa Alcott," she said pleasantly. "I recognize that day gown from a description I have heard." Well, so much for my pondering on how thorough the gossip of Walpole was.

"I am. I gather you are Helen?"

"Helen Kittredge," she said with a nod. "I would extend my hand, but as you can see it has a previous engagement. Do not tug so, Walter; you will separate my hand from my arm."

Walter was the boy who struggled with both his hands to hold one of Helen's, to keep her from falling farther into the chasm. I inched closer to the edge and saw that she stood on the large jutting rock onto which she had fallen. I also noticed that there were no other footholds between her and a fall of forty feet, and that the rock seemed to be loosening under her weight, for it tilted a little even as I watched.

"Hold her tight, Walter," I said. "Llew, bring the rope that tied our picnic basket!"

Llew, already right behind me, ran for the rope and was back in less than ten seconds, so quick was his pace.

"Helen," I said, forcing a calmness I did not feel, "can you take this rope with your free hand and tie it about your waist?"

"I think so," she said, and now I heard fear in her voice. She struggled for some minutes with this chore, and when the rope was around her we all held our breath, for the most dangerous moment had arrived: She must balance on that small, rocking foothold, release her other hand from the safety of Walter's grasp, and tie a secure knot.

But she tied the knot quickly and with such efficiency I deemed her to have some knowledge of amateur sailing.

"Ready," she said, smiling up at me once again.

"Then we will pull, and you must push yourself away from the edge so that you are not injured on the rock," I explained. "Push out with your foot and hold the rope with your hands."

A moment later Helen was resting at the cliff's edge, and though she laughed, her face was uncommonly pale.

Walter raced to the stream to bring her a cup of water; Myrtle offered her smelling salts.

But Helen would have nothing to do with such ministrations and instead sat up and offered her hand to me.

"Now we are properly introduced," she said.

"What are you doing here?" The male voice behind me was unsuitably harsh to address a young woman whose life had just been endangered.

I turned in surprise. Clarence Hampton stood there, glaring. "This is private land."

"And not of your ownership," said the young man named Walter. He rose from his knees beside Helen and glared back at Clarence. The two men were dressed similarly, in country tweed trousers and jackets and shirts loosened at the collar, yet there was such a striking difference between them I thought how little of our nature is revealed by clothing. Walter seemed boyish and trembling with the shock of this escapade; Clarence was chilly, aloof, indifferent to all but his own rights.

"It so happens this property is my godfather's, and I and my friends come here often. I turn your question back on you, sir," Walter replied. "Why are you here? Though I must add, Miss Alcott, I am grateful for your assistance."

We are here because for some reason Clarence Hampton did not wish us to be near his own campsite, I thought, waiting to hear his response.

"My mother secured permission for a picnic from Giles Cavendish," Clarence said.

"Then your mother is Mrs. Tupper," said Walter. "Godfather couldn't remember what day he gave permission for. Believe me, I would not have intruded had I known this was the day. I have no desire to make your acquaintance, sir." Walter turned on his heel and walked off to where his friends awaited, near a path that must have led to his godfather's country home, and that rudely turned back said much about what the native Walpolians thought of those newcomers, Ida Tupper and her son.

"Isn't this silly?" Helen said brightly. "Boys can be such imbeciles. Walter! Come back! It is too fine a day to end with a quarrel. I fell over a cliff and was rescued! Can you imagine a finer outing? We must write a play about this!"

Walter studied his boot tips, and his companions looked at us from over fluttering fans. The second young man, still nameless to me, had been silent all this time. Now he walked over to Llew and extended his hand.

"I am Thomas Kittredge, and I am pleased to meet you. You are from Michigan, I understand?"

"I am studying there." Llew shook his hand with great enthusiasm. Thus was the ice broken and the quarrel ended. Helen's group, added to our own, created a party of some dozen people, and we had no trouble finishing the remains of Ida Tupper's picnic hamper.

Clarence continued to glower and sit somewhat at a distance from us. I had recently reread Miss Brontë's ardent romance, *Wuthering Heights*, and it occurred to me that Clarence would make a fine Heathcliff: dark, brooding, inscrutable, solitary. Heathcliff had been a man of mystery, of unknown origin and parentage. He had also been passionate. There was the difference. Clarence sat aloof from us, indifferent to the considerable quantity of feminine charm present at this picnic. Sylvia, Helen, Anna, Myrtle—none seemed to stir his interest.

"How came you to fall over the cliff?" Anna asked our new friend, when the last of the shortbread and strawberry jam had been consumed.

"I was chasing after a piece of paper and did not watch my step," said Helen, blushing. "I prefer to think I am not usually of such clumsiness. I have studied ballet with Dame Petrovia of Paris."

"You had six lessons when she visited last summer," clarified her brother, Thomas.

"Seven, and she pronounced I had an uncommon gift for the lyrical," retorted Helen, again sticking that short and rounded nose into the air.

"Are you theatrical?" I asked.

"I am. And I have heard you are, as well. You must not blush, Miss Louisa. Small towns do gossip, as you know, and I have already heard that you are a writer and friend of the theater. I have been hoping to make your acquaintaince, and I offer you a proposition. Indeed, one could say our partnership was destined, considering the drama of our meeting." Helen leaned forward and gave me a wink, the sly gesture contrasting strangely with her cherubic face and girlish curls. "Write us a play. We will produce it here in Walpole."

"Do!" cried Anna and Sylvia simultaneously. "Louy, remember the fun we had in Concord with our theatricals?"

"I will try," I agreed, testing my own enthusiasm for the project.

This is what those who do not attempt to create with the pen do not realize: The muse cannot always be coerced. Say you want to write a play, and the imagination settles itself instead on a long poem, or series of letters. I was reluctant to take time away from my elves' stories and "The Lady and the Woman." But I could turn my hand to a script for a theatrical performance. "I will try," I repeated.

"It is settled," said Helen. "We will meet this next Thursday evening at six o'clock for further discussions. For rehearsals we will use the attic at my home, Elmwood. We are on the west side of the Common. You will have no trouble finding it." Again, that tone of a queen used to having her orders obeyed unquestioningly and promptly. She reminded me of my younger sister, May, also of cherubic face and tyrannic disposition.

"Settled," said Sylvia. "In an hour we must start home. What shall we do meantimes? Walk the path to the bottom of the chasm?"

Helen shivered. "I think not," I said. "We've had enough exercise for the day, and it is still a long journey home. Why not a game of cards?"

"Splendid idea," said Thomas Kittredge.

"Shall we play whist?" I directed this question to Clarence Hampton. *"Abondance déclarée?"*

Clarence looked surprised.

"Whist?" I repeated.

"I don't know the game," he muttered.

THE FAIR WEATHER of our picnic day was followed by two days of a grimly determined rain that saw my entire household, including myself, bound indoors. I discovered myself one afternoon spending an entire hour watching the house cat (for all country homes come equipped with a friendly mouser) similarly cabin-fevered, spring upon its own tail. Remembering my pledge to attempt a script for the amateur theatrical society of Walpole, I fled to my leaky cabin to see if a story for a small group of actors might arise from my sodden imagination.

Pen in hand, I wrote opening lines. *Angelo, did you see the mist coming over the moor? Did you hear the hounds bay?* and *They say the casket would not stay sealed*—only to cross them out in frustration. No romance sprang to mind, only a tragedy. Over and over again my mind returned to Shakespeare's *Hamlet*, the story of the prince who so hates his stepfather that the play ends with hardly a living person onstage. And such thoughts led me to think about Clarence Hampton and his stepfather, Jonah Tupper.

Murderers, I deemed, must be fine actors, since their survival depends on mixing into the populations of their community.

And then I remembered something that my beloved friend, Ralph Emerson, had once said: "Men are what their mothers made them." Perhaps if I knew more about Ida Tupper, I would know more about her son, Clarence Hampton. Perhaps then I would know the fate of Jonah Tupper. Somehow I believed Ernst Nooteboom, the healthy young man who had somehow fallen over a cliff in his town shoes, was connected to the two others.

I picked up my pen once again, this time to make a list rather than invent a story. I must learn where Ida Tupper had lived before settling in Walpole. I already knew she was a Unitarian, which knowledge was necessary for my plan, since I would need to write to her former parishes.

DESPITE THE RAIN, there was a fair in Walpole that afternoon, a small group of "travelers"—Irish immigrants who wandered from village to village, setting up their striped tents to tell fortunes and mend pots. They had set up in a marshy pasture next to the river. The women of this encampment were barefoot and much begrimed; their children were wiry and muddy but very gleeful. I sensed I would find the merry Ida Tupper there, and I did. She was sitting under a tent awning awaiting her turn with the fortune-teller.

"Why, Mrs. Tupper! What a surprise!" I said.

"Louisa! I am going to have my future read. What do you think of that?" she gushed like a schoolgirl. Her hair was more flamboyantly padded than ever, her gown was a determinedly youthful pink, and she smelled strongly of Hungary water. How does vanity affect a mother? I tried to imagine my childhood with Abba occupied most of the morning arranging her hair and spending the household pin money on fortune-tellers. Such a challenging scene defeated my ability to imagine it.

"Mrs. Tupper, I want to thank you for the picnic you arranged." I sat on the stool next to her.

"Why, Louisa, it was my pleasure. It is good for Clarence to be with other young people. He has become quite unsociable this year. Such a moody young person. What do you think the fortune-teller will see for me?"

"Lemonade," said Clarence Hampton, arriving with a glass in one hand and his umbrella in the other. As usual, he was dressed in polished boots (in a cow pasture!) with lace frothing at his throat and wrists, though most young men those days wore simple collars and cuffs. *Does vanity ever lead to violence?* I wondered. Narcissism. Ralph Emerson had been particularly fond of the classical tale of Narcissus and had told it over and over, about the boy who could only stare at his own reflection. That fable had ended badly, I recalled.

"Are you here to have your fortune told?" Clarence asked. His right eyebrow lifted, and there was a suggestion of a smile on his mouth, as if he thought the idea humorous.

"Are you?" I asked.

"A man's destiny is what he makes of it," he said.

"Really, Clarence!" said Ida Tupper. "You seem to think that there is no mystery, no romance to life."

Clarence's gaze grew hard. "Mystery? Romance? I thought you more practical than that, Mother." He turned away and stalked off through the crowd.

"Children," said Mrs. Tupper, sniffing. "I wonder some-times if they are worth the pain of bringing them into the world. Oh, excuse me, Louisa. I shouldn't speak of such things to you, you being unwed and such."

"It is quite all right, Mrs. Tupper. I know a little about childbirth." Last winter I had assisted in a home for unwed mothers. But this seemed a promising venue for our conversation, so I pursued it. "You must have been quite young when Clarence was born."

"A mere slip of a girl," Ida agreed. "My husband, Mr. Hampton, was an older gentleman. We were very happy together. He adored me, the sweet man. He passed over when Clarence was fourteen." She wiped away a tear. "His death was such a shock. So unexpected." Ida blew gently into a handkerchief. "I warned Billy to let the handyman take care of the roof, but he would attempt it himself. He fell, and left me with a boy to raise on my own." She blew her nose heartily into her flimsy lace handkerchief.

"My deepest regrets," I said. "I hope you had your family there to comfort you."

"No, Mr. Hampton and I had a house—oh, ever such a nice house it was, in Weymouth. Before that I lived in Manchester with my family, the Wattles. I come from good people. But they have all passed away, and so I was quite alone when I mourned my dear Billy. Alone, and in a town that was so unfriendly. You know how these small towns can be, Louisa. So Clarence and I moved to Worcester.

"Oh, how happy I was there!" She sighed, her tears for Mr. Hampton forgotten. "I met Mr. Sykes there—he was a lawyer, widowed—and he said, 'Ida, if you don't marry me I'll just jump off the bridge!' So I did, of course. So strange," she mused, growing thoughtful.

"Why was it strange?" I asked.

"Because he did drown, after all. He would go swimming too soon after lunch. He was a sporter, you see, and swam every day. He always said a brisk swim would keep him healthy forever. He took Clarence swimming with him."

"I was not there that day!" Clarence had returned from his perambulation about the pasture. Apparently whomever he sought was not at the fair, and he had crept up behind us with a second glass of lemonade in his hand. This he handed to me.

"Of course you were there, dear. Don't you remember?" insisted his mother. "I had gone into town with Brother, to see a specialist, and left you and Mr. Sykes together for the day."

"I was fossil hunting that day," muttered Clarence, whose lace cravat was suddenly too tight, for now he tugged at it in discomfort.

"Then we moved to Walpole and I met Jonah Tupper. Oh, how he courted me!" Ida fanned herself briskly. "Mr. Tupper did not care much for Clarence, I have to admit. Those two never hit it off."

"It does seem unfair," I commented. "To have been left a widow so young and so often, and now you are alone again."

"A man must earn his living," Ida said. "Oh, it is sad to think of the past. We must cheer up. Too bad it is so difficult to make a name for oneself in the theater. I understand you are to write a play, Louisa? Ah, you young people, so much promise, so much fun. I once acted, you know." Ida grew gay once again, her sorrows forgotten. She had a mind like a may-fly. "My day school when I was a girl had a teacher who was fond of theatricals, especially Shakespeare. 'So good for the memory, girls, so good for the memory,' she would tell us. My last year in school we played *King Lear*. Can you believe it, Louisa, dear? I was Lear! I had such a fine long white beard and really the best lines in the play. I still remember some of them."

Ida rose from her chair and struck a posture with one lace-mittened hand pointing up and the other at her nipped-in waist. She frowned, and even so I could not imagine a less Lear-like figure than the one before me.

"'Come not between the dragon and his wrath!'" she

growled, knitting her brows and stabbing her hand higher into the air. "'I lov'd her most, and thought to set my rest on her kind nursery. Hence, and avoid my sight! So be my grave my peace, as here I give her father's heart from her!'"

"Brava!" I exclaimed with feigned admiration.

Ida curtsied and blew kisses to me, arching them over the imaginary limelights of a stage.

At that moment the tent flap opened and a dreamy-eyed girl dressed in white came out. The fortune-teller must have given her good news, for she seemed to barely touch the ground as she walked away.

"Next," said the Gypsy with a tone of impatience in her voice. Her silver bracelets gleamed and clanked as she gestured at her opened tent flap.

"That's me," said Ida, clasping her hands under her chin.

"No. You," said the Gypsy, pointing at me. She squinted. "You, I think, are next. Those eyes. You live in two different worlds."

"You are mistaken," I said. "Mrs. Tupper was next." I pushed Ida toward the tent. As interesting as it would have been to spend time with a Gypsy fortune-teller, I could not spare a dime on such amusement. Besides, I had already acquired a considerable quantity of information.

CHAPTER TWELVE

A Cold Kitchen

IN THE MORNING before my run in the ravine, I sat down at the little desk in the room I shared with Anna and Sylvia and wrote a letter to the coroner's office in Worcester.

"What is that for, Louy?" asked Sylvia, still yawning but woken by the scratching of my pen. Anna slept on.

"To discover, if I can, whether or not Clarence was with his stepfather on the day he drowned. There is some confusion over it, and the detail seems rather important to me," I told her. "Will you take it to the post for me later?"

"Ummm." She turned over and went back to sleep, pulling the quilt over her head to keep out the bright dawn.

For good measure, I wrote a second letter to the Unitarian church in Manchester, Vermont, asking for details of the Tupper family and Ida's first marrriage. Such curiosity borders on low gossip, so I did penance for that sin by spending an hour with Father, weeding in the vegetable patch, after my run in the ravine. It was an unpleasant, muddy task, and the soil had a rotten smell that grew almost unbearable when it began to rain again and Father retreated to his study, still wearing his yard boots.

Absolved from further manual labor because of the rain, I decided to work on the play I had agreed to write for the theatrical group. First, though, I thought to quell the rattling in my stomach, for I hadn't eaten since the day before. A mystery often undoes my appetite, which renews once I have found an action that will forward my speculations. The letters gave me a sense of momentum, and that sent me to our little kitchen in search of a bowl of soup and mug of coffee.

The kitchen was damp and cold. The soup was chilly. "Abba?" I asked. She sat in a corner by a window, knitting a stocking. Rain pelted against the pane, making a crackling sound as if to compensate for a missing fire in the stove.

"It is a potato soup," Abba said. "Very good cold. I hear they eat it chilled in Paris. Try it, Louy." There was a dogged cheerfulness in her voice.

"What has Father done this time?"

Abba put down her knitting and smiled a little crookedly. "He gave away our firewood, dear. To a man who was in much greater need than we."

"I heard your voice, Louy. Are you done working for the day?" Sylvia came into the kitchen, wrapped tightly in a shawl.

"Have you had the *Potage de Pommes de Terre*?" I asked, laughing. "It is a French dish, served often on warm summer days."

"This is hardly a warm summer day," Sylvia complained. "What is it?" She stared into the bowl I had ladled for her. "Cold potato soup?"

Mother and I were laughing. Life with a philosopher had

its ups and downs. Father had given away all the wood, but at least we still had our rain capes. One previous spring those had disappeared as well, and I had had the uncomfortable feeling, during a stroll on the Boston Common, of seeing a young woman walk by in what I recognized as my own cape. Attached to the hands and knees of that young woman was a swarm of hungry-looking children. Father had been right: She needed a little warmth in a cold world.

"I will send to Uncle Benjamin for more wood," I said, kissing Abba's cheek. "There is more than enough in the shed to get us through this rainy spell."

"You might ask him for a pail of potatoes as well," Abba said. "It will be some time before the new potatoes can be dug."

"Now that is a strange thing, how well Father's vegetable patch is growing," I remarked. Sylvia sat next to me and dutifully swallowed cold soup. "Remember Fruitlands?"

"How could I forget it?" said Abba. Our months at the commune called Fruitlands had been a very hard time, and she, on her frail back, had carried all the practical exigencies of a community of philosophers and children. We had almost starved, since Father had refused to fertilize the fields and the harvest was a failure.

"I remember all too well," Abba continued in a tone as close to a complaint as that patient woman ever came. "It will not happen again. Seeing the ribs on my children stick out like that. Not again. Think no more on it."

"Think no more on what?" Llew came into the kitchen from the back stairway.

"Hard times," I said.

"Strange! I was just reading that volume when I fell asleep!" said Llew.

"You fell asleep over a Dickens novel?" I asked, stunned. "That is one of his best! It is excellent."

"Louy, you know I have little time for novels," said Llew, "so do not berate my lack of knowledge of current romance. Say, it's freezing in here! The fire gone out? They say there will be a death by misadventure when the kitchen fire goes out."

I shivered. "No misadventure," I corrected. "Only that Father gave away our firewood."

Llew laughed and rubbed his hands together. "I thought voices disturbed my study. Perhaps it was just the cold and damp."

"You heard voices?" I asked. "It must have been us, speaking here in the kitchen."

"No, they were men's voices, outside the window of your father's study. I admit to using *Hard Times* as a pillow when I rested my eyes. A very hard pillow, though of substantial thickness." Llew grinned sheepishly. "Then I heard a man's voice say something about Miss Nooteboom, and then, 'Louisa Alcott will know.'"

"You were asleep," Sylvia said.

"I was not," Llew insisted. "As a medical student I know the difference between asleep and awake. Moreover, I know the difference between the typical male and female voice and have learned to deduce intent. This was a man's voice, very angry. A young man's, I would say. And there was a second voice, another man's, deep as Mr. Alcott's. He said, 'It does not matter.' They seemed to be quarreling rather vigorously."

"Could you discern the subject of the quarrel?" I asked.

"Mr. Tupper's name was mentioned, but I could not tell if they referred to father or son." Llew rose from the table and paced, rubbing his hands together to warm them.

"Were you in the chair by the window, and was that window open?" I asked.

"Yes and yes," said Llew, sitting at the table and tasting the cold soup. He frowned. "I will fetch over more wood before supper," he told Abba, and he gave me a wink. He put down his spoon after the first mouthful and patted his stomach to indicate he desired no more.

"Could one of the voices have been Clarence Hampton's?" I asked. Llew nodded thoughtfully. Walpolians do not take "shortcuts" through other people's gardens. But if Clarence and the second man had been standing by the hedge that separated our house from Ida's, their conversation could have been heard in Father's study. Who was the second man? And what did they mean by "Louisa Alcott will know"? Somehow even more ominous was the other statement, that it did not matter.

"Louy, I forgot to tell you," said Sylvia. "When I posted your letters, Clarence Hampton was in the office. He saw them in my hand and I think he read the addresses. He had such a funny look on his face."

THE NEXT MORNING Mr. Dill, the unemployed railroad worker who had inherited our firewood, came by to give his thanks and to bring us a half dozen eggs from his hen coop. He stood on the back step rather than broach the kitchen, because his boots gave pungent evidence of his recent venture into a farmyard. I hoped it was his own, and the eggs were properly his to dispose of.

"Is the mister here?" asked Mr. Dill, cap in hand.

"He is," said Abba. "Bronson, you have a caller!" She raised her voice somewhat, despite her disapproval of such rudeness, but she was at that crucial moment of porridge stirring when the pot cannot be left.

"If you are what is meant by a philosopher, then I approve, I approve," said Mr. Dill when Father appeared. He shook his benefactor's hand with such lengthy enthusiasm we thought that appendage might drop off. Father, still in his nightshirt but with a volume of Cicero in his left hand, beamed.

"If it was philosophy made you send over the wood, then philosophy is a fine thing," asserted the man.

"It was nothing," said Father. " 'Give all thou canst; high Heaven rejects the lore of nicely calculated less or more.' "

"Say," said Mr. Dill, scratching his chin. "Now, is that a piece of philosophy? I'll have to remember that."

"It is Wordsworth," said Father.

"Well, well," said the man. "Fancy that. I'll be off, then. I've got work for the morning, sweeping out the town hall, since there's to be a hearing today."

"A hearing?" I looked up from the loaf of bread I'd been slicing.

"Town fathers have decided to officially question Mr. Tupper about Ernst Nooteboom's death," said Mr. Dill. "Seems his sister found a piece of what they are calling evidence."

Abba looked at me and sighed. A detective word had been used.

"Evidence?" I asked, handing Mr. Dill a slice of buttered bread. He stretched for it from his place on the step.

"She was cleaning out her brother's things and getting

ready to sell his Sunday suit when she found a note in the pocket from Tupper, asking Ernst to meet him by the ravine for a conversation."

"Who is this Mr. Tupper?" asked Father, who had been in his shop a half dozen times but had not yet noticed the sign overhead.

"Ida's father-in-law," Abba said. "It is an uncommon family, though. Mrs. Tupper and her father-in-law do not care for each other."

"Ah." He shook his head in disapproval. Father had adored Abba's family. "It's those horsehair pads in her hair, I suspect," he said. "Makes for a strange daughter-in-law." He wandered off with a plate of bread and jam.

I did not dismay Father with the news that Mr. Tupper senior also seemed to hold a grudge against Uncle Benjamin and had made domestic trouble for Lilli, as well. Mr. Tupper in all ways seemed at odds with his own community.

"Could I attend this hearing?" I asked Mr. Dill.

Mr. Dill stared unhappily at his boots. "Well, with you being a girl and all, and an outsider . . ."

"Louy, perhaps you should visit with Lilli instead, after the meeting," Abba suggested. She was right, of course. A stranger at such a meeting would cause considerable discomfort and perhaps even delay whatever truth might be available. Lilli would have to provide the information.

AFTER THE NOON meal of fish chowder (served warm, thanks to Uncle Benjamin's woodpile), Sylvia and I went off together to meet with Lilli Nooteboom.

She was in Mrs. Roder's back parlor with a cold compress on her forehead.

"Oh, dear," said Sylvia. "You look all-in. May I help?"

Her eyes were red. "I don't see how," she said.

"It is a temple massage I have learned," said Sylvia. "My mother suffers the most frightful migraines. Sit up here, with this pillow behind your back, and let down your hair." Lilli did as instructed, and an arm's length of white-blond hair fell over the harsh black of her mourning dress. I would use that image, I knew, in one of my "blood and thunder" stories about heroines in danger. Sylvia stood behind her and began moving her fingers in gentle circles over Lilli's forehead and the top of her head.

"That is better," admitted Lilli some minutes later. "I feel almost well, and the pain has gone. You want to hear about the meeting. It was as I knew it would be. They believed Mr. Tupper, not me. He denied the note was in his handwriting, or that he had sent for Ernst that day. They think I wrote the note to lay blame."

"May I see the note?" I asked.

Lilli took it from the little drawstring bag of black leather she wore tied to her waistband. It was a small piece of inexpensive brown paper, the kind merchants use to wrap purchases, and it contained very few words:

Meet me at the ravine. I have a better offer. Tupper.

"It is in script," Lilli said, "and Mr. Tupper wrote to Ernst in block letters, because we were foreigners and he made fun of our English, said it was children's English. But maybe this time he forgets."

Or maybe it was son, not father, who wrote the note, I thought. Or maybe someone who only claimed to be Tupper. Whoever it was, they had written on the same paper I had found at Clarence Hampton's camp.

"So we are back at the beginning, with Miss Nooteboom's word against Mr. Tupper's," said Sylvia as we made our way back home.

"Not quite at the beginning," I said. "Think, Sylvia, who else would profit from the acquisition of land wanted by Mr. Tupper?"

Sylvia frowned and puffed a little, trying to keep up with me. I was walking quickly by then, using the long-strided pace that often accompanies my worried moods.

"That would be his partner, which he doesn't have," she guessed. "Or his heir, who is not here."

"Jonah Tupper," I agreed. "Where is Jonah Tupper? But remember, Sylvia, there is more than one potential heir. There is a daughter-in-law, and she has a son."

"Clarence Hampton," said Sylvia.

"The first is missing, or at least his whereabouts are not known, and the second is . . ."

"Very strange," supplied Sylvia.

BY THE EVENING of the second Thursday after the picnic, I had the beginnings of my play ready for the Walpole Amateur Dramatic Company. Since I must wait for the mail to bring responses to my inquiries about Clarence's family, I had gone back to my writing shed with renewed energy.

The play scenes were not as humorous, when humor was

desired, nor as tragic, when tragedy was the mood, as I had hoped to produce, but there was time yet to further work them. It is my experience that initial attempts often fall short. It is in the second and third and fourth renditions that value might be mined in prose, another lesson learned both from Father and Mr. Emerson, who used much ink crossing out misshapen phrases and straightening them into a lovelier form. Meanwhile, we had an initial set of lines to rehearse.

However, the faults of the plot and characters became even more apparent once we had gathered in Helen Kittredge's attic for rehearsal.

Our rehearsal room was a beamed area brightened with oil lamps and as large as a barn loft. One end had been cleared of the usual leather and wooden trunks, woven baskets and boxes of chipped china, and ancient shoes that accumulate in attics, and a large rose-colored curtain put up to mimic a stage area. The effect was rather romantic: an island of possibility set into the debris of the past, rather like one of those gloomy and mystical paintings of the German landscape school.

The new Walpole Amateur Dramatic Company was there, a half dozen expectant faces.

Helen beamed. "Well, then, shall we start?"

There was a shy shuffling of feet among the young men and a giggling among the young women.

"Perhaps Louisa should tell us about the play we have commissioned," Helen suggested after a moment of deep thought. "Sit here, Louisa." She pulled forward a chair into the middle of the gathering and held an oil lamp over my shoulder.

Feeling horribly self-conscious, having thus been made the center of attention, I untied the string and brown paper that held the first pages of *Thornton and Emmeline: A Colonial Tragedy*. I cleared my throat.

"Thornton is the son of a cobbler, poor and ill-respected by the town because of his poverty and because his father is often seen publicly inebriated," I began.

"Ah!" exclaimed Helen, frowning to indicate deep thought. The others nodded.

"But Thornton," I continued, "has several qualities that will eventually redeem his reputation. First, he is brave, braver than most. Second, he is loyal."

"Loyal to Emmeline," Helen said.

"Exactly. He loves her, and she returns his love, but fears her own father's wrath for her misplaced affection. They must never speak in public but only steal a few moments of joy when Thorton measures her feet for new boots."

"How romantic!" sighed Sylvia.

"How racy!" said Helen. "There must be bare feet on-stage! And then what happens?"

"I don't know," I said truthfully. "I have only the first act."

"Then we will read that, and spur you on," Helen said. "I myself will play Emmeline, unless there are objections." No one dared object, of course. "Anna, you can play my mother, and, Thomas, you can play my father. Walter will play Thornton." She looked at him from under her long lashes, and that poor young man, already branded and trussed and ready for the altar, though he did not yet know it, ran his finger around his shirt collar.

The readings were dreadful. The young men were wooden

and muttered their lines; the young women giggled and poked each other in the ribs. The amateur group had earned its name, indeed. Painfully we struggled forward, turning page after page of my "blood and thunder" story.

When it was again Helen's turn and she exclaimed, "'Oh, Thornton, I shall never love another but you, and die a maiden rather than betray you!'" I knew the play would not do. Helen had declaimed her lines by putting one hand over her heart and shrieking with what she thought was a fit of passion. As Sylvia later described, she sounded more like a cat with its tail being pulled.

"I think a comedy will suit us better," I said, rolling up the pages. "Let us put this play aside for a later time." *Ten or fifteen years later*, I said to myself.

BEFORE SLEEPING THAT night, I spent an hour alone on our front porch, gazing at the full moon, round and white as a mercury glass globe. The rehearsal made me laugh at how dreadful we had been, but also saddened me because of how dreadful we had been.

I hugged my knees and tried to think of nothing, for there were too many thoughts in my head at once.

Footsteps shuffled down the sidewalk and I saw, in the moonlight, a man, awkward and slow, coming toward our house. No, the house next door. Clarence Hampton. He saw me just as I recognized him.

"Ah! The lovely Miss Louisa," he said. His speech was very slurred, the S's sibilant and hissing. "May I join you? Yes, thank you, I will."

I hadn't agreed, yet he sat next to me on the step. "Lovely night," he said. "Lovely."

"You have been celebrating," I said.

"I have," he admitted, giving me a broad wink. He hiccuped.

"Why?" I asked.

"I'll tell you a secret," he said, leaning so closely to me that I could smell the gin on his breath. "I have made a decision. An important one. I am going to run away from home. Enough of family."

"You already seem to spend quite a deal of time away from your family."

His drunken smile turned to a snarl. "Not enough," he said. "They confuse me. Make me doubt my own senses. That's how it's always been."

"That is harsh," I said. "May I ask you a question about other matters?"

He looked at me with slightly crossed eyes. "You may," he said.

"How is it that your stepfather paid a deposit for a new bell order out of his own family bank account? Doesn't the church usually pay?"

"Ah," he said. "You have been snooping. Thought you might. But Mother will tell you that it is not uncommon for commercial travelers to make such transactions. It is a kind of loan, you see. From him to the church, to encourage the bell order if they are at all undecided. And now, Miss Louisa, I'm going to turn in. If I'm lucky I'll make it upstairs without waking her. She doesn't approve of the company I keep, you see."

He rose unsteadily, with laborious and slow gesture unbuttoned his boots, and tiptoed home in his stocking feet.

I watched him go, fearing for the safety of his mother, for I remembered those murderous glances he often gave her.

CHAPTER THIRTEEN

Lady Macbeth Comes
for Dinner

"THIS WILL DO nicely for a summer comedy," I said to Sylvia, who found me sitting cross-legged on Uncle's Turkish carpet the following day, surrounded by volumes of plays and stories as well as a book of engravings of European locales. I had spent a lovely afternoon scouring Uncle's library for a suitable candidate, and found—rather refound—Sheridan's *The Rivals* and decided we could stage a production of that very humorous eighteenth-century play.

Sylvia sat next to me and opened the book of engravings. "Paris." She sighed. "Wouldn't it be lovely to walk along that bridge over the Seine? Mother, as you know firsthand, has not a large stock of principles, but those she has, she abides by sternly. She insists I cannot tour Europe until I am wed."

"She is afraid you will run off with a handsome scoundrel and end up running a vineyard in Sicily or an Alpine inn," I said.

"Doesn't it all sound exquisite?" Sylvia sighed again, and then looked dazedly at the volume I placed in her hands. "What is this?"

"It will become our comedy," I told her. "Just enough roles for the group, the lines are not overly long to learn, and it will make Walpole laugh."

"I almost forgot," said Sylvia, peering at the volume. "A letter has come for you." She reached into her pocket and retrieved the correspondence. "Abba sent me over with it. She knew once you were in a library you would be gone for many hours."

I studied the envelope. The paper was of good quality, though thin enough to indicate a certain thriftiness when it came to supplying stationery needs. The handwriting was thin and spidery, very old-fashioned, as a town recorder's should be. "It is from the coroner in Worcester," I said. "About Mr. Sykes, Ida's second husband." I hesitated, then tore the envelope and read quickly.

"Well?" asked Sylvia when I had finished and returned the letter to its envelope. "Well?"

"It is polite and official," I said. "It gives dates of Ida's marriage to Mr. Sykes and his death. He died just six months after the wedding. And the coroner writes one other thing: It was almost a double tragedy, for Mr. Sykes's stepson was swimming with him the day he drowned, and the stepson almost drowned as well."

"Mr. Hampton never mentioned that he once nearly drowned," said Sylvia.

"Just the opposite. I heard him say he wasn't swimming at all that day."

❊   ❊   ❊

WE FOUND ABBA in the kitchen as usual, stirring a pot of fish soup for supper.

"Lake trout," she said happily. "Caught this morning. Benjamin sent them over."

The scrubbed wooden table was covered with fish heads and tails, and the cat and her kittens were wild with appetite, meowing and dancing figure eights at our ankles. Abba gave them a plate of milk and one of the fish heads and put the rest of the unusable fish pieces into a covered pail. She poured lemonade for Sylvia and me and sat down to rearrange daisies and ferns in a long-necked vase. Abba loved flowers, and when Father had a garden he always planted a row for her. This summer the flowers, like the vegetables, were growing at an astounding rate.

"You look like little girls again"—she laughed—"come to tell me about a broken cup or scraped knee. What are these glum faces?"

"I need your advice about Clarence Hampton."

Abba stopped smiling. "That strange young man. Advice about what course of action?"

"That will depend on how you answer my question," I said. "What do you think of him?"

"Are there any biscuits?" asked Sylvia, who was always hungry. Abba took the tin from the shelf and put it upon the table.

"Mr. Hampton is a mystery," she said. "And people so young as he is ought not to be such a mystery. He is hiding something. I hope you are not . . . ?" She could not even bring herself to say aloud what all mothers fear, that her daughter has formed an attachment to a man so promising of heartache.

"I have no feelings for him, Abba, only an awareness that affairs are not as they should be between Clarence Hampton and his mother and his stepfather, indeed, that entire family. Ernst Nooteboom has died violently, and Jonah Tupper seems to have disappeared. I would like to know how you assess Clarence Hampton's character."

Abba poured herself a glass of tea and gave me a long, steady gaze, all the while stirring her fish soup with her other hand.

"When I was young," she said, stirring, "and still living in my brother's house in Connecticut, a boy came calling on me. This was before I had met your father, you understand. After I met Bronson . . . well. That was that. But this boy was different."

"In what manner?" asked Sylvia, leaning forward. She loved stories of Abba's youth.

Abba's usually soft gaze grew hard. "He carried an air of something about him, something unpleasant. He visited us often, since my brother was tutoring him in Greek, so that he might enter divinity school. My brother, Sam, was interested in new educational theories. That's how I met Bronson, you know. He and Sam corresponded, and then Bronson arrived one day on the stagecoach. He was wearing that funny old beat-up hat he kept for so long." Her eyes grew dreamy as she looked into that long-ago romance still so fondly remembered.

"The other young man," I prompted Abba.

"Yes," she said. "Mr. Crawford. Dick Crawford. He had

a fine mind, but always seemed unhappy, as if he carried a tremendous burden. And he didn't know the difference between mine and thine. Several times he brought me flowers he had taken from the neighbor's garden when no one was looking. He took one of Sam's stocks, a good lace one, and never returned it. As if everything were his by right. And there was gin. Much like your Clarence Hampton. My brother soon had to forbid him the house, and ask him to pursue his studies elsewhere. He caught him in the kitchen with Sally, the cook's daughter. Oh, how she cried, so afraid we'd dismiss her without a character, but we could tell the fault was Mr. Crawford's. I wonder what happened to poor Sally?" Abba grew soft-eyed again with nostalgia.

"Did you ever learn the origins of that cloud under which Dick Crawford walked?" I asked.

"Not really. But I guessed at it, sometimes. He had a mother who had had several husbands, and she had sent him away to be raised mostly by distant cousins. I suspect they practiced the 'spare the rod, spoil the child,' philosophy. Stepfamilies can be so cruel." I knew what Abba was thinking; in the darkest moments of the Alcott family she had had to consider sending her own children to live with others, or choose hunger and want for them. She had decided to keep us together at any cost. She had been right.

"What happened to him, Abba, do you know?" I asked.

She gazed sadly at her fish stew. "He was hanged, after he had stabbed a girl who, at a party, had refused to dance with him."

"Anyone home?" a fluting woman's voice called from outside our kitchen door.

Abba shook her head and put down her wooden stirring spoon.

"Coming, Mrs. Tupper," she said. "Will you take a glass of lemonade?"

"Why, that sounds lovely, Abba," said Ida, breezing in before Abba could open the door, and sitting down with us. Ida had that way about her; doors were for strangers, not her, and she did not wait to be asked.

"You all look frightful," said Ida Tupper. "Whatever have you been talking about?"

"An old beau, that's all," said Abba, turning back to the stove. "I was speaking of an old beau."

Ida gave Mother's back a funny look, and suddenly I knew exactly what she was thinking: There was Abba in her stained apron, her gray hair pulled back into a stern knot low on her neck, her hands red from housework. What had she to do with beaux?

"Abba was famed for her hair when she was a girl," I said. "She never had to fill it out with horsehair pads."

Ida blushed. "I'm sure Abba was the belle of whatever balls she attended, and had many beaux."

"I had not," said Abba, half-offended, stirring her soup somewhat more vigorously than required. Sylvia and I twirled the lemon pulp in the bottom of our glasses and said nothing.

Mrs. Tupper cleared her throat. "How are the rehearsals coming?" she asked. "I think it is so charming that you are bringing some culture to little Walpole, Louisa."

"Walpole seems quite cultured already," I said. "But I am pleased that the theatrical group has welcomed us into their midst."

"I had hoped Clarence might join you. I suspect he has inherited some of my own talent for playacting. Did I tell you about my King Lear? Yes, I see I did. I also played Cleopatra. Such a lovely costume! Too bad only the schoolgirls saw me." She giggled.

"Is Clarence interested in the stage?" I asked.

"He is interested only in fossils, I believe," said his mother. "I tried to raise him to appreciate the good things of life, but he digs in the mud."

"Has he considered serious study of science at Harvard?" I asked.

"I'm sure he has no aptitude," Ida said. "He is a dilettante in everything, and it would be a waste of money to send him to school. Think of the trouble he'd get up to without me to look after him. Why, he'd be chasing after servant girls, although Mr. Wattles seems to have convinced him of the wrongness of that error. I shouldn't speak so of my son, but he does try me."

Ida sipped her lemonade. "Of course, my own playacting days are past," she added. "Now I am old, married. Why, I have a grown son! I could never again appear before an audience in costume. That is a pleasure for the young." She sighed heavily.

Her hint was too lacking in subtlety to be politely ignored. "Perhaps, Mrs. Tupper, you would accept a part in the forthcoming production of the Walpole Amateur Dramatic Company?" I suggested.

"Oh, I couldn't." She looked at us from under her long lashes. "But, of course, I wouldn't want to appear standoffish. By the by, Louisa, I've received another card from my Jonah. In the morning's post."

"Let me guess," I said. "A penny card with just a few words of greeting."

"Since you know so much, there is no need to tell you what my dear husband said."

"I'm sorry, Mrs. Tupper. Please have another glass of Abba's lemonade and tell us about the card from Mr. Tupper."

"Well, if you insist. He says he misses me, of course." She looked at Abba and gave her a schoolgirl sort of smile. "Such a sweet man, my husband. Business has not been good for him. There have been no more orders for church bells since that last one came in from Grand Rapids, but he assumes that once all this potherill about Whig and Republican dies down, the commercial world will improve."

"He is still in Detroit, then?" I asked.

"Yes," she said.

"Strange that he would spend so much time in a city where his business is not successful," I commented.

Ida Tupper frowned. "I hadn't thought of that," she said, twirling a string from her shawl. "Well, Jonah can be strange and stubborn. I had to plead with him for ever so long before he would purchase our little honeymoon cottage. Men worry so much about money. Why, if you can't buy yourself a little home, what is the point of working your fingers to the bone?"

Abba smiled wanly. Mrs. Tupper's "honeymoon cottage" was a Walpolian mansion, larger than any house Abba had lived in since her marriage to Bronson Alcott, philosopher, and certainly larger than any she ever expected to inhabit again. But there was no bitterness in her smile, only patient amusement.

Ida blushed prettily. "Well, I must be on my way."

✳   ✳   ✳

OUR LITTLE THEATRICAL group rehearsed *The Rivals* that evening, and I grew optimistic, for our group was well equipped for comedy, with Helen in the role of Lydia, the pretty ingenue and ward of the dragon dowager, Mrs. Malaprop, and Charles as her disguised beau, Captain Absolute. In these romance comedies beaux are always in disguise, and Charles was hard-put to play both the dashing captain and the penniless Beverly, but he managed, for love of Helen.

I was Mrs. Malaprop, a widow trying to advantageously marry off her ward. No one else had wanted the role, for the widow is past youth and was never beautiful. But, dear reader, how could you not want to play a woman who utters such lines as, "I would by no means wish a daughter of mine to be a progeny of learning; I don't think so much learning becomes a young woman; for instance, I would never let her meddle with Greek, or Hebrew, or algebra, or simony or fluxions, or paradoxes, of such inflammatory branches of learning— neither would it be necessary for her to handle any of your mathematical, astronomical, or diabolical instruments."

I added geology and undergroundology to Mrs. Malaprop's list of things not to be meddled with. Llew laughed; Clarence Hampton, who attended a single rehearsal at the urging of his mother, did not. He had not left home, as he had insisted he would when in his cups, and I was both relieved and disappointed. Relieved, for I felt he somehow was involved in the tragedy of Ernst Nooteboom and should be made to answer for it, and disappointed because I had come to realize that his mother had a very negative influence on him.

I had other worries that night, and a different sort of problem. Anna had missed the same cue several times, and I had to face what could no longer be ignored, something that explained the cloudy distance I often felt between my beloved older sister and the rest of the world: She had lost some of her hearing.

After Clarence had stormed out, I whispered something to Anna, whose back was turned to me. She did not respond. "Oh, Anna," I said, putting my hand on her shoulder and turning her around to face me. "How bad is it?"

She saw at once that I had discovered her secret.

"Not very, Louy. Now, you are not to worry. Don't tell Abba. Not just yet. She is so happy in Walpole. Let her enjoy this summer. You promise me, Louy?"

I kissed Anna's smooth brow and thought back over the past weeks when I had thought my older sister was preoccupied or in some state of mind that disallowed full attention to conversation. She had not been hearing us.

"I promise," I said, "though Abba has probably already noticed and has not found the proper moment to bring it up."

"Let her find the moment. Now, Mrs. Malaprop, you are required in the stage area of the attic." Anna, with her resolute smile, gave me a little push and propelled me back into the clearing between the trunks and baskets.

A LETTER ARRIVED from Detroit in response to my telegram. Sylvia was with me the afternoon I picked it up at the post office, and she caught her breath when she saw the return address.

I tore it open and read the two lines it contained. Father O'Connor of the parish of the Immaculate Conception was, indeed, planning to order a bell for its new construction, but had not yet done so. *I admit to much confusion over this matter, Miss Alcott,* he had written. *I know nothing of the bell nor of the personage you refer to as Mr. Jonah Tupper.*

"He's not in Detroit," I told Sylvia. "Nor has he been, I would guess."

"Then where is Jonah Tupper?" she said.

"That is the question," I agreed. "I fear the worst. Too many lies have been told; too much is being hidden."

BUT I COULD not dedicate myself fully to those lies and mysteries, because on a fine Saturday afternoon, exactly as promised in her earlier correspondence, Fanny Kemble arrived in a blaze of glory.

Uncle Benjamin, agog to meet the famous actress, had rigged out and polished his old, rarely used brougham and hired a team and driver from the town stable for the day, so that we might meet her at the train stop and not require her to finish her journey by public coach. The old brougham, charmingly equipped with brass lanterns, yellow silk cushions (now somewhat moth-eaten), and a canvas frieze of cherubs painted on its interior top, held only four, so Uncle, Abba, and I went, leaving room for Fanny on the return. We left Lizzie, Sylvia, May, Llew, Ida Tupper, and Cousin Eliza fuming in Uncle's best parlor, each convinced she or he should have had a place in the coach; only Father and gentle Anna had expressed contentment to let others have a carriage seat.

In our haste and anticipation we three of the arrival deputation were early, and so waited half an hour in the afternoon heat, gazing out over fields and pasture and that strange gash in the earth where the tracks abruptly ended. Abba brought out her knitting and finished a stocking, while Uncle Benjamin read from a volume of poetry. I paced outside the carriage thinking of Mrs. Roder's white, square-framed boardinghouse, and wondering if Lilli was hemming linens or whatever her sewing task for the day was. I wondered who her secret beau was, and if she had one at all.

It was breezy that afternoon, so I took off my straw hat for fear of having it blown away. The wind clawed at my skirt, making it difficult to walk. I had a presentiment of evil despite that musical, strangely ebullient chugging sound of steam-driven wheels grinding over steel tracks. The noise grew to a roar as the train approached, its steam billowing against the blue sky and green fields. When the train ground to a stop, a black-suited conductor jumped down and unfolded the metal steps; six passengers alighted, including our own Fanny, who had brought not one maid, but two, as well as a footman whose sole task seemed to be carrying around her little spaniel. The servants would have to follow on the public omnibus. Fanny traveled with enough trunks to clothe the entire village; Walpole would talk about her visit for months.

She was dressed entirely in white linen embroidered with vines; her summer boots were white leather, and the plume in her hat was white. "Isn't it divine? Parisian, of course," she greeted me, twirling so that we might better admire the costume. "I thought white linen would do well for a country week." For Fanny, any city smaller than London or Rome was bucolic. She had once described Boston as "quaintly rustic."

Uncle Benjamin, hat in hand, gallantly dropped to one knee (emitting a worrisome groan of pain as he did so) and kissed the diva's white-kidskin-gloved hand. I felt queasy whenever I saw Fanny's white gloves, for I was in terror that I would inherit a pair or two and then be required to wear them. What can one do when gloved in white? Very little, I suspect, other than proffer one's hand for adoration.

"I have driven through thunderstorms and blizzards to be at your Boston performances," Uncle Benjamin said, panting from exertion.

"Then you shall be rewarded, sir." Fanny solemnly placed her hand onto his right shoulder, knighting him. "Will you take tea with me tomorrow?"

I wondered what Ida Tupper, who needed to be the center of all conversations, would think of this. There might be some stormy tea hours ahead.

"IS SHE HANDSOME?" asked Llew once we had left Fanny at her inn and returned home to Abba's supper of fish stew— again!

"I think we should go back to eating only vegetables," said May, dipping her spoon into the thick yellowish broth. "I'm tired of fish."

"The most beautiful woman in the world," I said in response to Llew's question, "next to Abba."

"Maybe only of her generation," Llew said. "There are younger persons possessing much greater beauty; I'm sure of it." Gallantry must have been in the air that day. Llew took my hand in his own and kissed it quickly, when he thought the others were busy with their meal.

But May saw and dropped her spoon on the floor in shock. I hastened to crawl under the table to pick it up, to hide my burning cheeks.

We gave Fanny a day to settle into her rooms at the inn and rest from the journey, and during that day only Abba and Uncle Benjamin were allowed to visit: Abba because she was full of common sense about such things as unpacking and moving furniture, for hotel rooms were never arranged to Fanny's liking, and Benjamin because she had accepted him as her rustic knight.

When Mrs. Tupper heard that her cavalier was paying homage elsewhere, her merry visage darkened visibly, and then quickly brightened again. "Oh, well." She sighed. "I know Benjamin will not desert me for long." She was standing at her back door holding a pair of knitting needles borrowed from Abba, for she had lost the first pair. A six-cent pair of needles gone, and not even a single stocking to show for it, I thought. Not so much as an "I'm sorry" from this lax student of the knitting arts.

"Perhaps Mr. Tupper will return home soon, and you will not be so lonely," I suggested, baiting her for information.

"Perhaps, though Clarence thinks his stepfather will be away longer than usual. Abba, could you show me again how to make that seed stitch?" Mrs. Tupper asked.

ON THE SECOND day, as promised, Fanny arrived at our humble cottage for supper. And what an arrival! All of Walpole must have lined up to watch as the world-famous Fanny Kemble made her stately way from the inn to our little cottage.

Fanny had dressed in her "rustic" white linen suit with a very large hat adorned with a dozen or so white plumes that bobbed at each step, and to contrast with her immaculate suit she carried a blue basket filled with bright red cherries. Her two maids followed behind, each carrying a brown-wrapped package—books, we would discover, one for each of us, chosen by Fanny herself. Her footman followed the maids, and he had in tow a very, very large turtle pulled on a cart, and on that same cart a cage of live pheasants.

"Oh, my," exclaimed Abba, opening the door to this exotic vision.

"Oh, my!" exclaimed May, running out to examine the turtle. "Is it to be a pet? Has he a name?"

"I rather thought he was for Sunday dinner," said Fanny, laughing. She handed the huge basket of cherries to Abba. "Mr. Tupper wished to carry them himself and said he was coming this way, but I thought they made an interesting prop for my entrance."

"Oh, my," said Father, disapproving as he looked over Fanny's shoulder at her entourage. "Fish, yes. Turtle, no. And as for those birds, you might as well set them free at this moment. They'll not be butchered in my house."

Fanny sighed. So did Abba, I admit. She'd had roast pheasant as a girl and would not have minded renewing that acquaintanceship. The cage was opened as Father requested, and the startled birds danced about in the front garden for quite a while before taking advantage of their freedom and winging off into the dusky sky.

Fanny's huge audience of Walpolians applauded, and the pretty actress curtsied.

"Surely you don't expect the turtle to fly off," said May, still hoping she might have acquired a new pet.

"I must think about the turtle," said Father, ascending into his transcendental mist.

Chaos took over our blue parlor, and it seemed to protest the arrival into its modest measurement of a dozen people, including the Alcotts with Llew and Sylvia, Uncle Benjamin and Cousin Eliza, and Clarence Hampton and Mrs. Tupper. Even Cousin Frank, who had so far spent the summer repairing roofs and henhouses, had made an appearance, looking somewhat harried but handsome, with his hair slicked down and his best jacket dusted and pressed off. I had wished to invite Lilli, but Abba had wisely said it was too soon for her to attend supper with such a crowd; she was still in deepest mourning.

May and Lizzie wanted all the news of Boston, Sylvia and Anna wanted the news of Europe, I wanted the theater news, and Llew wished to know if any new papers on geology had been printed at Harvard. We quite overwhelmed Fanny, who grew stumped when it was time to answer Llew's question.

"Let me see," she said, holding her chin in one elegant hand, a cordial glass in the other, for we were in the parlor having sherry before dinner. We did not normally have sherry before dinner or any other hour of the day, but this was a special day. "Ah, yes," she said with gravitas. "I did attend one meeting of the Harvard Geological Society where they decided that it was not true that the moon was made of green cheese."

"Mr. Willis might well believe the earth is made of cheese, if it be evolutionary cheese," said Clarence Hampton.

"Mr. Hampton would believe people were made of cheese, if it said so in scripture," Llew retorted.

"Gentlemen," warned Abba. "The purpose of any study should be to bring us closer together, not push us farther apart. There are already issues enough in the world to estrange friend from friend and brother from brother."

"Hear, hear," said Father.

Llew and Clarence looked daggers at each other.

CHAPTER FOURTEEN

Potatoes Are Requested

ABBA LOOKED WONDERFUL the night of our dinner with Fanny. She had brushed her gray hair smoothly into a silk snood and pinned a new lace collar onto her old bombazine dress. I studied her closely that evening, for I was close to finishing my story of "The Lady and the Woman" and sought exactitude of gesture from my muse.

Anna, who followed the conversation by watching our faces, now rerouted us into discussions of the novels being published that summer and who was reading what. Lyman Beecher's daughter, Harriet Stowe, had published *Uncle Tom's Cabin* two years before, and the book was flying off the shelves and still the center of most literary discussion. The lamps were lit as darkness fell, and our crowded parlor was lively with animated shadows.

"Mrs. Alcott, do sing for us," said Fanny.

"Yes, Abba, yes!" we agreed. Lizzie quietly took her place at the piano.

"My voice is quite gone," protested Abba, but she smiled with pleasure at being asked. There sat Abba in her old bombazine with an apron now tied over it, for every ten minutes she had jumped up and gone into the kitchen. Beloved Abba could have been a concert singer. Instead, she fell in love with a philosopher and gave him four daughters and all her heart.

"Please, Mrs. Alcott," said Fanny in a voice no one could resist, and to add to her plea she knelt before Abba in supplication. She was, after all, theatrical.

"Lizzie, do you remember the chords for 'Believe Me, If All Those Endearing Young Charms'?" Abba asked.

"I do." And to prove it, Lizzie played the opening bars. When she started the second time, Abba joined in and sang those lovely old lyrics with a voice as strong and true as an angel's. "'It is not while beauty and youth are thine own, and thy cheeks unprofaned by a tear, that the fervor and faith of a soul can be known, to which time will make thee more dear!'" she sang, looking at Father and trilling the final *dear* with so many grace notes we thought she must surely run out of breath. But she did not. The song died away as gently as it had started.

Llew cleared his throat and gave me a glance. Mrs. Tupper was, for a change, speechless. Clarence Hampton made a point of appearing unmoved by such sentiment, but his eyes had reddened, and I wondered if his conscience smarted.

Dear Fanny rose to her feet and applauded. "Mrs. Alcott, I've not heard a finer voice in this country or Europe!"

"Perhaps you would honor us with a declamation," Mother suggested.

"Well," said Fanny. "I think I could get through a speech

or two without much trouble. How about Gertrude from *Hamlet*?" (Reader: I had asked in advance for this particular section. The play's the thing wherein to catch the conscience.)

"Excellent," I said. "Mr. Hampton, you can read from Hamlet's role to complete the scene." I gave Fanny the book carried in my pocket.

"Charming," said the actress when she and Clarence stood face-to-face. "I see from where Louisa has opened the book that we are to begin in the scene after Hamlet has murdered Polonius." She paused, and I saw all her concentration move inward, searching, and then as her energy moved out again it was as if she were a different person, a woman who had seen much of life and understood none of it.

"'O Hamlet! Speak no more. Thou turn'st mine eyes into my very soul; And there I see such black and grained spots as will not leave their tint.'"

Fanny's voice was always thrilling, deep and lovely and rich, but for Queen Gertrude she made it higher-pitched, the voice of a woman who denies her own maturity until too late. I could not help but look in Ida Tupper's direction. Confusion showed on her face, and I suspected she was unfamiliar with any Shakespeare except *King Lear*.

Clarence cleared his throat. His face turned sullen and angry, as I imagined Hamlet's would have looked. "'Nay, but to live in the rank sweat of an enseamed bed, stew'd in corruption, honeying and making love over the nasty sty—'"

"'O! Speak to me no more—'" began Fanny.

"No more indeed," said Abba, rising hastily.

"What is an enseamed bed stew'd in corruption?" asked May.

"None of your concern. Louy, I do not like this choice of yours," Abba chastened.

"Perhaps it is inappropriate," agreed Fanny. "Though I must say, Mr. Hampton, even your abbreviated reading surprised me with its authenticity. You might have a future as a tragedian."

Clarence Hampton returned the volume to me. "Is there a future for villains? Ask Miss Louisa what she thinks."

Fanny stared at him, then at me, and I could not tell what she was thinking. "Well, since I have warmed my throat, I will do a little speech for you. Lady Macbeth," she announced.

"The spot speech!" cried Lizzie with delight, pulling her ottoman closer to the hearth, where Fanny stood.

Fanny drooped her head, as people do when much aggrieved in their minds, indeed just as Clarence often stood. She pulled loose one of her prettily dressed side curls and loosened the lace jabot of her dress; she pulled up her sleeves to reveal her arms all the way to the elbows. She closed her eyes and took a deep breath, which she held for a very long time. When she opened her eyes again she was Lady Macbeth, sleepwalking, much disturbed in mind over the blood she had caused to be shed.

"'Out, damned spot! I say! One; two: why, then, 'tis time to do't. Hell is murky!'" Her voice began as a quiet growl; it rose to a shriek with the word *hell*. Fanny—rather, Lady Macbeth—turned and faced Clarence Hampton and cast her gloomy gaze upon him. "'Fie, my lord, fie! a soldier, and afeard? What need we fear who knows it, when none can call our power to account? Yet who would have thought the old man to have had so much blood in him?'"

Clarence blanched.

"'Do you mark that?'" I said, for I knew this scene and could cue the lines for Fanny.

"'The Thane of Fife had a wife: where is she now? What! Will these hands ne'er be clean? . . . Here's the smell of the blood still; all the perfumes of Arabia will not sweeten this little hand. Oh! Oh! Oh!'" And with the final *oh* Fanny collapsed onto the carpet, sobbing.

"Oh, don't cry so," said Lizzie, her own eyes brimming. "Fanny, here, let me help you up."

When Fanny raised her face, we saw that she was laughing and quite gay!

"Tears and laughter are so close they can substitute one for another onstage," she said. I would remember that.

Supper began with steamed clams, progressed to oyster chowder, and moved on to a baked halibut. We wondered if Abba weren't perhaps feeling a little unsound. She hummed as she passed around the plates and hugged Father, who seemed somewhat stupefied by so much company and so much food. His blessing before dinner had been unusually brief:

"Bless the roof that protects the family beneath it."

"Hear, hear," answered Uncle Benjamin, raising his wineglass. "Though in a heavy storm the roof leaks somewhat in the southeast corner."

"That is to remind us that life is never certain," said Father solemnly.

"Nor always dry," said Lizzie, who shared a bedroom with May in that corner of the house.

After dinner, Fanny required "the young people" to entertain her, since she had entertained us. Anna, Sylvia, and I agreed to play a brief scene between Mrs. Malaprop, Lydia Languish, and the maid, Lucy. Clarence Hampton, with a great lack of enthusiasm, agreed to be, for the evening, Lydia's suitor, Captain Absolute, disguised, as he is for much of the play, as impoverished Ensign Beverly.

"Then we will disguise you," said Anna with great determination. "Uncle, may I?" And she fetched from the hall coatrack his Turkish hat and cape.

"Here, here," said Uncle with consternation. "See it comes to no harm."

"What harm can come to it?" replied Anna cheerily, placing the cap on Mr. Hampton's head and the cape about his shoulders. He cast angry looks about the room.

"Ready?" asked Sylvia, who donned one of Abba's aprons to signify her role as a maid. She carried a tray with a tea set on it. Abba's face was solemn with worry for the china, but she said not a word.

"Places," I instructed. "The parlor door will now be the entrance to Miss Lydia Languish's sitting room, where she awaits a secret visit from her lover, Ensign Beverly, to be announced by her maid, Lucy, while her guardian, Mrs. Malaprop, lectures her on the duties of youth."

I had tied a pillow round my waist and covered it with a coat to simulate the bulk my slender figure lacked; I stooped to hide my height and walked crablike, jutting my chin unpleasantly, encouraging laughter, and the scene went better than I had originally feared; we earned our applause and bows despite Clarence, who muttered his lines with obvious distaste.

"Bravo!" cried Fanny, when we finished. "Anna, I have never seen a more enchanting ingenue give a lover more difficulty! And Louy, if your Walpole audience doesn't hurt from laughing at your portrayal of Mrs. Malaprop, well, then we will have a measure of their lack of humor, for you are humorous in the extreme."

"Port all around!" cried Uncle Benjamin, for he had laughed loudest of all.

"Not all around," protested Abba, looking at May and Lizzie.

"A sip won't hurt them," insisted Uncle.

"Indeed it won't, Abba," said May hopefully.

"No," said that wise mother. "Not even a sip until you are twenty-one."

"But I have no port!" protested Father.

"Clarence, there is a bottle stored in the potato cellar. Would you fetch it?" Uncle Benjamin said. "And while you are there, bring up a basket of potatoes for Mrs. Fisher's Sunday roast. Make sure they haven't sprouted, mind you."

"Yes, sir," said Clarence, so eager to be away from the group that he neglected to remove Uncle's hat and cape.

The potato cellar was the traditional kind based on colonial housekeeping, just large enough to store a few baskets and barrels and dug outside the house, so we heard the kitchen door slam behind Clarence as he went out.

"I must powder my nose," said Ida Tupper, heading for the same door to the outdoor conveniences. Father snorted with displeasure. He did not like to hear of women powdering their faces.

As we waited, we discussed the performance of that evening, and the performance to come, when we would appear before the good people of Walpole. Fanny looked at my script and suggested a few changes in lines and exits, and Lizzie and May began to yawn. Mrs. Tupper returned. We waited fifteen minutes for the sound of the back door to open once again, for Clarence's step in the hall. It did not come.

"Perhaps I should go see," said Uncle Benjamin. "That last step is tricky."

"Perhaps he had a call of nature," said his mother. "Give him time."

We waited another fifteen minutes.

"Something is wrong," said Abba, rising from her chair by the hearth.

"I am sure he has taken offense and returned home," said his mother. "He is thin-skinned, and the girls had fun at his expense tonight. He often behaves in this manner, coming and going with no regard for others."

"I will check the cellar, to be certain," said Llew. He was unenthused about his chore, for we all knew his antipathy to Clarence, yet he disliked seeing Abba distressed. Llew returned four minutes later. "The cellar is empty," he announced.

"Why didn't you bring back the port and potatoes?" grumbled Uncle Benjamin.

"Forgot them," said Llew, grinning sheepishly.

It was growing late, and Cousin Eliza, too, began to yawn. We all made little stretching movements of fatigue. Anna and Abba went to the kitchen to begin the washing-up. Lizzie and May went upstairs to their beds.

Mrs. Tupper rose. "I'll be off. So charming to have met

you, Mrs. Kemble. Perhaps sometime when I am down to Boston we might have tea together."

"Perhaps," said Fanny noncommittally. "I, too, will be off. Louy, will you ask my servant to meet me at the front door with a lantern?"

I went to the little pantry off the kitchen where the man was having a pint of lager and making conversation with Fanny's maid.

Uncle rose to go, and scratched his head with great distress.

"The young scamp has gone off with my hat and cape," he complained.

CHAPTER FIFTEEN

The Ravine, or a Long Way to the Bottom

THE NEXT MORNING, though I was fatigued, I rose at dawn as usual and dressed for my run in the ravine. When I returned, I spent several hours in my writing shed, working with only a modicum of success, for I admit my thoughts were elsewhere than with the words marching uneventfully across my pages of foolscap. The morning had menace in it, somehow.

At midmorning, when I returned to the kitchen for a cup of tea, Ida Tupper knocked at our cottage door. Her hair was undressed and looked skimpy and dull; she had not rouged her cheeks and lips. In fact, she was still in her nightdress, with a thin coat thrown over it.

"He did not come home last night," she said. "Clarence did not come home. I woke up and went to his room and he was not there. Oh, I just know something is wrong!" She gave a little shriek and would have fallen to the floor in her faint, had Abba not caught her by the waist.

We lifted Ida by her ankles and arms and carried her to the parlor. She was small, and the task was not difficult. We put a compress on her forehead and passed smelling salts under her nose several times, bringing her to.

"It is my fault, my fault," that strange mother sobbed. "I should have been ever so much better. My poor boy!"

"Now, now," crooned Abba. "Mothers always take the blame for their children. Even so, we have no reason to believe he has come to harm. Why think so? Young men sometimes find places to rest other than their own beds."

Sylvia came in then, carrying her book of Confucius and looking dreamy-eyed, which meant she had again been attempting meditation.

"Clarence Hampton has disappeared," I told her.

"Ah. Fled," she said knowingly.

"Fled?" Ida Tupper began to wail.

"Louy, make us a pot of chamomile tea," said Abba. "We must wait this out."

Llew heard the commotion and came in from Father's study, where he had been at his work of classifying rock specimens gathered from the ravine.

He looked at Ida Tupper, swooning on the settee, and then at me.

"What has Mr. Hampton got up to now?" he asked.

"He did not come home last night," I said.

Llew paused and considered. He stroked his chin, the way Father did when deep in contemplation. "Perhaps I should give the cellar a better search," he said.

"You searched last night." I chafed Mrs. Tupper's wrists.

"Well, I peered in through the door," he admitted. "I was

certain he had gone on home, so I didn't actually go past the doorway."

"Oh, Llew," I said.

"Should I fetch the sheriff?" he asked.

"Check the cellar first," said Abba. "Take a lamp so you can see all the corners. Maybe he fell on the bad step and hit his head."

Llew returned minutes later, bloodied on his hands, his feet, his knees, his face. I couldn't help but think of Lady Macbeth: "Who would have thought the old man to have had so much blood in him?" Llew seemed all in blood, and what we could see of his face beneath that blood was bone white and dazed.

"Mr. Hampton is found," said Llew in a strange voice.

Some presentiment of doom brought Father out of his study. He lowered his reading glasses halfway down his nose, and eyed us with great misgiving. He flinched slightly when his gaze landed on Llew.

"Well," he said calmly. "I see you have found some trouble." Transcendentalists, I have observed, tend to be fond of understatement.

"Trouble," repeated Llew stiffly. He lifted his right hand, and in that hand was a walking stick dripping with blood and gore.

Ida shrieked, and this time her faint was complete. She lost consciousness.

I realized, at that moment, that I had been purposely misled by some evil greater than a young man's vanity and stormy pride. The evil had been there, close to me, and I had not identified it. I had let my desire to know human nature be misused by false starts and leads. My search to discover the whereabouts of Jonah Tupper had blinded me to the fact that another young man was in great danger. And now he was dead.

With a great sense of failure mixing with my horror, I went to Llew and closed the parlor door behind him. But my sisters, who had been sitting in the garden, had heard Ida's scream and gathered now in the doorway, pale and frightened.

Abba hastily took May and Lizzie by the hand and rushed them upstairs to their rooms. "Anna, sit with them and read," she ordered my older sister. "Do not let them come back down the stairs." Anna left, her eyes wide with terror.

Abba, that true and wonderful woman, had already recovered from the first shock and was ready now to begin to repair this situation. Trouble, for Abba—whether it be a fallen cake, an unwed girl cast out from her home, or a new widow with six children to feed—was to be cleaned up, in much the same manner that smudges are wiped from windows and mud removed from carpets. It is part of the process of restoring the world to righteousness.

"Bronson," she said, "go and fetch an officer of the law. Some abomination has been done in our home." Her voice already carried absolute conviction that Llew had been victimized by the situation, and was not the cause of it. She never once doubted his innocence.

"I will do just that." And Father took his cane and hat from the hall coat stand and, to hearten Llew as he passed, he gave him a gentle shaking of the shoulders and called him "My boy." Llew did not respond, but only looked down at his bloodied hands.

"Sylvia." Abba turned to my companion. "Fetch Dr. Burroughs for Mrs. Tupper." Without a word, Sylvia was out the door and running down the sidewalk after Father.

Abba then suggested I take Llew into the kitchen, while she saw to Mrs. Tupper.

"Now, Llew, sit," I said when we were alone. I wiped his hands and face with a towel. He was as passive as a child, and once the blood was removed his face was deadly white.

"Tell me what happened, Llew," I coached.

"It was horrible," he said, his eyes wide. "I pulled open the door and went in, past the doorway and the rotted step. I tripped on something. I tried to get up, but it was soft and slippery. I could not get my footing. It was when my hand touched another that I realized I had fallen over a body. A body!"

Llew started to shiver so forcefully I feared he would fall from his chair. I took the decanter of sherry from the cupboard and poured all that was left from yesterday's festivities into a glass. Last night Clarence had gone on an errand to that cellar and never returned. Had the body been there for almost a day already? The dampness would have kept the pooling blood from drying, making the floor slippery.

"Drink, Llew," I said. "You look so pale you may lose consciousness."

"Never!" said Llew, flailing with his arms the way some people do just before they fall into a dead faint, as if they are besieged by a plague of flies.

He finished the sherry with difficulty. There was blood caked under his nails, and I scraped at it. I had seen other men look that bloodied, in country autumns when hogs are slaughtered. Poor Clarence Hampton.

After Llew was somewhat restored and had discarded his stained jacket into the sink, where I would later try to remove the rusty stains already drying on the tweeded flannel fabric, we returned to the parlor. Dr. Burroughs was there by then, and he was half lifting, half carrying Ida Tupper, with Sylvia's assistance.

"Miss Louisa," he said, smiling at me through his thick white whiskers. "Your guest has taken quite ill. We must see her home to her own bed."

Abba gave me a warning glance. She had not told him about the body in the cellar. That was the sheriff's business; it was too late for the doctor.

"May I assist?" I asked.

"No, no, your friend and I will see to it." Ida moaned, and when Sylvia waved the salts under her nose she flailed and shrieked once again.

"Her brother is an invalid and unable to care for her," I told Dr. Burroughs. "Will you stay with her till she is sleeping? Then you might come back here. There is another matter that will want your attention."

His expression grew stern. "I will return," he promised, walking slightly bowed under the weight of Ida Tupper's arm around his shoulders.

Abba scrubbed at a red spot on the floor. Her face was thoughtful and worried, and now that she had gotten us through the first moments of the nightmare, she seemed at a loss.

"I must go into the cellar," I said.

"No!" said Abba and Llew simultaneously.

"But if the murderer—"

"Returns? All the more reason for you not to go alone into

that place," Abba insisted. She was right, of course. So we waited, and fifteen minutes later Father reappeared with Sheriff Bowman.

The tall, gangly Walpolian man had thrown on his coat and trousers over his nightshirt, some of which still stuck out the sides, and he wore a tall beaver hat over his uncombed black hair. He must have had a late evening and slept in, for it was near noon by then.

"I understand you have found a body," he said after giving Abba a brief nod of greeting and removing his absurd hat.

Llew looked up. Oh, his expression was horrible.

"I found it." Llew could barely speak.

Mr. Bowman studied him for a moment. The man looked comedic, but I could see by the sharpness of his gaze that he was no fool.

"Well, we'd better go see this body, hadn't we? Can you walk, boy?"

Llew rose to his feet and cast down the blankets with which we had wrapped him. Mr. Bowman saw then the dark stains on his cuffs and knees.

"Probably a dead raccoon," said Bowman, frowning. "They are fierce fighters over territory."

"It is no raccoon," said Llew darkly.

"I will come with you," I said.

"No, Miss Louisa, you will not," said Officer Bowman. "Stay in the house with the women."

I took a deep breath to protest, but Abba gave me a nudge. I knew what she was thinking, and she was right: The more I protested, the longer it would take to complete the process now begun, the hideous process of identifying the dead.

The men—Llew, Father, and Officer Bowman—took Abba's lamp and went back out the door. From inside the parlor, where I opened the window, we could hear their steps crunching on the dirt-and-gravel path, hear the creaking of rusted hinges as the cellar door was opened. There was a moment of silence, and then I heard Officer Bowman say, "Mother Mary and all the saints. It's Clarence Hampton. At least I think it's Clarence Hampton. Hard to tell."

CHAPTER SIXTEEN

The Son Returned Home

THE REST OF that day grew even more horrible.

It was decided by Abba and myself that Clarence would be removed from the cellar and cleaned up as best we could before sending his battered body back home to his mother. I left the group and went to the dining room for a minute, knowing already what had to be done. Wasn't this how my vacation in the country had begun? With a body, Ernst Nooteboom, being carried to the last stop before its final resting place. I took the cloth and saltcellar off the table and spread an old, thick blanket over it. I fetched a bucket of hot water and soap.

Dr. Peterson Burroughs had returned by then, and was in the parlor with Father, Llew, and Sheriff Bowman.

"A body?" he said, plainly stunned. "Clarence? No wonder his mother is in that condition. I had to give her thirty drops of laudanum to calm her, and another ten to get her to sleep. Well, let's have a look at this body. Bring it in."

I was glad he was there, with his stern, practical manner and his medical experience. Perhaps his examination would reveal more about the murder, for it was obvious that Clarence Hampton had been murdered. No simple fall could have so devastated the body that Llew and Father and Sheriff Bowman now laid on the dining room table.

Anna stuck her head back downstairs, and we shouted that she was to stay up there with May and Lizzie; on no condition was she to come down or allow them down. Abba closed the curtains tightly and brought a lamp over to the table. Its light made the red poppies on the wallpaper seem to wink in and out of focus, and that was how I knew her hands were shaking.

Clarence was still dressed in Uncle's cape, which trailed on the floor as they carried him, but the Turkish cap was missing. Of course, it would have been knocked off by one of the many blows that had killed the young man. Tomorrow I would go into the cellar myself and find that cap.

Carefully, as though he might come to further harm, Llew and Officer Bowman placed the body on the table. I could see how bloody was that body. I sighed heavily, feeling pity for the young man in death, though in life I had neither cared for him nor trusted him.

We did not speak, but several times I walked around the table, thinking that the order of the wounds might reveal the merciless murderer. I knew so little. I had seen women give birth, but otherwise the body was all secrets. Perhaps, I thought, looking at Clarence, perhaps someday I should train as a nurse.

His head had several different wounds, bloody dents and

welts obviously caused by the metal-headed walking cane Llew had carried in with him and dropped by the door. One blow had been so fierce it had almost severed his right ear. Another blow—the first, I suspected—had smashed his windpipe, and another his mouth and teeth. Clarence had been rendered silent before he had died. Whoever struck Clarence had meant to kill, that was certain. The killing stroke was a slice across the throat that almost severed the head.

"Most unusual," said Dr. Burroughs, "most unusual. I have seen violent crimes, but the thoroughness of this one is shocking, don't you think?"

I nodded.

"Miss Louisa, bring your sewing scissors. And then go and sit with your mother." He placed one of his hands over Clarence's, and I saw the difference, the gnarled, thin angles of the older hand, the smooth, strong one of the young man. And yet age had survived, while youth lay dead.

"I will stay," I protested.

Dr. Burroughs's bristling side-whiskers moved a little higher up his face in a tight smile. "I read the Boston papers and know of your involvement in the Dorothy Wortham murder. But you will not be in this room when this body is laid bare as his creator made him," he said. "Have some decency, young woman."

I would have argued back that there is worse indecency in this world than a human body, but knew I would waste my time and his. I went and sat with Abba, Father, Llew, and Sylvia. Mr. Bowman stayed with Dr. Burroughs; Llew sat next to me.

Sylvia stared into the hearth. She looked exhausted, and

so did Abba. Llew had withdrawn into himself, as people in shock often do. When I asked him if he wanted a glass of water, he looked at me as if I were a stranger, and then the look changed, and it seemed he was drowning before my very eyes.

An hour later, a very long hour later, Dr. Burroughs came to us carrying a basket filled with bloodied cloths: Clarence's suit, which had been cut away. It was the habit to save the clothes of the dead and give them to the living needy, but Clarence's expensive suit had been past saving, so torn and bloodied was it. Uncle's cape, which had fallen off after the first strokes of the beating, was folded and handed to Abba.

"The cape is stained but still usable," Dr. Burroughs said. Then he sat heavily in a chair close to the fire, drying his hands on a towel.

"It is Clarence Hampton for certain, and I know he was not among the saved," said Dr. Burroughs. "But he has been murdered before he could find redemption. The man was beaten and then his throat was cut, but of course you know that. I would say he has been dead for a day. The blood had begun to pool in the body. Gravity, you know. Rigor mortis had set in."

I remembered how the body had angled when carried, how stiff the legs had been. A day. Clarence had died the night before. He had been sent to the potato cellar for Uncle Benjamin's secret supply of port and a basket of potatoes for Mrs. Fisher's roast. We had thought he had run off on one of his escapades, but he had been lying in the cellar all the while.

Dr. Burroughs continued, "The first blow was probably to the head, cracking the skull and causing great bleeding.

Further blows were administered, including one to the windpipe, rendering him speechless. When he was fallen and already dying, his throat was cut, to finish him off. The first weapon used, before the knife, was heavy and pointed. Have you found it?" Dr. Burroughs asked.

"What of the weapon?" said Officer Bowman. His hair had been unruly before; now it stood straight up.

Llew groaned and stumbled out of the parlor. He returned carrying the walking stick he had brought back with him when he first announced the body in the cellar.

"I found it by the cellar door. On top of . . . on top of Mr. Hampton."

Officer Bowman's beady gaze changed. "Let me clarify," he began. "You discovered the body. You admit to having the murder weapon. There's talk in town of how you and Clarence Hampton were at loggerheads."

Gossip from the picnic, I thought. I rose, protesting.

"Sit down, Miss Louisa," said Officer Bowman. "This is men's work. I ask you and your mother to now depart the room."

"We will not!" said Abba. "This is my home, and this is my family. I stay, and Louisa stays."

Officer Bowman took such a deep breath of exasperation his shoulders rose with it, then fell as he breathed it out. During my walks down Main Street I had sometimes seen this man with his wife and daughters. He strutted as he walked ahead of them. They followed meekly, heads bowed.

"Llew is your son?" Officer Bowman directed his question to Father.

"In a manner of speaking," Father said. "We have known

him many, many years. He is a good boy, a thoughtful boy. He is a scientist and a philosopher," said Father, as if that proved beyond all doubt that Llew was incapable of violence.

"Well, this is a murder, and charges will be made against someone," said Officer Bowman. "The next grand jury meets in three weeks' time. I'll ask you to stay in Walpole until then. You are under house arrest."

That last comment was made to Llew, who nodded.

"You will vouch for him?" he asked Father.

"I will."

"Then take Clarence Hampton home. We are done here."

"Not quite," I said, standing between Sheriff Bowman and the door so that he would be forced to listen. "There is one other element that must be mentioned."

"And that is what, Miss Louisa?" The sheriff all but sneered.

"Clarence Hampton was dressed in Uncle Benjamin's cape and hat, and it was dark in the cellar. What if the murderer struck the wrong man?"

Abba collapsed onto the sofa with a little shriek. "He wanted to kill Benjamin Willis? My brother-in-law?" she asked faintly.

"I think it must be considered a possibility till proven otherwise," I said.

Sheriff Bowman dangled his hat in his hands and studied his shoes. When he looked back up, there was a new gleam, almost of respect, in his eye.

"You've got a point," he admitted.

"Who?" asked Abba, dazed, when the sheriff had gone and it was again just family and close friends in the parlor.

"Who could do this?" She rose stiffly and went back into that dining room to sit with the mortal remains of Clarence Hampton.

Who?

It was dusk by the time Abba had finished repairing Clarence's body as well as she could. Dusk, and already a crowd of curiosity seekers had gathered before our front door, gawking. A stone was thrown at the door, and a boy's voice cried, "Let us see the murderer!" Llew cringed.

Word spreads even faster in towns than cities.

AT EIGHT O'CLOCK, Dr. Burroughs and Mr. Bowman returned with six men to carry Clarence Hampton back to his mother. The Alcotts and Sylvia walked behind that covered litter in a show of respect for the deceased and sympathy for the mother. Llew had been required to stay at the cottage, under house arrest, forbidden to even step onto the front porch.

Ida Tupper was waiting for us in her doorway.

She threw herself at the litter when it arrived, and began to wail. Her eyes were large and dark and luminous from laudanum. She looked stunned, even surprised, as if the death of a son were a grief for other women, not herself. I suppose all parents feel—and hope—the same until the cruel discovery that they and theirs are mortally assailable.

Mr. Wattles, from his wheeled chair, directed the carrying in of the body of his nephew, Clarence Hampton. He muttered to himself and stroked his beard, and held his arms open so that Ida might weep on his breast, but in her agony she turned from him and buried her streaming face in her hands. I thought I had never seen a family so devastated by grief.

"I will stay with her," said Anna, taking Ida by the arm and guiding her back into the house.

CHAPTER SEVENTEEN

Jonah Discovered

WE NONE OF us slept well that night. I tossed and turned, all too aware of the grief emanating from that house next door to ours and aware of my failure: I had sensed danger and had not been able to forestall it. In my mind I went over and over the details of the two mysteries, the murder of Clarence Hampton and the murder of Ernst Nooteboom, for the violent death of one made me more convinced that Ernst's death was also no accident, just as Lilli had maintained.

As a young girl I once took a dancing lesson at Sylvia's house with an Italian dancing master. He was all the rage in Boston at the time and making a fine living, going from mansion to mansion on Beacon Hill and Commonwealth Avenue with his little black bag full of his slippers, gloves, and metronome. He had waxed mustachios and little black eyes as dark as his black patent dancing shoes. I thought of him and how he would tap our ankles with his cane if we did not quite leap high enough. "Higher," he would say, as if we were circus animals. "Girls, you must jump higher."

Louisa, I told myself, you must jump higher. *You have let your wits grow dull with this concept of vacation, and now someone else has died.*

Just before dawn I heard another sleepless person moving about downstairs and guessed it was Llew. Sweet, poor Llew, now under a dangerous cloud of suspicion. I knew how it looked to Sheriff Bowman: Llew had gone to the cellar looking for Clarence Hampton, and come back to tell us he wasn't there. Next day Mr. Hampton was discovered dead in that very cellar by Llew, who returned covered in blood and carrying the murder weapon.

Of course, no hard-hearted murderer would return carrying the weapon and therefore giving himself away in such a manner, but I wasn't convinced Sheriff Bowman would see it that way. Finally, I slept, my head aching and heavy with violent dreams.

WHEN I AWOKE later the kitchen downstairs was empty. Abba was spending the day at Ida Tupper's house, and Anna and my younger sisters were in the garden, drawing and reading. Llew was in the library, pretending to study, and Father sat next to him, likewise pretending. The philosopher was rarely so distracted with the affairs of this world that he could not concentrate, but today was one of those days. He realized the full danger for Llew—circumstances pointed to his implication, a trial might find him guilty, and murderers are hanged. That we, the Alcotts, loved him and trusted him explicitly might not prevent that worst of all possible miscarriages of justice: the execution of an innocent man.

Jump, I told myself, peering in at them. I went back to the kitchen to make our noon meal and my plans. This I had learned from Abba: Delicate and complex arrangements are best made over the dicing of carrots and peeling of potatoes—though I suspected none of us would have a taste for potatoes. For our soup that day I rolled a batch of egg noodles.

And I thought.

Who. Not Llew. The blood on his hands, the weapon in his possession, that he found the body—those facts meant nothing, for Llew's innocence would be the basis of my investigation. Who would want Clarence Hampton dead? He had a fast reputation and there had been suggestions of a secret liaison, but fathers rarely beat young men to death for that. If the flirting had turned to actual seduction? I must look and listen more closely to this community. Were any Walpolian maidens looking plumper than usual?

I poured flour onto the table and began rolling biscuits, after the noodles were cut and left to dry a bit.

I thumped away at the biscuit dough—they would be none too tender, but I was thankful the Alcotts had sound teeth because sweets were usually beyond our means.

Along with the why and who, I realized, was a third question: How did the murder of Clarence Hampton connect with the murder of Ernst Nooteboom? It was beyond the possibility of coincidence for two young men to die in a small town, so soon within each other, and not have those deaths be connected. Mr. Tupper Sr.'s voice called through my thoughts: *He fell. It was an accident.* Mr. Tupper was the connection. He had tried to force business dealings onto Ernst, and he was Clarence's stepgrandfather. He might have been worried that his daughter-in-law's child would inherit all he worked to accumulate, and he made it plain he did not care for his daughter-in-law. The two had not exchanged visits all the while I had been in Walpole.

I gave the biscuits another pounding. Who else would murder Clarence Hampton? A business rival. Greed, rather than revenge or passion, as the motive. But Hampton had no business except his small trade in fossils and handy jobs. I sighed. That could again implicate Llew, who also was a fossil hunter. It was not a motive, but it was another connection. *Look elsewhere*, I told myself. *Jump.*

The land. That wounded gash in the earth where the railroad ended. Mr. Tupper had wanted to buy it, but how did that connect to Clarence?

Ernst Nooteboom, who had fallen from the cliff so close to Clarence's campsite. Had that been murder, and had revenge now been taken? I tried to imagine Lilli with a knife, with blood on her white hands. I could not. But then . . . perhaps. I knew so little about her, really. She had accused Mr. Tupper of the deed, but perhaps that had been a decoy. And accusations had been made about Lilli, about a beau her brother would not accept, quarrels with that brother.

A red cardinal chirped outside the kitchen window and peered in at me, tilting its bright head. Lilli's land. Everyone was attempting to gain ownership, it seemed, every male of Walpole except Jonah Tupper, who was missing.

Jonah Tupper. I put down the flour sifter so hastily it thumped, and a cloud of flour rose up like a volcanic eruption, then settled down over the table. Maybe father and son were in on this together. Maybe all of his so-called commercial traveling had been a way to establish alibis.

I looked at the uneven, lumpy mass of dough on the table before me. I had never been known as a good biscuit cook. Perhaps it would be wiser to purchase a dozen from Tupper's General Store.

Sylvia came into the kitchen wearing her strange high-collared costume and looked surprisingly serene for a young woman who had participated in the recovery of a brutally murdered bachelor from the potato cellar the day before.

"I do not know how men got along without good faith. 'A cart without a yoke and a carriage without harness'—how could they go?" she said, tilting her blond head much in the same manner that the cardinal at the window had tilted hers.

"That is Confucius, I suppose."

"It is."

"What does it mean, Sylvia?"

"I'm not quite certain."

"I think it means we must find our own answers; they will not come to us."

MAIN STREET WAS subdued that afternoon. Everyone in town had heard, by then, of the dead body of Clarence Hampton found in our cellar, and I admit that more than a few women pulled their skirts aside as we passed, so that we would not touch them. Guilt by association.

Mr. Tupper's counter girl suggested we look for him in Crabtree's Tavern House, the next street over.

"We can't," Sylvia protested, pulling at my arm to slow me down.

"We will," I insisted.

Reader, I knew the rules as well as any woman. Unescorted women do not go into pubs, and even escorted ones sit in the females-only room, having been deposited there by father, brother, or son. But rules that stand as hurdles to truth beg to be broken. I broke that one. I pushed open the double swinging doors and entered Crabtree's, followed by loyal Sylvia.

The single large room was surprisingly dark for midday, perhaps because the walls, floor, and ceiling were all wooden and stained by years of thick cigar smoke. Sylvia and I wove our way among the tables and chairs, several of which contained card games in progress, looking for Mr. Tupper. All conversation in that room ceased. A burly-looking counterman knit his brows and came out from behind his workstation, barreling at us like a runaway carriage. I knew we were about to be forceably expelled from this male bastion. I spied Mr. Tupper in a far corner, and called his name loudly.

He looked up. There was no surprise on his face, as one would have expected, only irritation.

"Here comes trouble. I knew it when I first beheld you," he muttered. "I'll handle this, Sam. Save my beer for me. Outside, ladies." He pointed at the door.

"You have heard of the discovery," I said, when I had reversed my path through the swinging doors and stood in the bright sunlight again.

"Who hasn't? The famous Alcotts of Boston have a murdered man in their cellar." His voice was gleeful. "Soon as you said you were a guest of Ben Willis I knew you'd be no good."

I chose to ignore that last statement for the moment. But I would get back to it. "Then you know it is Clarence Hampton who has been murdered. Your daughter-in-law's son."

"He were a no-good layabout, and the family is better off without him."

Well. That was harsh but sincere, I guessed. "Did you wish his death?"

Tupper glared. "I did not. I barely thought about him."

"Now that can't be true," I contradicted. "If your son and Ida do not produce children, then Clarence Hampton might well have become your heir. And I heard there will be much to inherit."

Mr. Tupper's eyebrows knitted and he peered menacingly at me from under them. "Leave this alone and go back to Boston, where you belong," he said.

"I cannot. Not yet. Did you hear that whoever killed Clarence might have believed he was murdering my uncle instead? Clarence Hampton was wearing Uncle Ben's cape and hat when he was murdered in the dark."

"Now wait a minute—"

"I distinctly heard you say, some weeks ago, that the town would be better off without him, that you yourself would prefer to see him dead," I said quietly but forcefully. "I will testify to those statements."

"I never," he began, greatly flustered. "Them were just words. I wouldn't have harmed Benjamin."

"Uncle Benjamin introduced your son to Ida Tupper," I continued. "That is the cause of your hatred. What we must learn now is what violence your hatred could produce."

Mr. Tupper tugged at his waistcoat. I looked at his huge,

dirty hands, the right one with its gold signet ring. Above the ring I saw a rusty stain on his shirt cuff. His eyes followed mine, and he jammed his hand, all the way up to the forearm, into his outer coat pocket.

"A bloodstain, Mr. Tupper?" I asked.

"I was slicing up beef this morning," he said.

I looked him straight in the eye. "Mr. Tupper, have you had any word from your son? Do you know where he is?"

A group of women doing their morning marketing approached us on the sidewalk. When they saw Sylvia and me, they crossed the street, whispering behind their fans, their long skirts trailing in the dust of the street and leaving patterns like waves. Waves. Water. The river was so close by, yet Clarence had been murdered and left in the cellar. The murderer had wanted him to be found, had wanted us, the Alcotts, to be implicated.

"No." Mr. Tupper, his face red with emotion, turned back to Crabtree's before I could ask any more questions. "Stay out," he called over his shoulder.

Sylvia picked nervously at the lace trim on her gloves. "It appears even his son dislikes Mr. Tupper, to be gone so long from home without sending a letter."

"Is he gone?" I asked Sylvia.

I looked over my friend's head to the mountains beyond, to the forests and ravines and riverbanks and all those other places I had so admired upon my arrival. They could be hiding a murderer. Jonah Tupper would inherit the Tupper estate. Were father and son both trying to expand their holdings by violent methods? With Ernst Nooteboom dead, they had thought it easy to buy Lilli's holdings cheaply, through intimidation. And with Clarence dead, there would be no rival for the inheritance. I had suspected Clarence of hating his young stepfather enough to do violence to him. Perhaps it had been the other way around.

Or perhaps I had been right the first time: Clarence had murdered his stepfather, and Jonah's father, suspecting this, had now murdered Clarence. Oh, it was getting too Shakespearean, all this revenge, greed, deceit, passion.

Another unrelated—or was it?—matter was bothering me. The stench from Father's vegetable patch grew stronger each day. It increasingly stank as if something were rotting there. There, where the earth had been disturbed but not planted, where Clarence had been spied poking about with his walking stick. I thought of Dr. Burroughs's stories of the finding of bits and pieces of Dr. Parkman in Boston, and my stomach turned.

Jonah, where are you? I thought for the hundredth time.

Was Jonah the strange, tall man occasionally seen in Walpole in early morning or at dusk, walking alone, the one O'Rourke had described? That man had a limp. But any actress knows how easy it is to fake a limp.

FANNY KEMBLE ARRIVED to share our noon dinner, trailing her own retinue and a large group of townspeople as well.

"Such a lovely day for a walk!" she cried out as I opened the door to her. "Will you offer a meal to a hungry wayfarer?"

"The biscuits are heavy and the soup too thin," I said. "Abba was busy and I cooked today, but we will gladly share the meal with you."

"Because of the body in the cellar," said Fanny with astounding complacency, once the door was closed on the curiosity seekers now standing outside our door. "Such a thing will throw a household routine all out of order."

Llew, who had been sitting alone in the little parlor and heard this, came out to us with a look of disbelief on his ashen face.

"You jest?" he said.

"My dear boy, I have come to ease you through this difficult situation with some light comedy," Fanny exclaimed. "I have read enough scripts to know that you will not be tried and hanged; it just is not good plotting. No audience would allow a youth as charming and obviously innocent as yourself to be the villain. They would not stand for it."

Father, just in from his vegetable patch and still in his boots and overalls, scratched his chin.

"Fanny, you have been wrong on other matters," he said.

"Bronson, you will never allow me to forget that disastrous marriage, will you?" She pouted prettily over her white silk fan.

"I pray you are correct, Fanny, for we know Llew to be completely innocent in this," I said. Llew gave me a glance of gratitude, and I thought there was even more in his expression.

Despite Fanny's attempts at humor, the meal was a somber one, and grew yet more somber when, after the plates were cleared, the doorbell sounded and Abba opened it to Ida's little maid.

"Mrs. Tupper says I am to give you this," said the child,

handing me a note. Once it was delivered, she scampered back to the path that connected our house with her own.

"What does she say?" Abba asked, after giving me a moment to decipher Ida's uncertain handwriting, made even more quixotic by the laudanum with which she was dosing herself.

"She asks me to go to her son's campsite and bring back his personal items," I said. "She cannot do it herself, nor obviously can Mr. Wattles."

"I do not like this," said Abba. "It is unfair of her to ask this of someone who is not family."

"But obviously her brother, Mr. Wattles, cannot go up the mountain in his wheeled chair, and she has no one else to ask," I said.

"Well, I wish Llew could go with you," Abba said.

"He cannot, else Sheriff Bowman may lock him up completely, if he breaks house arrest. No, I will do this, Abba. I have a presentiment that the danger is over."

I was lying to Abba—a rare sin, indeed. I donned my running clothes. If I were to look through and gather up a dead man's belongings, I wished to be unencumbered of the skirts and hoops and high heels and tight waists that keep the female population moving at such a slow pace.

It had stormed during the night, and the stream that bubbled through the ravine now roared and was brown and frothy. I stayed close to the side of the path on the cliff rather than streamside; a fall into that raging water would be deadly. The steep hill to Clarence's campsite was slippery with mud and broken ferns, and my progress was slow.

The campsite, when I arrived, was despoiled by rain and abandonment, the tent sagging and the ashes of the circled campfire cold and black. The rain had made of the previously inviting camping area a devastated area of storm-flattened weeds, broken tree branches, and impromptu muddy paths and puddles slanting to the cliff's edge. It was evident that Clarence Hampton had not been there for several days. I gathered together his possessions: fish-boning knives, a fishing rod, tin plates and cups, hammers and chisels of all sizes, a volume of poetry, and two penny-dreadful novels.

He had kept no journal, indeed nothing that could be said to be of a personal nature, and I wondered that his mother would place sentimental value on such impersonal objects. But when I lifted the volume of poetry, a piece of paper fluttered from it. *My dearest Clarence*, I read, but before I could read more a stray gust of wind took it from my fingers and blew it toward the cliff.

The paper landed on the cliff's edge and balanced there, half over the edge already.

Cautiously, on my hands and knees, I crept close to the cliff, to the very spot from which I had estimated Ernst Nooteboom had fallen. Just as I reached for the paper, another gust of wind carried it away, over the edge. I reached, but it escaped my grasp. I looked down. The height, combined with my fatigue from the climb up the path, created a dangerous vertigo.

A twig cracked underfoot. The birds, which had been calling from the tall pines, grew silent. Someone was behind me. Another twig cracked, closer.

Still perilously close to the cliff edge and prostrate on the ground, I felt my body tense. I rolled up and on my hands and knees quickly backed away from the cliff's edge, thankful for Father's cast-off trousers, which saved me from the bondage of a woman's cumbersome skirts.

The birds began to sing again, and I knew that whoever had been there was gone. Who? The answer was so obvious I frowned at my own simplicity. The murderer. Clarence's murderer. Or had I imagined that sinister presence?

My lungs hurt from holding my breath. Perhaps I had simply imagined the encounter? I decided the best course was to think about it later, in Abba's kitchen. I felt a sudden urgency to be away from there.

The tent and bedding would be too heavy for me to carry, but I began placing his fishing knives, the tin plate and cup, and the volumes of penny thrillers into my rucksack.

Dark clouds hovered overhead. It would rain again soon. I sniffed the air, searching for that hint of green miasma that fills the air before a storm, and trying to gauge whether I could make it back down the mountain before the downpour began. But the wind was coming from the southeast, turning the leaves inside out, showing their fish-pale undersides. Branches overhead groaned.

I caught an unexpected scent, and my stomach turned. Decay. The wind blew it in my path and I followed, trying to find the source.

Just a hundred yards beyond the tent, I saw the mound that had, on previous visits, been camouflaged by thickly growing ferns. The storm had bent them and revealed the unmistakable long, mounded shape of a burial.

I approached slowly. An animal had been digging there, and the heavy rain had eroded a portion of the hasty burial. I saw bones. Human bones. And on those bones a signet ring, just like the one worn by his father, Mr. Tupper.

Here, at last, was Jonah.

CHAPTER EIGHTEEN

Young Love Revealed
and Destroyed

"LOUY, YOU LOOK a sight! What has happened? Quickly, out of those wet clothes. You'll catch your death."

Abba met me at the kitchen door, where I was gasping and bedraggled, for the storm had begun again during my descent from the mountainside, and I had fallen several times.

Llew was in the kitchen as well, and Anna and Sylvia, for it was the warmest, driest room in the house. They gazed upon me openmouthed, Llew with horror for my muddied, gasping condition, Anna with dawning realization that there was trouble, and Sylvia, who knew me well, already reaching for her coat.

"I can tell from your face that you wish me to fetch Sheriff Bowman," said that young woman with great complacency.

"Yes. Oh, how I wish Llew could go with you!" I exclaimed, giving vent to a little anger.

"Is it dangerous, Louy? Should I go as well?" Anna offered.

"No. The danger is not to your own being, but to your credibility. Sheriff Bowman is just as likely to dismiss the story out of hand if it is brought to him by a woman."

"Then I will go with her." Father stood in the doorway. Father, who had spent the summer with his cucumbers and radishes and Cicero and Plutarch, oblivious to much that was happening outside of his own deep thoughts, now put his gentle hands on my shoulders and held them so tightly my shivering stopped.

"Tell me what I am to say to him," Father said. "And if he takes my words lightly because they originated from my daughter's mouth, then I will lecture him on the steadfastness of the female intelligence until he does pay attention."

"Father, tell him he must also bring Dr. Burroughs," I said. "This requires a medical examiner as well as the law. Jonah Tupper has been buried just beyond Clarence Hampton's campsite. From the tent, look east, to where the ferns grow under the stand of pines, and you'll see the place."

"Oh, dear," said Abba, sitting down at the table. On the stove, her unstirred pot began to smoke and then burn.

ABBA INSISTED I spend the rest of the day in bed under thick blankets, for as soon as Father had released me I had begun to shiver again, so hard that my teeth chattered. My hair, released from my boy's cap, hung to my waist in dark rivulets, and my clothes were soaked through to the skin. There were several cuts and scrapes on my legs.

"You can do no more today," Mother insisted. "If you try, you will take ill, and what good will that do?"

She was right. I felt exhausted—more than just physically exhausted, but morally and imaginatively as well. I had suspected Clarence Hampton of doing evil, and he had been murdered because my imagination had found a path and ignored all other possibilities in this maze of deception and violence. I had suspected Jonah Tupper of evil, and now he, too, was dead. Three young men were dead. I fell into a troubled sleep muttering their names—Ernst, Clarence, Jonah. Had one person murdered all three? Or had there been a sinister geometry of revenge and payback?

IN THE LATE afternoon, after several hours of drifting in and out of sleep, I rose again and went downstairs. Fanny was in the parlor, murmuring quietly with Abba, and they both looked up with great concern when I entered.

"My poor darling," said Fanny, coming to me with open arms. "And this was to be a vacation! A quiet time in the countryside!"

"I admit to a certain disappointment in this turn of affairs," I said. "It would be pleasant to wonder about someone's whereabouts and not have them turn up dead."

Abba and Fanny exchanged glances; Abba always grew worried when I resorted to gallows humor. She knew it meant I had fallen into the Slough of Despond, a depression from which it was difficult to climb back out.

"Where is Sylvia?" I asked, and then quickly wished I hadn't; at that moment it seemed bad luck to ask about a friend's location.

"Still with your father and Sheriff Bowman. They went

and saw . . . what you said they would see . . . and then had to come back down the mountain to gather up more men, shovels, and a litter to carry the remains back down." Abba picked up her knitting. She was making a new winter shawl for me, with a pattern of blue and green waves, and for years after when I wore that shawl I thought of graves.

The knitting reminded me: "Has anyone spoken with Ida Tupper?" I asked. "How will she deal with this new tragedy? First her son, and now her husband."

"She seems a woman of singular ill luck," agreed Fanny. "I hear she has lost other husbands as well."

"Anna is with her," Abba said. "I went over with her and checked the laudanum bottle to make sure Ida did not accidentally kill herself with that poison. A small dose was administered, and then Anna took the bottle. Now Ida is sleeping, and Anna is watching over her."

I sighed heavily and sank deep into the blue settee, letting dark thoughts swirl about me as I drank Abba's strong tea and let the gentle murmur of her conversation with Fanny sweep over me. Jonah, it would seem, had died first, many months before. Then Ernst Nooteboom. Then Clarence Hampton.

Why was Jonah Tupper killed? He was young and wealthy—at least, he stood to inherit his father's wealth. And his stepson, Clarence, would have been the next to inherit, if the marriage between Ida and Jonah produced no children. I had suspected Clarence, for there had been an angry violence about him. But then why would Ernst have been murdered? There was no ability to profit from that murder, except for his sister, Lilli, who now owned the lands they had purchased together. Could sister murder brother? And Clarence. Who profited from his death?

My head began to pound.

At six o'clock, Father returned with Sheriff Bowman.

"Well," said that man of the law, giving me a cryptic glance. "Well."

"This time," I said, "you cannot accuse Llew. He was not even in Walpole until some weeks ago, and that poor young man was killed—"

"Six months ago, at least," said another voice. Dr. Burroughs, who had been taking off his muddy galoshes in the hall, now also entered the parlor. "Miss Louisa, this really will not do. No man of good repute will want to marry a female scribe who keeps finding bodies. It will put you beyond the pale."

Abba cleared her throat, one of the only predictions of anger that gentle woman made. "I am sure it is absolutely unfair to reprimand my daughter," said she. "You had better spend your energies discovering who put those bodies in her path."

"Well said," agreed Sheriff Bowman, with a smile at me that was almost—not quite—approving.

"How did he die, Dr. Burroughs?" I asked.

"There wasn't much left to work with, but I did discover a crack in the skull and signs of a knife cutting across the windpipe," he said.

"Then he died as Clarence Hampton died," I said. "Beaten over the head, and then his throat slit."

"Ayup," said Dr. Burroughs. "That's the essence of it."

"Was there a suitcase anywhere near him?" I asked. "Had he been traveling, or about to go traveling?"

Sheriff Bowman looked at me with a glimmer of new respect. "No suitcase that we found," he said. "But there was a train ticket in his pocket. He never got to use it."

"No," I said. "That's right. There would be no point of bringing his suitcase up the mountain. But he was lured up there, for it would have been too difficult to carry him if he were already dead. He was lured up the mountain somehow, and murdered there, near Clarence Hampton's campsite. He went up to perhaps say good-bye to his stepson."

"And never came back down," added Sylvia.

"I admit to being at a loss," said Sheriff Bowman. "Who is left to question?"

"It's very much like a Shakespearean play," said Fanny. "The stage is left littered with corpses."

"I will take my leave. 'Sufficient unto the day is the labor thereof,'" said the sheriff, rising stiffly from his chair. That walk up and down the slippery mountain path would make even young bones ache, I knew. He made a courtly little bow to the ladies in the room and then stopped short, facing in Fanny's direction. She had sat quietly, paying close attention but not interrupting. I knew that later, back in her rooms, she would note in her journal how the sheriff had moved, how voices had sounded when certain statements had been made. There was a reason why she was acclaimed for verisimilitude in her technique.

"You are . . . ?" the sheriff asked, already knowing. Who in Walpole did not know?

"Fanny Kemble," said she with a little smile and a nod of her lovely head.

"May I have your autograph? Er, for the missus, of course."

THE NEXT DAY, after an hour of contemplation, I went to visit Lilli. I knew there would be no lies, no more half-truths, this time.

Mrs. Roder showed me up to her attic room; Lilli no longer came downstairs to the parlor. "She hasn't eaten in days," Mrs. Roder anguished. "I fear she'll waste away to nothing. And she's behind on her orders. Soon she'll lose her customers and then . . . Well, I can't give charity. I've got my own family to think of."

I had such a sense of doom then, of time passing and me caught up helpless in it. It was late summer, and the zinnias in Mrs. Roder's garden were tall and straggly and looked faded.

"Give me half an hour with her, and then bring up a bowl of broth and a piece of bread," I said. Mrs. Roder shook her head but promised she would.

"Lilli! Open the door!" I banged loudly.

Silence. But I knew she was in there. I could sense her behind that door, frightened and alert.

"Open, or I shall have the sheriff force it open!" I said.

A key turned. The rusty hinges groaned. Lilli's small, white face peered out at me.

"What do you want, Louisa?"

I hadn't seen her since before Clarence Hampton's death, and the change in her shocked me. She had grieved for her brother; now she was like a woman harrowed and broken.

Her tangled hair hung loose upon her back, and dark shadows under her eyes gave her a sepulchral appearance.

"We must talk about Clarence," I told her.

She hung her head and studied the floor. She looked back up at me with tears rimming her eyes. "Come in, then," she said.

Lilli sat on her bed. The faded red-and-blue star quilt was rumpled and the pillows bunched up against the headboard. I suspected she had lain down to rest and jumped back up again, over and over, unable to sleep. I sat on the only chair in the room, a stiff ladder-back. No wonder Lilli had preferred to do her sewing in the garden. Her room was dark and damp, and even during the day mice scurried in the rafters overhead. Strange to be wealthy, and yet live in such poverty, for that land had made her wealthy.

"What will you do now?" I asked.

"Now?" She looked up, pretending not to understand.

"Now that Clarence Hampton, your fiancé, is dead."

She looked at me with wonder.

"My dear," I said, "I guessed, but your eyes give it away. The signs were there. It just took me too long to put them together. Clarence had been known as a rake, but this summer he had shown little interest in the young women of Walpole and even refused to court a wealthy heiress, my friend Sylvia. He had been aloof, preoccupied, and in a strained emotional state. He was in love with you, wasn't he? Did you meet at Tupper's General Store?"

The tears now overflowed. She sobbed so hard her shoulders worked up and down. She gasped for breath and turned pink from the effort. I put my arm around her and gave her a handkerchief.

"It is time to tell someone," I said. "Tell me, Lilli. Do not carry this weight all by yourself; it will break you."

"Not at the store," she said, blowing her nose and smiling as she remembered. "At the mountain. I had gone to the little clearing where the water pools—you know the place, Louisa? Where red columbines grow? I was sewing and he came, looking so funny with his new feathered mountain hat and shiny boots and that silly polka-dot tie. I laughed at him.

"Have you seen him smile, Louisa? He smiled at me the day that I laughed at him. I think first he likes me for my yellow hair and because I am a working girl that he can play with. But then I saw there was more that he buried deep inside, that he wanted to be with me because there was a kind of peace between us, an understanding. Do you see that?"

"I think I do," I said. "Many people think that in love, like attracts like. But Abba says that opposites are more likely to attract. I think Clarence could have loved you just for being so very different from his own mother."

"Yes," Lilli said. "He is not in good relations with his mother. For me, he says he will learn to farm, to like simple. He was to make a vegetable garden. But he never did."

I thought of the turned-over patch where Father had planted his own garden, the same place where Sylvia had once seen Clarence poking at the ground . . . the garden Clarence had not finished. That part of the riddle was solved.

"Your brother did not approve, did he?" I asked Lilli.

Lilli twisted the damp handkerchief. "He had a friend in Holland who was to come over and marry me. I had agreed before we left home, but I was just a little girl, you see. And then I met Clarence."

"My dear, I am so sorry." It was all I could think of to say, and Abba had taught me that sometimes it was enough.

Lilli rested her head and sobbed for a long while. When she grew calm again, I gently pushed her away so that we were eye-to-eye.

"Lilli, think carefully before you answer. You have already met with so much tragedy that a lie could make life unendurable. You will survive this, but only with truth. Tell me: Do you think Clarence could have wished to harm Ernst? So that you might wed?"

Lilli's blue eyes darkened. "No," she said. "Clarence would not do that. He would not hurt me so much, to kill my brother."

"Even if you could wed afterward?"

"No. Because there was Clarence's family, too. His mother wanted him to marry a rich girl. We kept it a secret from them. Clarence said we must wait for the right time or . . ." She hesitated. "Or something terrible would happen."

A knock sounded at Lilli's door. Mrs. Roder, with the broth.

"Go away!" Lilli said.

I opened the door and took the tray from the landlady's hands. I set the tray on a small table, and opened the curtains over Lilli's one window, letting in a little light. "Both Ernst and Clarence loved you," I told her. "You must live—for them." I broke the bread into the broth, and after a few attempts Lilli let me spoon-feed her.

After she had eaten she grew sleepy, so I pulled the quilt over her and left. The truth does more than set you free. It allows you to rejoin the living, to eat and sleep and pick up the threads of a life come unraveled, so that it may be made whole again.

I HAD PROMISED to sit with Ida Tupper that afternoon, to relieve Anna. My sister greeted me at the door when I arrived, and she looked thankful to see me.

"This is a strange house, Louy," she said. "Mrs. Tupper sleeps mostly from all the drops she is taking, and Mr. Wattles refuses to speak to me, or even see me."

"He has returned to his misanthropic ways," I said. "And . . . Clarence?"

"In the dining room. Abba helped me with the laying out."

"Mrs. Tupper did not assist?"

"In honesty, we did not wish her to. She either sleeps or raves."

"Go home and get some rest." I kissed Anna on the forehead and gave her a little push in the direction of the Alcott cottage. She looked at me thankfully over her shoulder and disappeared through the hedge.

Mrs. Tupper's house smelled musty and unused, the way large houses do when too few people inhabit them. The little maid seemed to have disappeared, so I hung my linen coat and straw hat on the hall rack. I moved quietly down the hall, over the expensive Turkish rug, noticing the new wallpaper, the new pictures hung over the wallpaper, the new little figurines on the bric-a-brac shelf. Mrs. Tupper and her brother seemed disinclined to favor old and sentimental memorial objects over the new and stylish.

The door to the library was closed. I knocked. "Mr. Wattles?" I called.

A long silence, then a gruff voice: "I do not wish to be disturbed" came from deep within that room, from behind the locked door.

"I thought you might want some tea and toast," I suggested.

Another long silence. I heard papers being rearranged, the squeak of his wheeled chair.

"Come back in half an hour. If you don't mind," he added.

I found Ida upstairs in her bedroom. On the dresser was the same tintype picture of Jonah Tupper that hung in the general store; it was the only masculine element in a room that was a frenzy of pink chintz and lace.

Ida herself was sleeping on her back, her mouth open and moving as if she talked in her sleep, though no sound came out. I looked down at her, and for the first time felt the compassion that is the essence of human friendship. Without the horsehair rolls to fill it out, her hair was limp and thin; without the rouge, one could see all too clearly the papery complexion of a woman past her youthful beauty.

The water glass with its dregs of laudanum was on her night table. I washed it and filled it with clear, health-bringing water.

Then I went into the parlor, to where Clarence Hampton had been laid out.

No candles had been lighted here; no sister or mother or uncle knelt in prayer. Clarence was alone.

Abba and Anna had done an excellent job, combing his dark, wavy hair carefully over the spot in his skull by which he had been felled, and tying a lace cravat over the long gash in his throat. His hands were folded over his chest. He looked dissatisfied, I thought. And so he should be, to have been young and in love and have all that destroyed, all that taken from him.

"I am sorry, Clarence," I said to him. "I suspected you of being a villain." But I felt dissatisfied, as well. There was still the chance that he had been; being in love does not always guarantee a person will forever more do only good, and who is a more likely suspect to want to do away with an interfering brother than a lovelorn suitor? This is one of the greatest evils of death—it cuts short the truth, the possibility of discovering the truth.

Half an hour later, Mr. Wattles opened his library door, and I carried in the tea tray.

"Ah, Miss Louisa," he said. "It was kind of your sister . . . What is her name? Anna? It was kind of her to come and attend to my sister, but I admit to some discomfort at having a stranger in the house, even if the stranger is a woman. Of course, you are harboring some unusual guests at the Alcott house."

He was in his wheeled chair, with a lap robe over his legs and a shawl over his stooped shoulders. His white beard gleamed in the dim light.

"If you mean Llew, then be reassured he is as gentle a man as you could hope to find. May I put the tray on that table? It won't disrupt your papers. His involvement in the death of your nephew is accidental, I am convinced. He found him, but had no hand in the violence that . . ." I paused.

"That killed him, you were going to say," said Mr. Wattles. "You are a writer. Don't shy from the words, Miss Louisa. And don't try to spare my feelings. They were destroyed long ago."

I poured tea for both of us, though I could not drink mine. I paced, as I do when preoccupied with unresolved thoughts.

"Did you love your nephew?" I asked Mr. Wattles.

"Why, my dear, of course I did," he said. He stroked his beard. "I have known him and helped Ida care for him all his life. She has had such misfortune with husbands. Clarence was a difficult child, unaffectionate and unbending, but he was family. One must love them, despite their faults, especially when we are the only ones who will probably ever love them." He seemed very sad, very alone.

"I'm relieved to hear you say you loved Clarence," I said. "He sometimes seemed very estranged from all of us. I often had the feeling that he wished to speak about something, but could not."

"He was independent by choice, my dear, by choice. Young men will have it so." Mr. Wattles finished his toast and yawned without hiding it. I took the tray into the pantry and spent the rest of the evening upstairs, on a chair in the hall, outside Ida's door, in case she should awaken. She did not.

Once, though, she did cry out, and I went in to check on her. She still slept, but fitfully, her eyes under their lids darting here and there, her hands making small grasping gestures, as if clutching at something. I lit a lamp, for sometimes even in sleep a light can bring some comfort. I spied a box on her dressing table, the kind in which women keep their sentimental trinkets and letters. My hesitation lasted only a moment; what was mere etiquette when lives were at stake? I lifted the lid. I found the telegram that announced the bell order that Jonah Tupper had never actually received. There were five or six penny cards in the box, all with much the same message: *Thinking of you. Send regards to Father. I am well.* Messages meant to reassure. Messages not sent by Jonah Tupper, but arranged by his murderer.

THE NEXT MORNING Sylvia arrived to watch over Ida so that I might go home and rest, and we had a hurried consultation. I walked outside to meet her on the porch, where we might talk. Dawn was turning the sky from gray to rosy, and the air smelled fresh and sweet, especially after the heavy atmosphere in Ida Tupper's house. I stretched and breathed in deeply, relieved to empty my lungs of the mustiness of Ida's house. I was physically exhausted, but my mind seemed to be dancing the same two steps over and over, to the music of Mr. Wattles's refrain, *We must love family.*

"Mrs. Tupper slept all night but will refuse food because of the drug," I explained to Sylvia, whose ramrod posture indicated displeasure with the task she was determined to fulfill. Others might deem Sylvia flighty—I knew her to be as staunch as Gibraltar. "Try to force her to eat an egg or two, or at least some bread and butter. And use this only if necessary." I gave Sylvia the bottle of laudanum.

"What about Mr. Wattles?" Sylvia looked terrified. Her own father had been so rarely present in her own life that mature men made her somewhat uneasy.

"I'll bring soup over at noon," I said. "Otherwise, leave him be. He prefers his solitude."

"Louy, before you go, I almost forgot to tell you. . . ."

"What, Sylvia?"

"Sheriff Bowman has arrested Mr. Dill. You remember him, the Irish laborer who was the recipient of the firewood your father gave away?"

I sighed heavily and felt, then, very tired indeed.

"On what basis?"

"That he was seen often in the neighborhood and he brawls on Saturday night. And they found some stolen things in his house. A silver cup and a garnet ring."

"But not Ernst Nooteboom's gold watch? Then he has the wrong man," I said. Sheriff Bowman had leaped to conclusions and made accusations on the flimsiest circumstances.

"He seems to require two murderers," Sylvia added. "Llew is still under house arrest."

UPON ABBA'S INSISTENCE, I slept late the next morning, and woke up just before noon to the sound of more rain on the roof and Father, housebound, pacing and muttering downstairs in his book-lined study.

"Isn't it the way?" he said, when he heard me come downstairs. "Deprive a man of work, make it impossible for him to care for his family and himself, and then accuse him of a crime. Where is the real crime here?"

I was barefoot and with my hair loose on my back, fresh from my morning rest, and Father gave me a peck on the cheek and tousled my hair, as he used to do when I was a small child.

"I think I preferred it when I was the sole suspect," said

Llew, who appeared behind Father. "Well, not really, if I am to be quite honest. I have a reasonable fear of hanging. What must you think of me, Louy? And I had so hoped for your highest esteem."

Llew took my hands. His eyes were dark and large and searched into mine.

"You have my highest esteem. I know you are no more guilty of this crime than I could be, or Father."

Father, seeing my hands in Llew's, cleared his throat. Llew and I stepped apart.

"I will always be your fondest sister," I told Llew. I looked at the two men I loved most in the world, my father and my friend, and felt a new urgency that all of this must be set straight, order must be restored, truth must be victorious; else there would be no peace in the Alcott household, or in my friendships, for once a man has been accused he must be proven innocent, even if he is never proven guilty, or the stain lasts his lifetime.

"Where are you going, Louy?"

I ran back upstairs to don my afternoon dress and linen coat.

"Remind Anna to send soup over to Sylvia," I answered.

CHAPTER NINETEEN

A Father Grieves

MY NEW WALPOLE acquaintances, those I knew by name and those I knew only to nod to as we passed, were friendlier that afternoon, since Mr. Dill had been arrested. He was, after all, one of theirs even if he was a fairly recent import from Ireland, not one of the "Boston crowd," and so my family had achieved an early vindication at Mr. Dill's expense. Hats were tipped and "good days" exchanged as I walked to the main square. Several people shyly inquired about Mrs. Kemble's health and indicated that they would be happy to host a party or dinner in her honor, but I gave the response that Fanny had required me to give: Mrs. Kemble was in the country for a rest, thank you, and too exhausted for calling, but I would relay the kind thoughts to her.

"Such a shame about Jonah," added one woman. "Such a terrible shame. We thought something strange was going on, but never thought he might actually be dead." The woman shuddered with a kind of delight.

I nodded. *It's difficult to believe that someone is dead when his penny cards keep arriving in the mail,* I thought to myself. Whoever arranged that had a cruel heart, indeed. Again I thought of Clarence and wished with all my heart that on those occasions when he had opened his mouth to speak, and then decided in favor of silence, why, I wished I had forced him with all my ability to say what was on his mind. It was not inconceivable that Clarence had been involved in Jonah's death. And if I thought so, so would Jonah's father, and he was a man of anger and violence, the kind of man who would require revenge. Both young men had been beaten and then had their throats slit; either they had been killed by the same man (and I could think of no reason why that should be), or the second murder had been an imitation of the first, as part of the revenge.

Of course, the problem was that the murder of Jonah wasn't discovered until after the murder of Clarence—unless Mr. Tupper had discovered that grave himself earlier, and had decided to take his own revenge rather than going to Sheriff Bowman. Mr. Tupper could have waited for the right moment, and found it when so many had gathered at our house for dinner, when Clarence stepped out alone to go to the cellar.

Mr. Tupper, as did many shopkeepers, lived in rooms above his store. I went through the double door that separated storeroom from front display room, up the narrow, creaking wooden stairs. The stairwell walls were papered over with old flour and rice sacks and an occasional picture calendar from previous years, to keep out drafts. A few newspaper pages were glued up as well, with various advertisements circled in grease pencil—all advertisements of land for sale. The only light came from one small glazed window that was murky with years of dust and dead-fly speckles.

At the top of the stairs I knocked at the only door. "Go away," his deep voice answered my knock. The words were slurred.

I knocked harder. "It is Miss Louisa," I called.

Silence. Then heavy steps approaching in an irregular pace. The door opened. Mr. Tupper glared out at me, looking almost demonic. His red hair stood on end; his mustachios were drooped over his lip, looking more like monstrous teeth than hair. His red-checked shirt was hanging out of his pants, and his suspenders fell past his hips, revealing the gray long johns that some country folk wear even in summer. He looked old.

"You," he growled. He took my arm, pulled me into the room, and slammed the door shut. I looked around for some weapon and settled on an empty bottle, which I picked up and grasped in my fist.

He laughed. "You think I would hurt you? I could squash you like a fly." To make his point he stomped his boot on the floor and ground it into the carpet. "But why would I? Why?" He started to weep. "Why my boy?"

He wept as though his heart were breaking, with big gasping sobs and rivulets of tears staining his distorted face. I did what I thought Abba would do. I put down the weapon-bottle, knelt beside him on the floor, and forced his head onto my shoulder.

He quieted after a while, snuffling and wiping his nose with his fists. I gave him my handkerchief.

"Thank you," he said in a small voice. "Please take a chair, Miss Louisa."

I sat in the chair. He sat across from me in the other. I studied the room while he struggled to further regain his composure. It was poorly furnished, as if its occupant gave no thought to his own comfort. The collected objects and disorder—hunting rifles leaning against the wall, a bow and arrow, a set of horseshoes for gaming, several decks of cards, and empty bottles—made it clear there was no Mrs. Tupper to care for the home, nor had there been for quite some time. Only the faded red-checked curtains, the yellowed lace trim on the shelves, indicated a wife had once shared these rooms; only a carved wood bassinet, now filled with old ledgers and papers, indicated there had once been a child to bring comfort and joy to husband and wife.

Gone. I wondered how Mrs. Tupper had died, but knew it was not the time to ask. Mr. Tupper had other griefs weighting him down.

"I am so sorry about your son, Mr. Tupper," I said when I thought he was calm again.

"What was he to you?" The bristling anger was back.

"It's true I never met him. But any death wounds us all, and I fear you have been greatly wounded by this loss."

"Is that philosophy? From your father?"

"No. From me. From my heart."

He sighed again, so heavily, so raggedly, I could almost hear the tearing of his own heart.

"Yes. I am wounded. A man works to acquire a home, a name, a business, money, land. Why? For his son. And his son's son. Now what?" He stared out his window, a glazed pane as murky as the one in the stairwell. "Now what?" he repeated in a dead voice.

"Mr. Tupper, it is time for the truth," I said.

"And what truth would that be?" He sneered, then looked at my handkerchief, which he still held, and his face softened again.

"The day Ernst Nooteboom died, were you there?"

Again that ragged, heart-tearing sigh. He ran his fingers through his disordered red hair.

"I was. I asked Ernst to meet me there, to talk about the land. I wanted to buy the lot he had purchased two years before, and to sweeten the offer I was going to give him that piece of the mountain, where we met. Told him that someday the mountain would be worth something, that in Europe they build resorts and health spas in the mountains and we would too, once the summer visitors started to come, after the train was finished."

Mr. Tupper rose and walked to the window, and looked down at the busy square.

"He laughed at me," he said. "Said he didn't want a mountain. That he was a lowlander; he wanted his lowland for the railroad."

"And then?" I asked.

"And then I . . . well . . . I said some things, called some names best not repeated, and then I left."

"You left Ernst Nooteboom alive on the mountain."

"I did. But . . ."

"But what, Mr. Tupper?"

"Before I got far down the path, I heard him talking again to someone else. I thought I heard a shout and a scream."

"But you never said anything to Sheriff Bowman about this?" I asked.

"What was there to say? Someone up the mountain quarreled? No, I didn't say anything. I was busy." He looked at his raveling shirt cuff and mumbled, "Busy time in the store, in the spring, and my business with Nooteboom was confidential. I aimed to keep it that way."

"Do you know who the other man was?"

"No. I only heard Nooteboom's voice, not the other."

ABBA WAS IN the kitchen when I returned home. She comforted me as I had comforted Mr. Tupper, with a shoulder to lean against and gentle reassurances that all would be sorted out, that the worst was over.

"But how can it be over?" I said, hanging up my coat and hat. "There is a murderer walking freely in this pleasant village, and no one is safe till that murderer is caught."

"Write, Louy," Abba said. "Empty your mind of all this, and work on your story. Sometimes things come to you that way."

"O wise woman," I said. "Keen-eyed enough to see her own and others' faults, and wise enough to find a cure for them. Abba, what would I do without you?"

So I took a pot of tea and tray of biscuits and locked myself in my writing shed, feeling safe there, feeling separate from the horrors of the past few days, from all the deaths, and concentrated on my story about Mr. Windsor, who must make a choice between the shallow beauty of Miss Amelia and the independent nobility of Kate. My emotions were in a turmoil; my thoughts roiled and stormed around the events of the past few weeks in Walpole, and the storm appeared in my story.

> *"Hark!" said Kate, suddenly dropping her work. "What is that?"*
>
> *They listened, and a loud, continuous roar like distant thunder was plainly heard.*
>
> *"It is the brook but it sounds very near," said Mr. Windsor, going to the window. A sudden exclamation brought his companions to his side, and they saw a dark flood rushing by where an hour ago there had been a grassy road.*
>
> *"This is a wild freak of your Undine's, Miss Kate. See how it washes away that bank opposite. I'm afraid the bridge will go, and then we are all prisoners here."*

I put down my pen and reread the words, and they seemed to have more than one meaning to me that afternoon. I had believed I was coming to spend a pleasant, quiet time in the country; instead I was in the midst of a dark flood of violence, and if I could not discover the truth I would always be a prisoner to the deceit, the violence, that was being wrought here.

I wrote for several hours, making what I thought was good progress with my story, when I was interrupted by a timid knock at the shed door.

"It's suppertime, Louy," said Sylvia when I opened the door. "Abba says you are to come and eat something, for you haven't eaten all day."

"How was your own day with Mrs. Tupper?"

"She slept, as you said she would, but in the afternoon she woke and ate bread and butter and drank a pot of tea. Her mind is all unraveled, I think. She kept looking at the door as if Clarence were about to walk in. She asked where he was."

" 'One woe doth tread upon another's heel, so fast they follow,' " I quoted.

"Is that from your story, Louy?"

"No, it is Queen Gertrude's complaint, close to the end of *Hamlet*. Let us go and pretend to eat Abba's supper to ease her mind, for I have no appetite."

We gathered about the table, Llew and Sylvia, Abba, Father, Anna, May, Lizzie, and myself, and the prayer before that meal was a long one, for we all felt the need for grace, for meditation upon powers stronger than our own. Supper was fish chowder again, and if I hadn't already lost my appetite I would have then, but I played with my spoon and dipped my bread and ate enough to convince Abba that body and soul would not be separated by starvation that night.

For dessert we had a bowl of peaches and cream, sent over by Cousin Eliza.

"Louy, I almost forgot," said Abba, spooning the peaches into our bowls. "Benjamin also sent a message. I have no idea what it means, but he asks if you have seen Anubis."

CHAPTER TWENTY

The Post Arrives

"Anubis!" I dropped the cream ladle with such careless surprise that I chipped it, I'm afraid to report, and sent a spray of cream down the table, so that a spot of white ended on Father's nose and another on Sylvia's frock.

"Louy, what have you to do with pagan gods?" asked Father, somewhat shocked. "What does this mean?"

"He means his walking stick," I said, rising and beginning to pace in our little dining room. "Remember the set of four from Egypt? Anubis! He would never let us play with Anubis, because it was sharp and dangerous, he said. 'You'll put out someone's eye,' he said. He was right. It was a walking stick that killed Clarence, and now one of Uncle's is missing. Oh, why didn't I take a closer look at it before Sheriff Bowman took it away?"

"Because it was covered with blood and gore," said Llew, who had grown pale at the renewed references to the murder of Clarence Hampton.

Abba put the bowl of peaches on the table with more care than I had shown the ladle. She looked confused and very worried. "But doesn't that then implicate Benjamin?" Father reached over and patted her hand for reassurance.

"It can't," he said thoughtfully. "Benjamin cannot be in two places at once. He was with us all that night."

"Besides," added May, "Uncle Benjamin would never ruin his cape with a bloody murder. If he intended to kill Clarence, he would have made him take the Turkish hat and cape off first."

"May!" said Mother, shocked.

"I was just trying to be logical, like Louy!" May protested.

"Oh, let me think!" I said, pacing furiously back and forth before the window that looked directly into the dining room window of Ida Tupper's house. The lace curtains were closed, but I could see the table was bare; Ida and her brother would be dining in their rooms, off trays, if at all. And then I remembered.

"Weeks ago," I said, "at tea with Eliza and Benjamin, it began to rain and Mrs. Tupper borrowed one of Uncle Benjamin's walking sticks. She must have borrowed Anubis."

I sat back down, overwhelmed. I stared at my hands, at the ink stains that never completely washed away. I looked at Abba, that good and gentle mother, and at Llew, whom she loved like a son. The room was absolutely still.

Sylvia broke the silence. "Are you saying, Louy, that Mrs. Tupper is the murderer?"

"How could it be?" I said. "How could it be? His own mother! I could almost understand marrying for wealth and dispatching the husband. . . ."

Father cleared his throat.

"Understand," I clarified. "Not condone or recommend as practice. But to murder one's own child . . . ! Abba, what should I do?" I looked to my mother for advice.

"There have been three deaths, not just the one," she said. "If you accuse her, you accuse her of more evil than I fear a woman could be capable of. Yet you cannot ignore what you know. Perhaps tonight it would be enough to send a message to Sheriff Bowman. Tell him you know the owner of the walking stick that was used to destroy Clarence Hampton, and let him know that the stick was in Mrs. Tupper's possession. Let the sheriff make of it what he will. Then think some more."

As always, her advice was perfect. The note was dispatched to the sheriff, written by Father himself, and then we all went to our beds.

There was no rest for me. I assessed anew Mrs. Tupper's nature, her coquettishness, her obvious delight in the company of men, her nature to take offense easily, to be mortally wounded by a slight; there was passion in her, and vanity and greed, as well.

"Are you thinking of her?" Sylvia whispered when the moon shone full in the room and I had tossed and turned for the hundredth time. Anna was fast asleep, her breath sounding like a gentle, soothing tide, but Sylvia was as awake as myself.

I watched as a cloud passed over the moon and the room grew dark; the cloud moved on and dim outlines returned, the curtains flapped, and Sylvia sat up.

"I am," I admitted.

"And to think that Mrs. Tupper wished her son to court me. For the inheritance, of course."

"He was already in love with Lilli. Does that wound you?"

"Not really. We would never have achieved harmony together. I suspect Lilli was the better choice for him. Oh, Louy, would she have killed him over that? Because he wanted to marry a poor girl? How awful!"

"To begin with, Lilli is not really poor. She still has the land she and Ernst purchased. No, I don't think that was the problem between those two. There is still something missing, Sylvia. We have an odd assortment of facts and motives, but I don't think we have the solution yet."

Anna made a little noise in the back of her throat and turned onto her other side. Dear Anna. I thought again about her hearing loss and wondered how severe it was, if it was a small matter, as she said. My family seemed changed this summer, with Lizzie growing up yet ever shyer, May becoming even more outspoken, Anna seeming distant though still loving. Abba and Father looked healthier, even younger, than they had looked the year before in Boston. The country air and sunshine agreed with them. Yet I had a sense of their changing as well, of Abba struggling with the need to let her Golden Brood fly free of her, and Father reconciling himself to his lack of great success by forcing himself to delight in small achievements, like his vegetable patch.

The vegetable patch. Now there was a relief. In the back of my mind had grown the possibility that the stench of that soil came from a buried body: Jonah Tupper. That had not been the case. The relief was short-lived. That nagging sense of failing my family returned. When I had the solution, I would devote myself completely to my family, I promised myself in bed that night. I would write stories for May to illustrate with her paints, and listen more carefully to Lizzie's piano exercises and compositions, and take long walks with Anna, as we used to do. When this was over. When this was over. I fell asleep, finally, to that refrain.

SINCE SHERIFF BOWMAN seemed to be a late sleeper, and I had no reason to expect a message from him till later in the day, if at all, I went for my morning run in the ravine the next day; a good run cleared my head so that my thinking was more productive, less rambling. Maybe I hoped that the stones themselves would speak of what they had seen.

As I ran, I listened in my head to Kate and Mr. Windsor debate the qualities of womanhood and wondered at what moment the handsome but somewhat fickle Mr. Windsor would finally realize Kate's worth. I had left them in the midst of a raging flood; now I sent Kate off to find help, while Mr. Windsor attended to the others of the group, being the protection and mainstay during the dangerous storm. Yes, Kate would be the heroine, bringing help when help was most required.

But what was I to do with Mrs. Tupper?

The run did not clear my thoughts but only jumbled them more. Disheartened, I climbed back down the slippery path of the ravine, almost oblivious to the prettily bubbling brook, to the birdsong and wildflowers and stands of pines that had so enchanted me weeks before. At the top of that ravine, one young man had been killed and buried; a second had fallen to his death; a third had been discovered in our cellar. How could I admire a stalk of Queen Anne's lace when somewhere in Walpole a murderer was walking free and perhaps preparing to strike again? Or had Clarence, the country bachelor, been his last victim? Or her last victim?

I returned home and wrote for several hours, stopping only when Sylvia knocked to give me a cup of tea for refreshment and a letter that had arrived from the post office.

I did not recognize the handwriting, but I knew the address. It was from the Unitarian minister of Manchester, Mrs. Tupper's birthplace and childhood home. I tore the envelope open and read. I had written to him out of curiosity; as I read I realized that my intuition had not been superficial, as I had first assumed.

> Dear Miss Alcott,
>
> I have delayed in answering your letter; I apologize. I hope it has not inconvenienced you. You must understand that I had to deeply search my conscience before answering your letter at all, for I am a soul who believes in forgiveness and fresh starts. But further thought suggested that perhaps it would harm Ida Wattles if I turned away from someone claiming a relationship with her. So I have decided in favor of answering your letter.
>
> I knew Ida from when she was born to when she left Manchester at the age of sixteen. Hers was not an auspicious home. Her father had a pronounced preference for the state of mind that occurs only when a cer-

tain amount of alcohol has been consumed. He was a carpenter by trade but often out of work because of his habits. Ida had eight brothers and sisters, and I must admit that not much thought was given to their education or their moral upbringing.

Given those circumstances, it was not surprising to any in the community when Ida took up with what was termed "fast" company. In particular, she spent much time with a youth of great disrepute, one Johnnie Dodge, a boy of good looks but no morality. He was suspected of burning down his own father's barn when the man refused to give him his share of his inheritance. To do so would have required mortgaging the farm, which his father was reasonably unhappy to do. Mr. Dodge was also suspected of breaking into several homes in the area and robbing them.

I joined Ida and Mr. Dodge in holy matrimony on her sixteenth birthday. She had indicated that a wedding was required to justify a certain situation that had arisen, and I thought a legal relationship might improve both of them. Only time will tell if I was right or wrong. Neither family offered any objection. Shortly after the wedding Ida had a confinement; the child was stillborn. Six months later, Johnnie Dodge was caught breaking into the home of Ida's uncle, a Mr. Edward Wattles, who was a middle-aged bachelor with a good job, and it was rumored that he had a nest egg hidden in his house. I don't know if that was true or not. What was true was that Mr. Wattles kept a shotgun, which he let loose at Johnnie Dodge, injuring him in the leg.

But he was his niece's husband, so Mr. Wattles let the young couple leave town without legal prosecution.

I heard some two or three years later that her husband had again been caught burglaring but that he had gone to jail. That is the last I know of Ida Wattles Dodge. If she is now among your acquaintances, please tell her she is in my prayers. I suspect she has need of them.

Might I ask if you are the daughter of Bronson Alcott of Concord? I am a great admirer of his philosophies of education.

Yours truly,
Reverend Titus Charles

Sylvia was sitting on the stoop, staring up at me.

"Louy," she said, "you should see your face. You have lit up like a lantern."

"I have it," I said. "I have the answer. Come with me, Sylvia." I ran back to the house in search of Father. He was in his study, and looked up with benign concern when he saw me standing in his doorway.

"Louy, my dear. What is it?"

"Time to send another message to Sheriff Bowman," I said. "About Mrs. Tupper again."

Abba was behind me, looking worried.

"Louy, I thought you had gone up to the ravine," she said.

"Why would you think that?"

"Because of this." She handed me a note, not post delivered, but one that had been slipped under the front door. It was written on familiar plain brown parcel paper, and the words were not scripted but scribbled in block format, like a child's—or like an adult with little education.

> Meet me at the top of the ravine. It is important. Please. Lilli.

"I was going to give this to you, but something started to burn in the kitchen and I got all distracted. I gave the note to Anna to put on your desk." Abba wrung her hands in her apron.

Suddenly our crowded little cottage felt very empty.

"Where is Anna?" I asked, fear rising in me.

Lizzie came out of the parlor, where she had been practicing her exercises. "She put on her hat and coat and went out," Lizzie said. "She said she would be back soon, and that probably Lilli Nooteboom would have supper with us."

"Oh, no," I said.

"Louy, what can be wrong with that?" Abba wrung her hands even more fiercely.

"That note is not from Lilli," I said. "It is not from Lilli, and it was meant for me. Llew, come; we have no time to waste!"

"I cannot leave the house!" he protested.

"That does not matter now. Llew, trust me; come with me. I need Sylvia to get Sheriff Bowman, and Father should stay here to protect Abba and Lizzie and May."

Llew looked at me. "I will," he said. "Lead the way."

We ran up the path to the ravine trail, moving quickly, without speaking, intent only on arriving at that place where I knew Anna waited. She expected to meet Lilli. Instead she would be at the mercy of the murderer. The murderer had thought to trap me in this way, knowing that I was getting close to the truth. But instead Anna had decided to relieve me of a chore, and in so doing was risking her life and did not even know it.

Anna would stand looking out at the breathtaking sight, at the babbling brook running through the ravine and the gray, green-ferned, steep walls of the cliffs. She would look, and wait for Lilli, not hearing the steps approaching behind her.

"Hurry!" I yelled to Llew. He was just behind me, his hands already bruised and bleeding from the rush of our ascent up that steep cliffside.

We were halfway up. Then we were only a third of the way from the top. We were just steps from the rise of the hill, beyond which all would be visible—the sad, emptied place of Clarence's campsite; beyond that the hill of broken ferns, now even more disrupted by the disinterring of Jonah; beyond that, Anna, standing at the cliffside, the wind blowing back her cape. Her blond hair was tucked tightly under her straw hat. From the back—where the murderer would approach, probably from that thick, shadowy stand of pines—there would be no way to know that Anna Alcott stood there, not Louisa.

"Look!" I pointed, panting, as a shape emerged from the forest. It was just yards away from Anna.

A black, hooded shape approached her. I yelled, but the wind carried my voice in the other direction and Anna did not hear. Two hands appeared from under the cloak, two hands reaching for Anna.

Llew uttered a cry such as I have never heard; he leaned forward, balancing his arms across his chest, and charged.

The two figures wrestled close, perilously close, to the edge of the precipice, but Llew was young and strong and furious at this threat of harm to his beloved adopted family. In minutes the caped figure was lying in the gravel and dirt, face pressed down, arms twisted behind him.

Anna was weeping with fright. I put my arm about her, steadied her, then went to the figure on the ground.

"Llew, turn him over," I said.

Mr. Wattles glared up at me, one eye already blackened from the brawl, the other glittering with menace.

"He has a formidable strength, for an invalid," Llew panted.

CHAPTER TWENTY-ONE

The Business Concluded

THE SHERIFF ARRIVED just minutes after Llew had managed to tie up Mr. Wattles with the ribbon from my straw bonnet. It was an old ribbon; it would not have held long, so the sheriff's promptness was much appreciated. Sylvia and Sheriff Bowman gaped for some time at the figure on the ground.

"Why, that's Ida Tupper's brother, without his chair. It would appear his rheumatism has significantly improved," Sylvia finally exclaimed. "Come to think of it, he is without his beard as well," she added.

"His identity has been a pretense," I said. "As was the relationship. Ladies and gentlemen, please meet Mr. Johnnie Dodge, Ida's first and only legal husband."

"Well, I'll be," said Sheriff Bowman.

"Oh, my," said Anna, and she fainted.

❊   ❊   ❊

THE WIND RUFFLED the long dried grasses of August, and a streamer tied to the top of Clarence Hampton's collapsing tent blew bravely. There was a hint of autumn in the air, I thought. I had both my arms about Anna, who was still only half-conscious. She and Sylvia and I leaned against an ancient oak, catching our breath. Llew and the sheriff had not so gently led Mr. Dodge-Wattles back down the steep path to town, to jail.

"It is over," Sylvia said.

"It is," I said. "Anna, can you walk yet? Should we send for a litter?"

"Don't be ninnies," she said, rising carefully to her feet and smoothing her muddied and crumpled dress. "I am more embarrassed about fainting than I can say. You are so very brave, Louy, and I—"

"You are the bravest of all," I said. "You came up here by yourself to help a friend without any thought of your own danger."

"But I fainted!"

"From excitement," I assured her. "Facing a fall of some forty feet down a cliff face can be overstimulating. Moreover, that faint of yours has just helped me out of a difficulty in my story. Oh, thank you, Anna!"

"You're welcome, I'm sure, though I've never before received enthusiastic gratitude for a faint," said Anna. "Come, girls, we must get home before Abba begins to worry."

ONE WEEK LATER, the parlor of the Alcott cottage was again filled to overflowing with family and guests, and the scent of fish chowder for supper wafted through the air. My lack of appetite for yet another fishy meal was shared by others present, as could be seen by the hostile glances that they gave their soup spoons. And to think that at one time I had actually feared that Jonah Tupper had been buried in Father's vegetable patch. Now there was a mystery still unsolved: that stench.

"More sherry?" asked Benjamin, passing a decanter and pouring when someone nodded yes. Uncle Benjamin had been up to his own attic and found an old trunk with souvenirs, and was adorned, once again, in exotic style with a Turkish robe and cape. Cousin Eliza looked tired but happy. One of her children back home was sniffling, and she knew that soon they would all be ill and she would be sleepless for days, but on that night she was out with her husband and friends and was enthusiastically conversing on subjects other than skinned knees and nursery rhymes and colic.

"Oh, what a summer it has been," she said. "When I met Mrs. Tupper—well, I guess we are to call her Mrs. Dodge—when we first met I knew she would be trouble, but I didn't suspect how much. Only Louisa could discover that."

"I do find her an interesting study," I admitted.

Abba beamed at me. "And Louy wasn't so much as scratched in the process, though her hands are a mess from climbing up and down that ravine trail," she said.

"I will give you a manicure, my dear," said Fanny Kemble. "I have all sorts of lotions and potions."

"No, thank you," I said. "Ink will soon cover all the bruises."

Lizzie, in a fit of joy, bounced up from her place on the old blue settee and dashed into the second parlor to her rented piano, and pounded out a rendition of "Darlin' Corey." Llew took my hands as Sylvia pulled Anna from her chair. May and Lizzie paired off, and we tried to dance but only tripped over each other in the congested space, and fell back into our places, laughing.

"Play 'Pretty Saro,'" Abba called to Lizzie through the thin walls.

"Will you sing?" Lizzie called back.

Abba, her gray hair tucked into her lace cap and an apron covering her much-mended dress, looked at Father with eyes soft and gentle and sang the old love song. He gazed back with a rare clarity of emotion; he adored Abba. I remembered something he had written to her once, in a letter, years before, when he was traveling and alone: *I was first attracted by your faithfulness to your brother and the intelligent vivacity of your conversation. But I soon felt the real nobility of your character, and loved you.*

My story "The Lady and the Woman" was finished and ready to be sent to William Warland Clapp at the *Saturday Evening Gazette.* I hoped readers, someday, might recognize that Abba, my own dearest mother, was the inspiration for feminine womanhood depicted in the story, for she was kind, patient, courageous, and wise. But it was thanks to Anna that my story was completed, for after Kate faints, she is wooed and won by Mr. Windsor, who recognizes her gentleness as well as her strength.

"Enough entertainment," said Fanny Kemble. "Though, Abba, I wish I had your voice. But I wish to hear how Louisa arrived at the solution to this puzzle. Who would have guessed that poor old Mr. Wattles was the scoundrel Johnnie Dodge?"

"You might have," I said with a smile, "if you had met him. Mr. Wattles's beard was always beautifully combed. Not the beard of an old man who has trouble eating his soup. I suspect it was the same beard Ida wore in her school play, when she was King Lear. But that's hindsight. I should have suspected he was not what he claimed when he interrupted our game of croquet in the yard."

"How was that suspicious?" asked Llew.

"Dear Llew, it is a new game, yet he knew the rules. How could he, unless he had played himself, and how could he have played croquet from his wheeled chair? Ida must have taught him. I suspect it was part of her efforts to make him more genteel."

"So the husband pretended to be the brother," said Anna. "But why?"

"Because Johnnie Dodge is still wanted for robbery in several places and did not wish to be recognized," I said. "And there was an even darker purpose. He saw that his pretty wife might earn more by marrying money than he could by stealing it. So the husband became the brother, and Ida married—several times, each time acquiring more wealth."

"I did perceive her as a woman of weak intelligence," said Father. "Weak morals often accompany that condition."

"She met Johnnie Dodge when she was quite young and easily impressed," I said. "I suspect she never broke the habit of attempting to fulfill all his requirements of her, even when they involved crime."

"But did she herself help dispatch those poor men who married her?" asked Sylvia.

"One fell from a ladder and the other drowned," I said.

"Perhaps we will never know the truth of their deaths, except that Johnnie Dodge wished them. Abba, do you think Ida Tupper-Dodge was capable of murder, or assisting in murder?"

"That is what most disturbs me," said Abba, frowning and sitting again. "I thought her silly. A grown woman who couldn't even knit. Was she guilty of deep evil? Did she help, or simply stand by and allow it to happen? I don't know."

"I think she helped," said Sylvia in a dark voice.

"I don't," said gentle Anna. "I think her sin was failure to act, to stop Johnnie Dodge."

"I think I must agree with Anna," I said. "She was in Johnnie Dodge's power, and there did not seem to be an excess of communication between them. Certainly, had she known that her husband was to kill her son, it would have roused her to action to stop him. Even as faulty a parent as she proved, I think she had an element of affection for Clarence. Once she realized Clarence had been murdered, she took her own revenge against Dodge."

"She did?" asked Sylvia, startled.

"Yes. By sending me to Jonah's grave, under a pretense of fetching her son's camping items. She wanted me to discover the murder of her husband, to avenge the death of her son. She helped hide the murder of Jonah by pretending those penny cards were posted by her husband who was supposed to be traveling for business. But when Clarence was murdered, she turned on Johnnie Dodge."

"Oh, my," said Abba, turning white in the lamplight. "Does that mean Johnnie Dodge murdered his own son?"

"Dodge's son was stillborn, and Ida married again after

Dodge went to jail," I said. "Perhaps Dodge assumed Clarence was not his son. We may never know."

"They did have quite different noses," said Sylvia. "Wattles's—I mean, Dodge's—was quite flat, while Clarence's was long."

"But what about poor Ernst Nooteboom?" Abba asked.

"Ernst Nooteboom would not sell his land to Mr. Tupper," I said. "So Dodge, perhaps in a fit of spontaneous anger, perhaps with premeditation, pushed him over the cliff. Sheriff Bowman found Ernst's gold watch in Dodge's pocket."

"Why did he affect that chair, Louy? It must have been irksome," Fanny said.

"Because of his limp," I said. "It was one of his identifying characteristics. He had been shot during a burglary. But he needed periodic release from that chair so that his legs did not completely atrophy. O'Rourke at the foundry said that a stranger had been seen occasionally walking in Walpole at odd hours. That was probably Dodge, going up and down the ravine path for exercise when he thought no one would see. After pushing Ernst, Dodge then tried to frighten the surviving sister into selling the land to Mr. Tupper Sr., by sending her menacing notes."

"But how would that enrich Mr. Dodge?" asked Anna.

"Through his wife, Ida. Once Jonah and his father were dead, Ida would inherit everything."

"Oh, heavens." Uncle Benjamin sighed. "So old Mr. Tupper was to die as well?"

"I think eventually he would have," I said. "I also think Ida had set her sights on her next husband."

Uncle Benjamin grew pale. "You don't mean . . ."

Cousin Eliza choked on her sherry, and Anna had to reach over and pound her back.

"But why was Clarence murdered?" Abba asked.

"Because like poor Hamlet, he had a conscience," I said. "I think on several occasions he wanted to tell me about the violent oddity of his household. He had discovered Jonah Tupper's grave, perhaps the very day I first saw him at his campsite, when he was drunk and raving. But he knew his own mother was involved, and how could one turn on one's mother like that? He went along with the pretense of the bell order to protect his mother."

"Indeed," said Fanny Kemble. "That is the tragedy of every Hamlet: how to accuse the king without also implicating the queen."

"That was my worst mistake of the summer," I said. "I saw Clarence's hatred, his violence and confusion. I did not see far enough to the reasons for his extreme disturbance of conscience."

"But what about the death of Mr. Sykes, when witnesses said Clarence was swimming with him and his stepfather drowned?" Sylvia asked.

"It could easily have been Johnnie Dodge with him that day. From a distance, who could have identified one man over the other?" I looked down at my bruised, ink-stained hands. If I were to write "true" stories, and not just "blood and thunders," not just tales for children, I would have to pay closer attention to those around me, to see the invisible as well as the visible. I would have to see into the depths of the human heart itself.

Sylvia read my thoughts. "You will, Louy," she whispered.

"But you say he had a conscience. What is the basis for that judgment?" Llew asked. "I admit that being thought guilty of his death was unpleasant, but a part of me could not grieve for him. He was arrogant and unpleasant."

"But he would not marry the girl he loved, Lilli Nooteboom. Not until he could hide her safely away from his family. He tried to protect Lilli," I pointed out. "The conversation you overheard, Llew, the quarrel between the two men, was probably Clarence arguing with Dodge."

Llew gave me another of those strange glances, and then looked away. I knew what was in his heart, and in mine as well. I took his hand and held it between my own.

"My friend," I whispered.

"No more than that?"

"No more."

Father cleared his throat loudly, and as we sat in contemplative silence, the sun finished setting on the long summer day, one of the last of summer. Abba moved quietly about the room, lighting lamps. We had more than one lamp that night, since it was a celebration and, we suspected but did not say, the beginning of a parting, for soon Abba's Golden Brood, all now gathered under this one roof, would separate. My purse had finally emptied and I had decided to return to Boston in the fall, to teach again, and sew, and write, and do what must be done to keep my family from financial danger and to keep creating my stories. I'd had enough of the quiet country life. Anna had accepted a job in Syracuse, at Dr. Wilbur's Idiot Asylum. "It will be calmer there, I suspect," she had commented.

But that evening the lamps cast flickering shadows and

the faded blue silk of the hand-me-down settees grew yet paler in the dimming light, as I looked from face to face of my beloved family and friends. What strange conversations that parlor had witnessed; what a strange cast of characters had tested the springs of those chairs and sofas!

"So once the itinerant court begins, I'm sure Johnnie Dodge will hang for murder," Llew said. "Mrs. Dodge will spend some years inside the North State Prison for Women, for bigamy if not worse."

"And now, supper," said Abba. "There's a dish of new potatoes and a salad as well, all from your father's garden."

"There's the real mystery," said Sylvia. "How ever did you get your late-planted garden to produce so much, so quickly?" she asked Father as she took his arm and headed to the dining room.

"The beneficent creator provides," Father said.

"Amen," said Llew.

I took Abba's arm and we walked slowly behind the others. "Tell me the truth, now that no one can hear us," I pleaded.

"Fish heads and tails," she whispered. "Best fertilizer in the world. Only don't tell your father. Oh, if only they didn't stink so!"

Louisa May Alcott has returned to Boston, living as a seamstress by day and writing her secret "blood and thunder" stories by night, when her friend Sylvia attempts to reach her long-dead father through a psychic medium and they are swept up in a murder investigation in. . . .

Louisa and the Crystal Gazer

Coming in February 2012 from Obsidian.

An excerpt follows. . . .

Gentle Readers,

In December of 1855 I found myself in Boston temporarily separated from my beloved family in Walpole, New Hampshire, and facing a Christmas, that most wonderful of seasons, without the comfort of my loved ones.

But drudge a living I must, for I was not yet the rich and famous author I later became. My stories, when they sold, earned little, and so I had sought employment and received an offer from Reverend Ezra Gannett, who wished me to complete an order of a dozen winter shirts for him, all to be finely seamed, buttonholed, and finished with pleats and embroidery.

I was an unenthused seamstress at best, but his payment would allow me to purchase Christmas presents for my family, so I accepted his offer, and a second one besides, for a dozen summer shirts of lighter fabric to be completed by April. These matters are relevant to my story. Trust me.

My dear friend Sylvia Shattuck was also in residence in Boston, fortunately, for more than ever I counted on her steadfast and amusing companionship. Sylvia, however, was in a strange frame of mind, one that set into motion a course of events that would involve us in murder, faithless lovers, and sad deeds of a dark past. Beware of boredom, gentle reader. It can lead one down dangerous paths.

"I miss Father," she sighed one morning as we took our walk along the harbor. It was a misty, cold day, and the harbor waves were tipped with frosty white.

"Unfortunately, your father passed away when you were a child," I answered gently. "You barely knew that long-enduring man, so how do you now claim to miss him?"

It was unlike Sylvia to yearn for any family member, dead or alive, and I had a vague presentiment that she was to introduce yet another faddish custom into my life. Sylvia lived in vogues, and had just relinquished Confucianism, which had not brought the enlightenment she sought. No use to explain to her that philosophers spent years at that task; Sylvia tended to give three months and then move on.

"My point exactly," my companion responded, turning upon me bright eyes filled with a passionate melancholy. "I feel the need for a masculine presence in my life, and would like to converse with my father. I will, with the assistance of Mrs. Agatha Percy. Please come with me to one of her sittings!"

I groaned and jammed my hands deeper into my pockets, despite the stares of several passersby; a lady did not put her hands in her pockets. She did if they were cold, I thought. Ship rigging creaked in the wind and bells chimed the start of a new watch, and I pondered Sylvia's statement.

Mrs. Agatha D. Percy was the newest fad in Boston, one of the recently risen members of that questionable group of individuals known as "spiritists," or mediums. One must feel a very heavy burden of ennui to wish to spend time at that dubious amusement, I thought.

"Oh, it will be such fun, Louisa. All of Boston goes!" Sylvia persisted.

"Then it must be quite crowded," I rejoined, walking at a faster pace to try to dissuade Sylvia from this topic.

But she turned pink with enthusiasm and fairly raced about me in circles, imploring that I join her in this new activity. "Please come with me, Louy; say you will! I have an invitation for you from Mrs. Percy." Sailors in their blue overcoats turned in our direction and grinned.

"I can think of better ways to spend time and money than sitting in the dark and watching parlor tricks. I would much rather, for instance, attend one of Signor Massimo's musical evenings." The signor, a famous pianist, was touring the United States from his home in Rome and had decided to winter in Boston. He was giving a series of performances—performances I could not afford, since the tickets were as much as three dollars apiece, even when they were available, which wasn't often, as he preferred private homes and small salons.

"Mother tried to get tickets and could not. She was furious," Sylvia said. I could understand; women with Mrs. Shattuck's family name and wealth were not accustomed to hearing no.

"Look, there is ice in the harbor," I said, putting my hand over my eyes to shield them from the glare.

"I will have your answer," Sylvia persisted.

I introduced several new topics of conversation, hoping to distract Sylvia from her mission—Jenny Lind, the Wild West, a newly published travel book about France that was flying off the shelves—but each topic she cleverly rejoined and detoured back to Mrs. Percy. Jenny Lind, accompanied by her American manager, P. T. Barnum, had visited Mrs. Percy. Mrs. Percy had published a "memoir" from a spirit who had visited her from Oklahoma. Mrs. Percy had toured France the year before and had been received by their umbrella-carrying Citizen King.

"Don't you see?" Sylvia sighed in exasperation, pulling at my hand to prevent me from taking another step. "The spirits themselves wish you to visit her. They put those very suggestions in your mind!"

"Then they should put a plot or two in my mind," I said, remembering the still-blank sheet of paper before which I had sat that morning at my desk. Being between stories was an unpleasant state for me, when no plot or story threaded the random thoughts of everyday imagination, no characters spoke to me in my head as I swept the parlor or stitched linens.

"They will," Sylvia said complacently. "I hear they become quite chatty and friendly in Mrs. Percy's parlor. You might use the scene in one of your 'blood and thunder' stories. Think what fun it would be to write about Mrs. Percy!"

"I am unconvinced that 'fun' is the correct word to describe an hour of sitting in the dark, pretending to speak with the dead," I said.

"Spirits," corrected Sylvia. "The dead don't like to be called dead. Such a harsh word."

Neither of us was yet aware of exactly how harsh that séance would become.

"I will think about it," I promised. "But now come with

me to Tremont Street, and let us look in the windows and begin to think of Christmas presents, and what we will give our families."

"I know what Mother wishes," said Sylvia. "A son-in-law."

"I have an easier shopping list," I laughed. "A ream of writing paper for Father, new Berlin wools for Auntie Bond, something frivolous for Marmee since everyone else is certain to give her sturdy handkerchiefs." Marmee, my beloved mother, was also known as Abba, but more and more in my imagination she was Marmee, and she was already the center of a story I had yet to write but often thought about, a story about four daughters, one named Jo, and their wise, generous mother. "A pair of gloves for Anna in Syracuse, and Faber pencils for Abby." Abby, the youngest Alcott girl, was the artist of the family.

"You've forgotten Lizzie," said Sylvia.

"No, I haven't." Lizzie was a musician, a quiet, shy girl who asked for little and was content with all she had, which was little enough. "But what can I give a sister who deserves a grand piano, a gift out of the question? I am at a loss."

"You'll think of something. Louy. You always do," Sylvia assured me.

About the Author

Anna Maclean is the pseudonym of Jeanne Mackin, an award-winning journalist and the author of several historical novels. She lives in the Finger Lakes area of New York with her husband, artist and writer Stephen Poleskie. Visit her Web site at www.annamaclean.net.